C000146690

ABOUT THE AUTHOR

James Crown was born in Australia and brought up in Canada. Since returning to Australia in the 1970s he has edited national magazines, daily newspapers, worked as a Foreign Editor, a newspaper executive and television commentator on foreign affairs. His special interest is terrorism and his study *The Terrorist Connection* was published in 1986.

Married with two daughters, James Crown lives in Sydney and now writes full time. *The December Conspiracy* is his second novel in the Julian Castle series.

THE DECEMBER CONSPIRACY

JAMES CROWN

BANTAM BOOKS
SYDNEY • AUCKLAND • TORONTO • NEW YORK • LONDON

THE DECEMBER CONSPIRACY
A BANTAM BOOK

Printing History
Bantam edition published 1989

Copyright © James Crown 1989

All rights reserved. No part of this publication may be reproduced, stored in a retrieval system, or transmitted in any form or by any means, electronic, mechanical, photocopying, recording of otherwise, without the prior permission of the publishers.

National Library of Australia
Cataloguing-in-Publication entry

Crown, James, 1946—
The December Conspiracy

ISBN 0 947189 31 9

I. Title.

A823′ .3

Bantam Books are published in Australia by Transworld Publishers (Australia) Pty Limited, 15-23 Helles Ave, Moorebank, NSW 2170 and in New Zealand by Transworld Publishers (NZ) Limited Cnr Moselle and Waipareira Avenues Henderson, Auckland.

Typeset by Midland Typesetters
Printed by Australian Print Group, Maryborough, Vic.

Cover illustration and design by Peter Bollinger

PROLOGUE

"Hello." The deep, cultured drawl belonging to the Australian who answered the telephone was tired and slightly blurred, as if he had been dragged reluctantly out of a sound sleep. He was sitting up in the large bed in the plush bedroom of the vast mansion that, from the exclusive hillside suburb of Vaucluse, overlooked the awesome midnight darkness of Sydney Harbour. "What did you find?" he asked, quickly forcing the sleep away in the time it took to speak the short sentence.

The American's voice was coming across the distance from the Philippines' capital of Manila. There was more than a slight hint of subservience in the caller's manner. "I have the information we've been waiting for."

"Marcos is moving the money?"

"Within the next couple of hours. By air from Clark Air Force Base."

"Destination?"

"Geneva."

"How much?"

There was the slightest pause before the American spoke. "Best guess is $50 million in US currency."

"Son-of-a-bitch!" It was an expression of genuine

surprise. "I didn't think there were that many greenbacks left in his country."

"There weren't. At least, not officially."

"Who's the courier?" the Australian asked, carrying the telephone across the room until he was standing by the wide, curtainless window.

"An aristocrat named Gerry Roa. A henchman of Marcos. Manages a steamship company."

"Can you carry out the mission as we planned?"

"No problem. I'm leaving now."

"Remember," the Australian cautioned, "you have to get to the money before this guy Roa has a chance to deposit it."

"*Or* get the number of the account."

"That's the hard way. Keep it simple. Get it before it's deposited."

"No problem," the American said confidently.

The conversation over, the Australian replaced the handset on the telephone's ivory cradle. He paused for a long moment by the window and looked out at the harbour. He had a grand vision and the $50 million would help make it a reality. They were really going to have to take notice of him this time. He would bring the wrath of Lucifer down on them if they didn't. But even more than this new $50 million would be needed to do what he wanted properly. The long sigh that escaped from his thin lips sounded almost melancholy. Slowly he crossed back to his bed, pausing and staring down at it and, for the first time in a few weeks, wishing there was a woman waiting there for him. He toyed with the idea of sending for Consuelo. The thought warmed him, but he dismissed it and climbed between the satin sheets, alone and wide awake.

* * *

The young woman was particularly beautiful. Hers was a classic beauty that had never revealed

itself during those seemingly endless and awf__
years as an awkward, skinny teenager. It had
taken maturity to bring forth the final perfect
shape and richness of the skin. Gracefully she
swung her long legs off the bed and stood up, naked
and trim, stretching as the warm sun streamed
through the bedroom to bathe her pale skin in its
reddish-yellow dawn tones. She moved her
nakedness closer to the window, not near enough
to be seen from the street outside but close enough
to see the glittering frost that liberally coated the
manicured lawns of the old houses ranged neatly
along the street of the Washington, DC suburb.
Leafless trees stood motionless along the empty
sidewalks.

She cocked her head to one side and listened
carefully. The big Georgian-style brownstone was
silent, its inhabitants still fast asleep. It was often
like this. Her aunt and uncle were a generation
and a half older. She always awoke well before
them and, when she was lucky, had left the house
before she had to start making excuses. They
didn't agree with what she was doing and they
never seemed to stop telling her so. She grimaced
as she dressed in faded jeans and a warm flannel
shirt. Marching around outside for the next eight
hours was going to be damned cold.

Her silver-haired aunt had tried to make her
point quietly at first, commenting on the obvious.
The scroll that labelled her niece a doctor, a
graduate with honours from one of the country's
top medical schools, had been framed and hung
conspiciously in her bedroom. But the parchment
made little impact. When she was cornered, she
argued that she could practise medicine any time.
Right now she had a more important role to play
out: trying to change the foreign policy of the
United States government.

She walked softly along the corridor and down the carpeted stairs. The back door creaked on its hinges as she opened it. She took a deep breath of cold, crisp winter air, feeling it burn into her lungs. It felt good, driving away the last vestiges of sleep. She walked more swiftly now, out to the garage, then inside to the placards. They all had the same kind of message: HANDS OFF NICARAGUA. She loaded them into the red Ford Pinto and drove off toward the scene of this day's protest march in the national capital.

She had no doubts that what she and her friends were doing was important. Her only concern was that she was not doing enough, that she should be doing something more active. Violence was out. Not only was she personally against violence, but the 1960s and 1970s had already proven the futility of taking to the streets against well-armed police. Still, she thought as she turned a corner and entered a four-lane highway into the heart of the District of Columbia, she could be doing something more. That thought stayed with her, nagging away, unable to be dismissed.

* * *

The colonel with the close-cropped hair and the strongly lined face looked around him at the men he was about to lead ashore. Peter Radcliffe-Jones still used the rank, even though he had been cashiered five years ago from Her Majesty's forces. His men were a good lot, perhaps among the best he had recruited during all the missions that had occurred since the time of his sacking. There was a hunger in their young faces, a quest for the kind of bloodthirsty violence he knew was going to unfold when he finally got them off the fishing trawler and onto dry land. The few older faces showed mere resignation for what lay ahead, an acceptance of the inevitable. If this was to be the final event, well, so be it! He grinned in the dim glow of the waning moon. Setting aside the Falklands, he could count all the battles he had fought since leaving the British Army, and realised he had seen far more action as a private enterprise soldier than he had encountered during two decades of loyal and dedicated service for country and Queen.

Granted, Northern Ireland had been particularly bloody but there had been too many restraints on him there and he had chafed—quite naturally, he thought—at all those rules that gave his IRA enemies a better-than-even chance of winning any engagement. His troops had forgotten the rules or deliberately set them aside a couple of times. They had successfully taken out the enemy on those occasions but the goddamn press had eaten him, their commander, alive. 'A question of civil liberties', Fleet Street had trumpeted, and the commanding general had carpeted him—offering clucking sympathy about the problems of dealing with the elusive IRA and then issuing less-than-muted threats about what would happen if the British Army lost the war with Fleet Street. That battle, the general concluded, went way beyond what was happening in Ulster and Belfast and Londonderry.

They had sent him back to England, to sit behind a desk for his sins in Londonderry. He had been rescued only when Argentina seized Port Stanley and everyone had scurried around to find a map that included enough of the South Atlantic to show the rocky islands of the Falklands.

The Falklands! He shivered in the warm, humid night air. His hands shook a little and he crossed his arms and gripped his elbows to steady himself. They'd told him it was a war and all around him it looked and sounded and even smelled like a war. He led his troops in some vicious fighting around Goose Green. They had overwhelmed their enemies in dangerous sorties and there had even been talk of a very important medal.

The fragile peace that followed the retaking of Port Stanley had shattered all the talk of medals. The Union Jack had been hauled back up the flagpole in front of the governor's residence and they had cheered. The Argentine prisoners had remained a sullen lot, uncooperative, surly— dangerous, he had thought—and he had taken the *appropriate* steps to see they would never again threaten his country and Queen. Once again the press had cried foul. He was shipped home, separated from the troops he had led into battle and flown home in the back of a big cargo plane. There were no cheering crowds or bands playing when he arrived.

"Colonel!" The voice cut through his thoughts and yanked him unceremoniously back to the fishing trawler.

He looked up. It was the German sergeant he'd recruited in West Berlin two years ago. He was a good soldier who had saved his colonel's life during those trying days in Ethiopia's wartorn state of Eritrea.

"Yes, Klaus. What is it?"

"Almost time for the recognition signals, sir."

He nodded, rose to his feet from his position in front of the wheelhouse and took the binoculars from the German. Lifting the powerful glasses to his eyes he peered toward the African shore, a dark forbidding landmass a few kilometres away. It looked even more ominous bathed in the sickly yellow light of the moon. He sighed as he thought of the impending battle. Africa! Eritrea! Lebanon! The place made no difference. It was just another battle for him. He felt invincible standing there in the darkness. Dangerous to think like that, so very dangerous. *Invincible* was such a stupid word—almost as foolish and empty a concept as country and Queen had turned out to be.

He picked up the red and green blinking lights quite quickly, only a moment after they were turned on by his advance party which had been ashore for the past week. It was time to move now, time to go to work . . .

* * *

The December Foundation had received honours from presidents, prime ministers and kings. There had even been rumours of a Nobel nomination. The foundation's logo—a stylised red heart with an equally stylised letter "D" in the centre—had been seen on every continent. Cartons of food, medicine, clothing, tents had all been unloaded in every conceivable kind of scene, in environments of disaster and need. Floods, earthquakes, drought, civil war—all these and more brought December Foundation workers in jeeps, boats and aeroplanes. The founder of this worthy humanitarian enterprise had summed it up many years earlier, before becoming a virtual recluse. *December* was an apt title to apply to his herculean efforts to alleviate pain and suffering, for December, he explained, encapsulated in one word so many different things.

He pointed out that in the northern hemisphere December brought the cold of ice and the biting chill of a winter wind, and Christmas emphasised the plight of those who had nothing. In the southern hemisphere December brought heat and exhaustion, summer drought and starvation. December was, in the calendar year, the final month—the last month of the dying year before the rebirth of the new year. It was a symbol to be applied to old men and new babies, so many of whom were suffering and dying in so many parts of the world.

The December Foundation, its founder explained, tried to lift some of the crushing burden from those who suffered, tried to provide a modicum of human dignity to those less fortunate. When asked how the foundation raised the massive amounts of money necessary to carry out all its good works, the man who had created it was coy, saying only that the money came from many anonymous sources—most of it from those who had it to spare.

PART ONE

THE 78
HOURS

CHAPTER ONE

DATELINE: MANILA . . . By Julian Castle

The sheet of white paper was still waiting in the portable typewriter on my small desk. The words were all I had been able to write before I went to bed. I had the kind of headache that was threatening to kill me and it had been two days since I'd had any sleep. The editors back home in Australia had the hard news story I'd sent; the feature piece they'd demanded for next Saturday's magazine section was just going to have to wait until I got some rest.

The insistent jangle of the telephone dragged me out of a deep sleep. I shook my heavy head. At least the headache was fading. The telephone rang again. I swung my legs off the bed and stood up. My eyes focused once again on the words in the typewriter. I had a feeling—my reporter's sixth sense—that Australian newspaper readers were going to be seeing that dateline and my byline a lot more in the next few weeks. This country was about to become a big story and I wouldn't be covering it alone. From all over the world journalists were already pouring in. Like hungry sharks lured in by the smell of blood, the scribes were homing in on the death rattles of the embattled Marcos regime.

I picked up the telephone on the third ring. "Castle."

"Come on buddy, up and at 'em."

It was Chester Price, one of New York's better reporters and a longtime friend. We went back a long way together: Vietnam, Cambodia. We were covering the developing crisis in Manila in a sort of unofficial partnership. While I slept he stayed out there in the streets, and vice versa. If anything broke, each would let the other one know.

"What's happening?" I asked.

"Enrile and General Ramos have just declared for the rebels—we've got a genuine coup attempt on our hands this time."

It had been building to this ever since Marcos claimed victory in those phony elections earlier in the month. Enrile was Marcos' former longtime defence minister and Ramos was deputy chief of staff of the army. But the key to the political solution was Corazon Aquino.

"Where's Cory?" I asked.

"In Cebu."

Cebu was an island about two hundred kilometres southeast of the capital, one of seven thousand islands, large and small, that made up the archipelago. "At least she's far enough away to have some time to think."

"She's gone into hiding, I'm told."

"Where are you?"

"The Defence Ministry, Camp Aguinaldo."

"I'll be there as soon as I can."

"We're all waiting for Enrile and Ramos to give a press conference." He paused. "Julian?"

"What?"

"Keep your head down. A lot of Marcos loyalists are out wandering the streets with guns. They're pretty jittery."

I chuckled. "Not to worry. I'm destined to get

4

run down by a little old lady in a Morris the day after I retire."

"Just keep your eyes open."

I hung up. Chester's warnings were common, but I'd have thought he'd hand out a throwaway line to my little old lady in her Morris. He was taking it all very seriously—and so would I. My eyes swung to the calendar below the tourist picture of Bondi Beach, my only visible link with home. It was Saturday, 22 February.

Outside my hotel it was quieter than usual. What movement there was seemed somewhat more frenetic and passed quickly. It was as if a typhoon was on its way, and people were battening down the hatches. Even in the constant heat and sweat of the Philippines' crowded capital, a cold chill swept back and forth across the streets of Manila, setting nerves on edge, making civilian and soldier alike suspicious of everything around him. The smell of revolution was in the air. I'd taken in that odour before, in other capitals, and unlike the earnest youngsters from Australian television who had arrived at my hotel a few days earlier, I knew enough to be frightened. Not paralysed; just scared enough to take those extra precautions that would keep me alive if the guns started firing. From experience I could tell the time for shooting was getting close.

There was a taxi near the front door. I'd never known a time when there wasn't. The Filipino driver didn't look too pleased when I told him where I wanted to go.

"You sure?" he asked. "There's been some shooting over that way."

I nodded. "Let's get over there."

For an instant he seemed to be counting up the odds. You could almost see the wheels turning in his head. Bullet holes wouldn't improve the

5

appearance of his small cab. I waved a Yankee twenty-dollar bill in front of him. That was enough. He pulled away from the kerb. American money still commanded a lot of respect here.

"What do you think's going to happen?" I asked the driver. Most of the time the street people had a better handle on what was going on than any official source.

"Marcos will fall if the army goes against him. Simple as that. Army stays with him, he'll continue to rob us."

That was the way most Filipinos seemed to be calling it. And no doubt whoever took Marcos' place would face the same dilemma. As long as the Army stayed on side, the government could cling to power.

"Hope Marcos leaves a few crumbs behind for us," the driver added.

I nodded. "Would be nice, but I hear he's got a fortune tucked away."

The cabbie laughed. "Not just a fortune. A few fortunes would be more like it."

We drove on. Legend had it—and the legend was fast becoming fact—that Marcos and his wife Imelda had salted away millions of dollars, one hell of a lot of pesos, overseas. I made a mental note to ask a Filipino friend who worked over at Treasury.

The cabbie suddenly stood on the brakes and the small cab skidded around in the middle of the road. A big army tank was parked ominously in the centre of the street. The lights had been turned out in the block and we'd almost run right into it. My heart popped up into my mouth. A little more nervousness and the tank crew might have fired.

Before I could react, a soldier stepped out of the shadows and yanked open the taxi door. "Get out!"

he ordered, aiming an M-16 in my direction. He didn't bother with the driver. Just me, the *gringo*.

I got out very slowly. This was no time for heroic moves. The soldier was young and tense.

"Where are you going?"

"Camp Aguinaldo."

"Why are you going there?"

"I'm an Australian newspaper reporter. I'm going there because that's where the news is right now."

He seemed to buy that. "Your papers?"

I took out my passport and my press pass.

The soldier called a superior with a flashlight and they looked at the passport and card, then shone the bright light in my face. I squinted against its glare.

The officer nodded. "Okay, you can go on. But go slowly. There are other checkpoints. We have to be careful these days." As if by way of apology, he held the door until I was inside, then shut it gently.

The driver had said nothing, staring straight ahead. When the door was shut, he asked, "You sure you want to go ahead? This is perhaps a good time to be in bed with a warm woman."

I agreed with him, at least to myself. "No, let's get in there and find out what's going on."

He moaned a little but drove on. There were more army tanks and personnel carriers along the way. There were also a lot of people. The momentum of Cory's People Power was well under way and I was feeling the effect of the assembling crowds. There was always something intensely attention-focusing about the sight of army tanks and armed soldiers sealing off the intersections of streets in a city where English is a language you can hear everywhere you go. The sight also tended to be very unsettling.

7

By the time the driver let me out, we were awash with Filipinos who had flocked around the two military camps, literally across the street from each other, which were now the final redoubts of the rebel leaders and their followers. I got out of the cab and started walking. There was tension in the air, but no hostility toward me. Just open curiosity. The few people who spoke to me seemed pleased when they found out I was a reporter.

There was no trouble at the gates and a soldier with a flak jacket and a machinegun whisked me off to the compound where the journalists were being herded together in preparation for the press conference of Enrile and Ramos.

Across the din and through the smoke of too many cigarettes and cigars I spotted Chester waving madly at me. He was a big guy, strong with broad shoulders and a nose that had been broken a long time ago. He could have been mistaken for a heavyweight boxer who'd lost one too many fights. I knew better—Chester had been a boxer and he took great delight in talking about how he'd never been knocked down. A wife named Marnie and a daughter named Jade had swept him from the ring. When Jade was born, Chester had been told to hang up his gloves or else. The referee had called it; the gloves went into an old trunk he still lugged around. They had been in the basement of their home in upstate New York until Marnie died. That death also knocked Chester out. He gave up his daughter, packed her off to live with an aunt and uncle in Washington and then hit the bottle badly. His editor was one of the better types. Picked him up out of the gutter one Saturday night, showered and shaved him, stuck a battered old typewriter under his arm and sent him off to war—to Vietnam. That's where I'd met him. Chester cleaned up his act out there. He'd had to in order to survive.

After some pushing and shoving, we got our heads close enough together to hear each other.

"Hell of a story, Julian," he said in his tough-guy voice, a cross between Eastwood's macho "Make my day" and Gable's putdown, "Frankly, my dear, I don't give a damn".

"It's shaping up," I agreed.

He nodded at the young men with the television cameras, microphones and fancy safari suit jackets that made them all look like underfed versions of the classic great white hunter. "The kids are all here with their travelling circus."

I grinned. It was an old joke. Electronic media, television versus print. "The airport's closed and NBC-TV's stuck in Hong Kong with a hundred boxes of gear."

"Serves them right."

"Enrile and Ramos have got themselves one hell of a defensive position. There are thousands of people out front. Marcos will have to kill a lot of civilians to get in here," I commented.

"Think he'll do it?"

I shook my head.

"Neither do I. While you were getting your beauty rest I talked with an old friend at our embassy. Apparently Reagan has let it be known that if Marcos uses armed force against civilians, the US will withdraw everything it can think of."

"That makes sense. But it's not Marcos I'm worried about. It's the chief of staff," I said.

He agreed. "General Ver's the danger point. But these guys here have got a couple of things going for them. Every hour that goes by gives them more support. Some of the air force have already declared for them. And, not least, Ver's still following orders from Marcos and I don't think the old man's up to a bloodbath."

There was some noise at the front of the room. A rebel officer stood on a table and shouted that he'd have something for us in about ten minutes.

Chester lit a cigar. "Sure wish my kid could be here for this. Might show her the real world for a change. She's always babbling on about the power of the people."

The last time I'd seen Jade Price she'd been a toothy teenager. Chester had been working out of the Hong Kong bureau of his New York newspaper and he'd brought her out to Asia for the school holidays. The two of them had stayed with me in Manila for a week. Uncle Julian, she'd called me. Big eyes, I remembered, and a lot of heart. Not only had she forgiven her father for dumping her but she had a well developed social conscience, particularly when she saw the slums of nearby Tondo. I figured she'd grow out of the social do-gooder side of things but she hadn't. Now she was all grown up and, by the looks of the pictures Chester had shown me, she was a great-looking lady.

Chester was still talking about her. "She's mixed up in street politics now. She got her medical degree and instead of going out and making some money, she's marching around the streets of Washington."

I'd heard these complaints from him before. "Any new causes?"

"Nicaragua now. Figures the White House is the cause of all of the ills of the Central American peasants."

I smiled. "She'll grow out of it."

"Jesus, Julian," he said, looking serious, "I sure hope so. Thought she'd finished with that kind of stuff when she left university."

There was a sudden lowering of voices and General Ramos and the former Defence Minister,

Juan Ponce Enrile, entered the room, surrounded by armed soldiers. The young soldiers were obviously elated, but Enrile and Ramos looked tired and tense. They were carrying the weight of an entire country on their shoulders and were about to tell a listening world what that weight felt like.

CHAPTER TWO

As the Boeing 707 lifted away from Clark Air Force Base north of Manila and climbed steadily into the cloudy night sky, Gerry Roa shook his head and stared out at the distant lights of the capital. He was not a particularly religious man, but he found himself muttering a quiet prayer. *Deliver my president from evil,* he said to himself. Then he stopped and corrected the sentence. *Deliver my country from evil, my God.* For a moment he considered the almost hypocritical position he was taking. In the large case sitting on the lounge suite across from where he was hovering by the window was $50 million American dollars. He was taking it to Geneva for the president—a president about to lose a country. He was supposed to deposit the money into a new numbered account in Geneva and then provide the president with the number. Why was he doing this insane act, stripping his country of valuable assets? The new government would need this wealth to rebuild the shattered economy the dictator—he had no trouble using that word—had created with all his stupidity and corruption.

Gerry Roa knew exactly why he was doing it. Because he had to. Because there was a chance Marcos might survive this latest challenge and if he did he would remember anyone who had refused to carry out his requests. And if Marcos fell—well, that was another scenario. Making this trip to Geneva would accommodate that eventuality as well. It was all so complicated, yet it seemed that he was flying straight into some simple scene, the final climax of which had already been played out during that massacre at Forbes Park.

He shook his head again, seeing in the reflection from the double-glassed windows of the big jet the strong, aristocratic bearing of the handsome forehead, nose and mouth. The skin was tight and firm, showing little evidence of the years of good living. The expensive treatments at the health club and the use of the president's own masseuse and doctor had kept the saggy skin at bay. It was in his eyes that he knew the truth lay and tonight they were deep and black, almost mournful. The dictator had hidden the final truth well. Their friendship had been phony all along. It was all a giant game of emotional blackmail. Being close to the president had given him great make-believe power and wealth but a price had always been exacted—he was a courier at this moment, nothing more nor less, taking away the president's future and his country's treasure like a common thief and secreting it where only the dictator could get at it. Roa wondered how many others were making similar journeys, paying their final debt to an evil old man who had pretended to be their friend.

He looked up, almost startled, as a thin, gentle hand was placed on his shoulder. Fatima was standing there quietly, looking down at him with all-too-obvious concern. He loved the woman. They had been together a long time, childless—not for lack of trying—then she had provided a son to carry forward the family's name. That act of giving

13

had meant a lot to him, much more than he could ever explain to her: perhaps even more than he could adequately explain to himself. It was one of the reasons they were together now, carrying the dictator's money. He would never, not even for the briefest moment, consider leaving the country without his wife and son. Not even for Marcos. Particularly not even for Marcos.

A gentle pressure from her slender hand brought him back. He smiled at her gesture. "It won't be long, then we'll be back home."

She sat down beside him, fingers playing nervously with her wedding band and diamond-studded engagement ring. "Are you sure we're doing the right thing?"

He sighed. "No Fatima, I'm not sure. With everything in such chaos I've no idea what the right thing is any more." He could talk this way with her. Part of his strength came from the openness of their marriage. They had few secrets from each other.

"Will Marcos survive?"

"If he is ruthless and uses his troops ruthlessly, he may win this round. Enrile and Ramos are bluffing, I think." He fell silent for a moment, weighing up the possibilities. "But the president will have to move quickly. Every hour he delays, the bluff will become stronger and there will come a point where Marcos will have lost the advantage."

"And lost the country," she added, not unhappily.

He studied her finely sculpted face. She had been a model before they'd met. It never ceased to amaze him that even after all these years her cheeks still had the same soft curves, and the nose and mouth had never shown any of the dozen or so years that had passed since she had last been in front of a camera. "You never have liked him, have you?"

"Never," she said with extra emphasis, her brown eyes flashing defiance. "He and that pompous ass of a wife. The Philippines was a plaything for them, a toy for their amusement. They had such power to do good and they frittered it away on trivialities, on false walls to shield them from what they didn't want to see."

"You don't think you're being a little harsh?"

"Not at all, Gerry. They were parasites, surrounded by a court of parasites."

"Including me, don't forget."

She reached over and took his hand. "No, my dear. The others were opportunists. You were never that."

He looked away from her. "Then what was I?" The words were sharper than he had intended. He felt her grip tighten.

"I think you were a guardian of your family's interests. You were their conscience brought to bear on Marcos, your presence reminding him of what he had taken from them."

What she said pained him. His father and uncle had owned a thriving steamship company— seven ships plying a multitude of trade and passenger routes. Five years ago Marcos had offered, through an intermediary, to buy a controlling interest in the line. The Roa family had declined the offer. Suddenly the successful company had been faced with a series of crises. Alleged communist terrorists planted bombs aboard the passenger liner that served as flagship of the fleet, and it went to the bottom in Leyte Gulf, taking with it 300 passengers and crew. The cargo contracts started to dry up. It didn't take long before the cash flow suffered. The company was in trouble.

Gerry Roa had been there when it was happening, recently returned from doing a business degree at the London School of Economics. The situation didn't need his expertise to define it. A first-year accounting student could have drawn a graph to show the declining fortunes of the once-proud line. When it was on the verge of bankruptcy Marcos made a new offer, toning down the original offer. No longer did he want a controlling interest, merely one-third. But there was a catch. As a temporary measure, until the Marcos loan of working capital had been paid back, the president required a codicil be written into the wills of both Gerry's uncle and his father. In the event of their deaths during the period of the loan, half of each of their stock holdings in the company would go to an individual nominated by Marcos. Gerry had argued against the deal. Simple arithmetic showed that Marcos' nominee could end up with control of the company if both father and uncle died. Marcos and the nominee would have two-thirds and Gerry Roa would be left with one-third.

His father and his uncle could both count. They could see the risk but, they argued, they were both very healthy and the loan period was only one year. They could also see no other way to avoid bankruptcy. The loan would carry them through the trading slump and they all knew, having seen it with other companies, that a business relationship with Marcos usually prospered. They made the deal.

The president was magnanimous. The contacts that had fled to other companies suddenly reappeared, wanting to do business with the Roas. Even more encouraging was the sudden disappearance of objections that had delayed the insurance payment on the sunken passenger liner. A cheque quickly arrived. Gerry argued it should be used to pay out the Marcos loan. The president argued it should be spent on a replacement liner and soon a new, much grander flagship was under construction—to be named after the First Lady, *Imelda*.

The tragedy Gerry feared came in the tenth month of the loan period. Communist terrorists, it was alleged, struck in the heavily guarded and exclusive Manila suburb of Forbes Park. The newspapers claimed it was a large-scale, coordinated attack. Certain homes had been targetted: a banker, the owner of a lumber mill consortium and the joint owners of the Roa Steamship Company had all been assassinated.

Marcos immediately set up an exhaustive search for the killers, two of whom were apprehended and shot to death by state security before they could be questioned. There was a state funeral for the respected businessmen at which the president delivered a moving soliloquy and the First Lady wept. A day after the funeral Marcos' nominee, Raymond Sanchez, claimed half of each of the father's and the uncle's holdings, giving him—when added to Marcos' existing one-third interest—two-thirds of the company. Gerry received the remaining third, was installed as chief executive and was ushered into the inner court of the president. He and Fatima were frequent guests at Malacanang Palace.

He stayed inside the court, ostensibly a follower but never falling completely for the paternalism the president tried to bestow on him. A day might come, he kept telling himself, when it would all be back in his hands.

Fatima pulled him back from his reverie. "You served your time," she said softly. "Now—take what is yours."

He smiled at her. She saw everything so simply. "It will take a while. He's still in the palace."

She shook her pretty head. "No, Gerry. Take

what's here now. Take this money." She nodded toward the case containing the $50 million. "You have a right to it. Take it and let's go somewhere far away."

He was surprised at how forcefully she was delivering the idea. The thought had already passed through his mind. They could buy a lot of security and anonymity with that much money. But not enough, he knew, if Marcos managed to hold on during this crisis. And the money would not satisfy the deep sense of revenge he knew he could exact if Marcos fell. He studied her eyes. They had never discussed his plan. Now was the time.

"We're not going to take the bastard's blood money," he started.

She tried to interrupt, not used to his harsh language.

He raised a hand to silence her. "We're going to do much better. We're going to bank the money and hold onto the number until we see if Marcos wins. If he holds onto his throne, then we give him the money and keep on waiting."

She shook her head.

He grinned. "But if he fails, then we move. We turn over the number of the account to the victor in return for the new government giving us back our company—*all* of it."

"But will they do that?"

"They will," he said slowly, "when I show them the proof that the president ordered the execution of my father and my uncle."

"You have proof!" Her shock showed.

"Absolute!"

"Tell me." She was excited and moved closer to him, expectant and conspiratorial.

"When Marcos nominated Raymond Sanchez to hold the shares in the line, he made the mistake

18

of telling Sanchez how he was going to get control. He laid out the plans to use his hit squads to murder my father and uncle. And they weren't the first or the last. Sanchez became a rich man as a front for Marcos."

"A crooked, wealthy man," she said.

He nodded. "Exactly. But he was also a very cautious man. He believed that some day he might have a need to show what Marcos had been up to, so he made tape recordings of his meetings with the president."

"He bugged Marcos?" she asked gleefully.

"He certainly did. I've heard some of the tapes. He played them for me."

She calmed a little. "Why you? Because he thinks Marcos will be toppled?"

He shook his head. "Not at all. He told me about the tapes before this latest crisis started."

"But why?"

"Because Raymond Sanchez wants to buy something."

She looked doubtful. "He's rich enough and powerful enough to buy anything."

"No. Not quite. He can't buy a clean conscience, final forgiveness for not speaking up before now. Absolution for his sins."

She didn't understand.

"Raymond Sanchez is dying of cancer. He's got three months more at the most. He wants to buy his way into heaven—a kind of confession, backed up by his electronic evidence."

Fatima was silent for a moment. "Where are the tapes?"

"Sanchez gave them to a couple of people he thinks will use them. He gave me the tapes that touch on Roa Steamship Company."

"You've got them now?" Her excitement was back.

"In a manner of speaking. They're with your father in Australia."

She grinned. "I don't believe any of this. My father, Miguel Santamaria, a man made rich by Marcos, is holding the tapes?"

"Ah, yes, but Miguel made his fortune on his own. Marcos might have funded him, but your father did the rest himself—and he survived long enough to break the connection to Malacanang totally."

She nodded her agreement. "So what are we going to do?"

He looked across at the bassinet in which his four-month-old son was lying, playing with a small rattle that masqueraded as a yellow duck. "Why don't you check Joseph's diaper? I'll get some sleep and we'll let this plane get us to Geneva. One step at a time."

"It's hard to wait."

"We've waited this long. A little while longer won't kill us."

She got up and crossed to the baby. He liked watching the two of them playing together. Whatever he did with those tapes, it would be for Joseph. Roa Steamship Company was going to be his legacy for his son. He drifted off to sleep. The *Imelda* would be renamed. That would be among the first changes.

* * *

They had been to many countries together but never to Switzerland. Geneva was their destination and Fatima had shown him the map as the aeroplane made its long descent. The city was at the end of Lake Geneva in a pocket surrounded on three sides by France and almost cut off from the rest of Switzerland. Everywhere they looked out the windows of the airliner there was snow and high mountains and vast forests. It was, they agreed, very different from their homeland.

Later, after they had cleared customs with their diplomatic passports at Cointrin international airport, they stepped outside into bright sunshine to find something else very different. The temperature was hovering around the freezing mark. Fatima clutched Joseph close to her, fretting about the cold while their suitcases and the case containing the money was put into the boot of the taxi.

The airport was only four kilometres northwest of Geneva and the taxi driver kept up a running commentary on the short drive to their hotel.

Fatima was pleased. The Hotel de la Paix, 11 Quai du Mont Blanc, was elegant and dignified and imbued with an old-world ambience. It stood facing the lake and, beyond that spectacle, the lofty heights of Mount Blanc. They passed quickly through the exquisite public areas and the entrance to the French restaurant. High above the street level their suite faced the lake. The views were magnificent.

Gerry settled his family into the rooms, then took the case of money downstairs to the hotel's vault room. He inspected the large vault in the presence of the manager. The case would have to be stored until the banks opened in the morning. It was all routine to the hotel's manager. Switzerland took great pride in providing efficient and very secure financial services. Few questions were asked; even fewer requests were denied. The manager was a proud Swiss. The Roa case would be secure, no matter what it contained. He would, he said in perfect European English, stake the honour of Switzerland on it. The Filipino was satisfied.

As he returned across the lobby, he caught the eye of a man sitting in the centre of the room reading a newspaper. It was only an instant before the man's eyes swung away to the floor. Gerry shivered and then felt foolish. One evening and a couple of hours in the morning and he would be rid of the money. He reached the elevators, pressed the button and waited. The doors opened, he stepped inside and swung around. The lobby spread out before him. The man with the newspaper was gone. He stepped forward without reason, searching the vast room. He spotted the man just as the elevator doors started to slide shut. The man was talking to one of the clerks at the reception desk on the far side of the room and they were both looking his way. His view was cut off as the door met. He stared at the shiny metal for a moment and then shrugged. It would all be over early tomorrow morning. He could live—would have to live—with his paranoia until then.

Back in the suite he turned on the television set to watch the evening news. It was worse than he imagined. Marcos was a virtual prisoner in his palace. Some of the army, part of the air force and what seemed like almost all of the civilian population had turned against the president. The situation was, the newsreader commented, precarious. It could still go either way, depending on whether or not Marcos decided to use force to end the rebellion at Aguinaldo and Crame.

They waited until Joseph was asleep. The hotel had provided a babysitter, a gentle old lady who explained that she was a great-grandmother and who smiled down on Joseph as if he was her own. Gerry and Fatima went out to dinner and, near midnight, strolled, hand in hand, along the concrete boardwalk of the Quai du Mont Blanc. There were stars and a moon that sprayed beams of fragmented light across the rippled surface of the lake.

They were almost alone on the *quai*. It was too cold for anyone except the most hardy of tourists. Gerry noticed the tall man some distance behind them as they stopped to admire the play of light on the waves. The man halted to light a cigarette. He walked on when they moved, matching their pace, always keeping a large gap between them. He wasn't the man Gerry had seen in the lobby and he forced himself to forget him. The new shiver he felt was from the cold, he told himself.

By the time they got back to the hotel, they were chilled to the bone. They bid the old lady good night and went to bed, making love—Fatima had only asked for a cuddle to warm her—and fell into a restful sleep.

* * *

He wasn't sure what had woken him. The baby was quiet in the second bedroom. Fatima had rolled away from him to the far side of the queen-sized bed. That was natural; she always did that. He lay still, watching the ceiling slowly appear in more detail as his eyes adjusted to the darkness. he looked for the moon but it had moved to a point where it fell only on Joseph's room. There was no light from it in their bedroom. He looked through the open French doors into the living room. It was dark in there, too.

But something had woken him! Without moving his head he looked at the numbers on the digital clock on the small bedside table close to Fatima's head. It was just after three.

There was a small click somewhere in the suite. He froze, holding his breath, straining to hear it again, to identify it. Nothing. His eyes were fixed on a spot on the wall in the living room, directly opposite Joseph's bedroom door. The sliver of moonlight reflecting off the wall was getting larger, growing. It didn't make any sense for a long moment and then he suddenly realised what was happening. The door to his son's bedroom was opening, letting more moonlight through. Now there was a large shadow in the middle of the yellowish light.

He rolled off the bed, hoping Fatima would stay asleep and not speak and warn the shadow. He glanced wildly around for some kind of weapon. There was nothing. And there was now no more time to look. The shadow was moving across the living room toward the door to the corridor. He launched himself through the doorway. The shadow turned, saw him and let out a startled cry.

Gerry heard Fatima call out but there was no time. The shadow of the man reared up and threw something at him. A bundle of clothing. Instinct caused him to throw out his arms and grab the bundle. He looked down at it just as it squirmed and let out a piercing cry of alarm. The bundle was Joseph. Gerry dropped to one knee, clasping the baby tightly. Joseph was howling and he was scared of dropping him. Fatima swept into the room. The man was opening the door. She screamed and the man ran out, slamming the door shut behind him.

He stood up shakily, handing the baby quickly to Fatima, and then ran to the door. He opened it carefully and looked out. The hall was deserted, as he had expected. Whoever had been in the room certainly wasn't going to linger in the corridor.

She was rocking the baby gently, sitting on the edge of a sofa, when he closed the door. She looked up at him, fear and worry written all over her face. "Why? Why the baby?" she asked in a strained voice.

The answer was obvious. "It was their only way

to the money. They kidnap Joseph and they ransom him back to us for the money. It's the only thing I can think of."

She nodded, silent for a moment before she spoke. "Who was it, Gerry?"

"I don't know. So few people knew about the trip."

"It's Marcos, isn't it?" she said.

He couldn't believe it. "How could it be Marcos? It's his money in the first place."

"That's just it—it's pure Marcos," she explained, still rocking the baby. "He sends you off with the money. He steals back the money and then says you were guilty of negligence, or worse."

"Why?"

"As compensation he claims the remaining third of the company."

He thought about it. Fatima was always able to find a point of focus. Would the president go to these lengths? "But it doesn't even look like he'll survive the coup attempt."

She almost grinned. "But he didn't know that when he decided to send you over here."

What she was saying was logical, he knew. He didn't know if it was true or not but at least it made sense. The only way he would be in the clear would be to bank the money. If Marcos held onto office and Gerry gave him the number of the account then the Roa family would be safe, at least for the moment.

"What are we going to do, Gerry?" Fatima asked.

"Make sure the money gets into the bank," he answered, walking across to the telephone.

He called the night manager and summoned the man to their suite. The night manager was as polished and as proud of being Swiss as the general manager had been the day before. He was aghast at the story Gerry told him. He wanted to call in the police immediately but demurred just as quickly when Gerry insisted the whole incident be kept quiet. It involved a great deal of money that might be hard to explain. The manager understood. This was Switzerland. Such transactions were common here. The manager had the right contacts and was able to follow Gerry's new instructions to the letter.

Within the hour there were two plainclothes security guards, one in the living room and one just outside in the corridor. Down in the lobby were two more guards.

There was no chance of further sleep. The only Roa who dismissed the incident was Joseph.

By dawn, the next stage of his plan was ready. A discreet phone call had ensured that the executive vice-president of the bank and his two assistants would be available two hours earlier than usual. An armoured car would be ushered into the basement entrance of the hotel and would be directed to an unobtrusive loading bay normally used for kitchen supplies. There would be two additional guards beside the normal complement of driver and two security men. The guards upstairs would stay with Fatima and the baby until after the deposit had been made.

Two hours later the operation swung into action. The case was carried to the service elevator by Gerry with guards on both sides, and front and back. The service elevator's controls were on manual and the hotel manager drove it himself, sending them quickly to the basement.

They remained inside the elevator until the signal had been given that it was all clear. Crossing to the armoured car took only a few seconds and once they were locked inside Gerry knew they were almost safe. The bank was the only other stop.

They drove through the early morning streets

without interruption. Traffic was light. It was going to be a fine day, Gerry could tell. He could see blue sky through the narrow, thickly glazed windows. For an instant he wondered how Marcos was faring. He choked down the uncertainty that welled up in his throat. This was not the time for it.

The radio crackled. A man on the point, at the bank, was reporting. "We've got a car with two men in it, parked about half a block down on the south side."

The man in charge of the security men looked at Roa. "Want to keep going?"

"Absolutely," he answered.

The security man smiled. "If they're after what you're carrying, I'd like to hear what they have to say when they see what we've got in mind."

Gerry grinned.

"Okay, send them out," the security man said quietly into the radio.

Gerry moved closer to one of the small windows as they turned the corner into the narrow street where the bank was located. They were coming in from the east. The car with the two men was farther down the street, beyond the bank. Suddenly, the front doors of the bank opened and two lines of men, each carrying a shotgun, jogged out to the street, forming a corridor into the bank. Gerry almost laughed. No one was going to get at the money. He saw the car move at the same time as the radio squawked.

"The car is doing a U-turn and pulling away."

"We see it," the security man answered.

The car sped off down the street.

"Beat you, you bastards," Gerry breathed.

The transfer was straightforward. The vice-president of the bank was from the same mould that had produced the managers at the Hotel de la Paix. There were minimal questions, some minor paperwork. As soon as the bank officially took delivery of the money, Gerry dismissed the security people, except for the two still at the hotel. He wanted to take over personally there. They had all done their jobs well.

A few minutes later, in the civilised atmosphere of the bank's boardroom, the vice-president offered coffee.

"You realise, sir, that this number is such that anyone possessing it can access the account."

"I realise that," Gerry answered.

"Do you think, sir, that whoever assailed you this morning also knows that?"

Gerry shook his head. "No. My guess is that they'll think they've lost out, that I've deposited the money into an account long established."

"That is the norm, of course," the banker sniffed. "This is somewhat irregular."

Gerry smiled warmly. "And my client and I thank you most profusely. The amount deposited, I am sure, will be of use to the bank."

The banker was obviously aware of the undercurrent in Gerry's words. "It is very much appreciated, Mr. Roa."

* * *

Two hours later he was back in their hotel suite. He wanted to get out of the city but the 707 had left Geneva for Frankfurt to pick up something for the First Lady. It would not return until this evening. Until then, they were on their own.

Gerry felt relaxed. He had beaten whoever it was. The two remaining guards had been dismissed. He listened to the news. Marcos was still holding on. There were about to be two inaugurations in the Philippines. Aquino was declaring that she had won the recent election. Enrile and Ramos and a lot of the armed forces were supporting her.

But at Malacanang Marcos and Imelda were also preparing for their own inauguration.

He shook his head. "You have to give him points for tenacity."

"That's not it at all," Fatima said. "He just doesn't have anywhere to go."

He nodded.

"Speaking of going," she added, "let's do just that ourselves. You've done what you came here for, now let's go out and look around a bit. I feel like a prisoner cooped up here."

He frowned. "You want to go shopping after what we've been through?"

She hugged him. "Hey, I'm a woman. Indulge me. Just a little trinket for my charm bracelet."

"Okay." He knew there was very little danger. The number was in his head. It was simple. He had chosen the ages of his family and their birthdates. But he kept it to himself. There was no need to burden Fatima.

They left the hotel, planning to return in time to pack before meeting the 707. A taxi carried them through the streets to a department store. Joseph cooed softly, bundled warmly against the biting cold.

Inside the department store, they went to the jewellery counter. There were so many charms to choose from. Fatima loved this part, he knew as he stood beside her, Joseph perched in his arms, watching his mother and the shiny metal objects she was picking up and putting down. She finally picked one. After it was wrapped and paid for, they browsed through the aisles. Joseph had been returned to his mother. Gerry had relaxed, the stress of the previous hours slipping farther away.

Fatima drifted away. Usually he would have been frustrated. She was like this. They could be walking through a store together and then he would say something to her, only to find she had moved off to look at something. It had happened now. He turned. She was half a dozen paces away, bending over a display of silk scarves. He grinned. There was lots of time.

He felt the hard metal poke into his back at the same time as he heard the voice behind him.

"One move, Roa, and you're a dead man right where you stand." The voice was brusque and spoke in English, British English.

He felt more disappointed than frightened.

"Don't even think of turning around. Just move off to the right, quickly. Very quickly. We're getting out of here." The metal barrel of the gun pushed harder and a hand gripped his elbow long enough to point him down an aisle that led to an exit.

Through the glass doors he could see another man watching him. It was the man from the lobby of the hotel, the one who had been reading the newspaper. The man had his hand in his jacket pocket.

There was a sudden commotion beside him. He spun around.

The gunman was falling to the ground, the pistol clattering to the floor as it fell from his hand. Gerry recognised the new man, the one who had clubbed the gunman with the butt of a revolver. It was the security chief who had organised the operation at the bank.

"I thought this might happen," the man said quickly. "So I took it on myself to keep an eye on you."

"You alone?"

"Yes."

Then he remembered the man outside. "There's another one . . ."

But it was too late. The man had come through

the door, his hand out of his pocket, a gun levelled at them. It fired once.

The security man was hit in the face. He flew backwards, smashing into a display which collapsed. There was screaming everywhere in the room as people reacted.

Gerry reached down and scooped up the gunman's pistol.

There was another shot. It went over his shoulder as he bent down, hitting an elderly woman in the shoulder. The screaming and bedlam increased.

The gunman was still coming.

Gerry held the pistol in two hands and squeezed off three shots. The gunman dived behind a counter. It was all the time Gerry needed. He swung around and ran back to where Fatima was standing, terror in her eyes. "Come on," he yelled, grabbing the baby from her and racing into an aisle where the displays effectively hid them from where the second gunman had taken cover.

They raced through the big room, elbowing people out of the way, taking advantage of the growing chaos around them. He was moving toward a second room. They went through the doorway. He took an instant to look back. Store security was moving in around the fallen men. He couldn't see the second gunman. He pushed Fatima toward an exit.

Outside, the street was filled with cars and trucks. There was a taxi rank at the corner. He slowed them down as they approached. "Keep hold of yourself," he said to her. "We can't alert the driver." The gun was in his pocket.

They climbed into the taxi.

"Where to?" the driver asked.

"The airport."

"Cointrin?"

"Yes."

The driver shrugged and pulled away.

He pushed her back in the seat, away from the window. As they passed the store the second gunman appeared in the doorway. He looked up and down the street, obviously angry at having lost them.

"Do you have the passports?"

She was recovering. "Yes."

"Good." He had counted on that. She always carried them when they were out of the country, keeping them in her purse. Without them they would have been trapped. They couldn't take the risk of going back to the hotel.

"Who was the man who helped you?" she asked very quietly so the driver wouldn't hear.

"One of the security men from this morning. He thought we were at risk so he followed us—thank God."

"He was shot . . ."

"I know." It had all happened so fast. There was nothing he could do about it now. Nothing at all.

"What are we going to do?"

"We're getting the first plane out of here."

"To where?"

"It doesn't matter. We've got to put some distance between us and whoever is after us."

She was silent for the rest of the ride.

* * *

At Cointrin they moved swiftly into the departure lounge. He scanned the departure boards. The only flight within the hour was a Lufthansa entry for Rome. That would have to do, he knew. At the ticket counter, his credit card and their passports were enough to get them tickets. First-class tickets, the only ones left. The clerk raised an eyebrow when told they had no baggage, but assigned them seats without saying anything. A sale was a sale.

They started toward the customs check-in and he stopped.

"What's wrong?" she said, alarmed.

He looked around. "The gun. I've got the gun in my pocket. It'll set the metal detector off." He hated the idea of leaving it behind, but he had no choice. He steered her to a seat and sat beside her. At his elbow was a small table and a discarded newspaper. He casually picked it up, pretended to read it for a moment. Then he folded it over and took the pistol out of his pocket and slid it into the fold. "Let's go."

They stood up and walked toward the customs check-in. There was a litter bin on the way and he deposited the newspaper and the gun into it. He felt naked without the gun. It was all that had saved him. Those three shots had sent the gunman for cover, giving them valuable seconds to flee. He shrugged. "Come on."

They cleared customs and moved down the long corridor to the boarding area. He felt safer now. The only way anyone could get at them now was to have a ticket for the same flight, and he was sure whoever was after him didn't know what they were doing. The thought only provided momentary solace: he could be wrong. He had made that error, believing they were safe, and look what had happened. They had got to him; they had almost had him. He shook his head hard, scrambling the thought.

Fatima was tense. Joseph was whining. She opened her purse and took out the one baby bottle she had with her. It had juice in it. The moment the nipple went into the infant's mouth, he sucked greedily.

A few minutes later the first boarding call came and they followed the other passengers aboard. At least it would be comfortable, he thought, fondling the first-class tickets.

CHAPTER THREE

I couldn't believe the flurry of activity. It was as if the whole city was living on adrenalin alone. People were waiting impatiently, noisy and expectant. There were so many places I could have been but Chester and I had agreed. We were still running our team effort. He'd stay as close to Enrile and Ramos as possible and I'd try to get through to Malacanang Palace. There were a few thousand people crowded around the Mendiola bridge leading to the palace, facing a couple of hundred soldiers who were supposed to be guarding the last approaches to Marcos' stronghold. The crowd, for the most part, seemed more festive than aggressive. But the soldiers facing the civilians looked nervous and among their ranks were many whose faces suggested outright fear. The whole scene had the tenuous feeling of a powder keg. The slightest spark would set off the explosion.

I'd had to walk the last four blocks to get to the bridge. The taxi couldn't get any closer because of the press of the crowd. By the time I'd worked my way up to the front of the crowd it was almost nine o'clock. The darkness was made even more eerie with the crowd starkly lit by extra security lighting that had been hastily manhandled into place.

Everywhere I turned there were rumours. Marcos had left the palace. Marcos was still inside. He and the First Lady had taken an overdose of sleeping pills. They were dead. They were in the gaudy disco inside the palace partying after the fantasy-like inauguration ceremony earlier in the day.

There was no way I could get to the palace. The gap between the noisy crowd and the waiting soldiers was a dangerous no-man's land. Everyone seemed to know it. Neither side made any attempt to occupy it. The soldiers were getting more and more restless. I felt cut off from the story I was supposed to be reporting. Around me important events were taking place and I couldn't get near enough to witness them unfolding first hand. I eyed the gap. It was only a few paces. Then I looked at the soldiers and held back. At Aguinaldo and Crame the soldiers Marcos had ordered in had backed down in the face of nuns and old ladies with flowers and had gone over to the rebels. But these soldiers, here at the bridge, included seasoned veterans, elite loyalists.

Suddenly a hush fell across the crowd. The thumping of helicopter blades was obvious in the night sky. There was a buzz of expectancy. The young woman beside me, holding a sleeping baby, looked scared.

"Gunships?" she asked me.

I shook my head. I had no idea, but if they were gunships and they were headed this way the crowds were sitting ducks. There were just too many people filling the streets for any kind of quick movement to cover. I peered into the sky. For an instant I caught sight of four dark shapes, navigation lights out, moving across the sky and then dipping out of sight into the palace compound. Marcos was getting visitors. Friendly or hostile?

Four helicopters were far too few to herald an invasion of the palace compound.

Across the gap the soldiers were fidgeting. A number of them were crowding around a jeep with a long whip antenna. There was some arguing.

I looked at my watch. Just after nine. The crowd remained quiet and expectant. A few minutes later, the helicopters could be heard lifting away. For an instant they appeared in the sky and then they turned north, away from the palace. Clark Air Base, I said to myself. I took a wild guess: the president and his lady were gone. It was almost over. It was just a guess—an educated one, though. Sooner or later Marcos had to recognise the incredible pressure being exerted by the people. His position had been untenable for hours now.

The crowd was buzzing. I wasn't the only one guessing the sequence of events. Across the gap the soldiers were looking even more uncertain. The movements around the communications jeep were more animated. The officer got into the jeep and waved at the driver. The jeep turned and started back over the bridge toward the palace gates. It was a signal. Other soldiers slung their rifles and started moving the barricades of barbed wire out of the way. One of them finally waved at the crowd. It was a wave beckoning the people forward. The time had come!

It was like a coming wave, racing up the sloping sand, almost sizzling. It grew until everyone was part of it. A hiss, a cheer, then more yells of delight. The whole street surged forward. I was carried along by the momentum of pressing bodies. If Aguinaldo and Crame had coined the phrase "People Power", then this was it in its raw, physical form. The soldiers disappeared into the mass. I saw a nun embrace one of the younger soldiers and then, arm in arm, they started forward joyfully over the bridge.

We rolled forward, up the rise onto the bridge until the palace gates could be seen in the distance. Everyone was starting to run. We passed Central Escolar University on the right, the buildings in darkness. There were more dark school buildings on the left. A bell started to peal and I couldn't escape the irony of it. The church, tucked in almost against the walls of the palace, was named for St Jude, the patron saint of hope—of the hopeless. It might have been hopeless once, for so many years, but here we were now, before the gates of the palace.

They were locked and sealed and obviously unguarded. There could be no doubt now. Marcos had fled. Everyone was giddy with excitement; hundreds of Filipinos literally scaled the walls. Before long the gates were broken down. The palace lay before us, the inside of which was a sight most Filipinos had always believed they would never see.

They swept through the Spanish-style buildings. This former seat of absolute power had been breached.

I followed the leaderless first wave and entered the grand buildings. Everywhere the opulence was staggering. It was the way I would have imagined Versailles or Buckingham Palace, where wealth could be displayed without appearing overtly ostentatious. But not here, not this way, not in this country where starvation was an epidemic and the poor and those with nothing were in the vast majority.

The walls were hung with rows of expensive oil paintings, the shining chandeliers were everywhere I looked—staggeringly beautiful at first glance and then turning, with my stomach, into mere symbols of decadence.

A young Filipino tapped me on the shoulder. "Julian, want a souvenir?"

It was Tony Sorrento, a good-looking kid who'd worked in the palace for a couple of years. We'd met once when I was interviewing Marcos and we'd stayed in touch. He had told me little during those two years, maintaining a loyalty to his employer that I'd come to admire even though I found it frustrating. Now he was standing in front of me, a silver candelabra in one hand and some kind of pearl necklace in the other. They looked expensive enough to meet his grocery bills for the next decade.

"What the hell happened?" I asked him, stepping aside as someone went past carrying a large painting.

"He's gone. Here one minute, gone the next. Took most of his relatives and aides with him."

"What about Ver?" I asked, referring to chief of staff Fabian Ver.

"He went too. No way he could stay here. They'd string him up for killing Benigno, whether he was guilty or not." Then he laughed. "And he was guilty!"

We stopped talking for a moment. There was a shout from an upper balcony and a couple of young men appeared carrying a massive oil painting of Marcos and his First Lady. She was dressed like a princess and painted to look far more beautiful than she'd ever appeared in real life, and he was wearing a uniform with more medals than he could have legitimately earned in three lifetimes. With great glee one of the men ripped a knife through the canvas, then they raised the painting up high and threw it to the marble floor below. The ornate frame fragmented and slivers

39

flew across the marble. The crowd roared its collective approval and then everyone was racing on to explore the myriad rooms.

"Come on, I want to show you a treasure that would make King Midas envious," Tony said, taking me by the arm and wheeling me off down a long corridor.

Tony had been at Malacanang long enough to know all the back routes. "I want you to see something before the rest of them get there."

I followed him, wishing I'd had enough brains to bring a camera.

He soon paused before a set of ornate doors. "This is Imelda's suite. If you think the president was a crook, you should see what his lady amassed." He elbowed his way through the doors.

Whatever I was ready for, it wasn't what lay beyond that entrance. The suite was a combination of the best boutiques, the most expensive department stores. There were two queen-sized beds on elevated platforms.

Tony threw open a door to a bathroom. The tub looked like gold.

"Solid," he confirmed.

There were rows and rows of shoes.

"And downstairs in a basement room there are more than two thousand pairs some of them not even out of the boxes they came in. All the same size. All for Imelda. There's five shelves of Gucci handbags, most of which cost more than your average Filipino makes in a year."

I was astounded. I'd heard the stories and I'd believed the First Couple splurged a lot, but nothing like this. Tony steered me into a room that looked like a vault filled with shelves of jewellery boxes, many of which were open. Even the lesser pieces that had been left behind, scattered as though they had been hurriedly appraised and discarded as sub-standard, would command a king's ransom. It was ostentation beyond bad taste. It was manifestly obscene.

The sound of the approaching crowd was loud on the level below. Somewhere raucous rock-and-roll music was playing.

"They've found the disco. They had some great parties in there with many well-known internationals," Tony explained as he led me down another corridor.

Here and there paintings had been removed from the walls. Only the special holders and the pin lights remained in place. "Where'd it all go?" I asked, as we clambered down a carpeted staircase, moving against an excited crowd.

"Overseas," Tony answered, "during the past few months. Marcos might not have known he was finished until today but he certainly stashed away enough loot in case this day ever really came."

"Plus what he must have taken with him tonight."

"Chickenfeed compared to some of the treasures and cash carried out of here by some of his friends."

We moved out into a courtyard. A torn portrait of Imelda floated, half covered with muddy water, in a fountain in the middle of the yard.

"Friends like who?" I asked, wondering how much Tony really knew and how much he might be making up just to impress me.

He named a number of men, most of whom I had heard of. Sycophants. I believed Tony. Those who had escaped had a reason to be away on this particular night.

"And Roa was sent to Geneva with a lot of cash," Tony added.

I was surprised. "Gerry Roa of the shipping line?"

"One and the same."

I'd met Gerry and his wife, Fatima, on a couple of occasions. I didn't know him well but he'd hosted a journey to the Hundred Islands, north of Manila, to show off the *Imelda* when she was commissioned. "When did he go?"

"Couple of days ago. Rumour in the palace had it that he took millions and millions in American dollars."

We were interrupted by the arrival of a jeep filled with soldiers. They were under the command of a colonel and they were businesslike, obviously there to take control on behalf of the new government.

"I think we'd better get out of here," Tony said quickly, obviously realising that former employees of the deposed president might be better off out of sight for a few days.

"Time I got out of here, too," I said. "Want to come with me?"

He looked grateful for my offer and nodded. "This way."

We had little trouble getting out. The farther we got away from the palace the thinner the crowds became. It was only a matter of a few hours, I knew, before the country would hear the news. Then the real party would start.

I turned to Tony. "Tell me about Roa's trip."

"Not much to tell, Julian. He was one of the couriers. They loaded him up with a case of money and he took off from Clark with his wife and kid."

Tony didn't know much more than that. But it was enough to suggest a good story when the excitement of the revolution and Cory's People Power died down. I filed it away for future reference.

CHAPTER FOUR

Gerry Roa was still trying to figure out what to do next as he cleared his family through customs at Leonardo da Vinci airport and started the 30-kilometre taxi journey into Rome. They had been here before. It was a city they had both fallen in love with. It had been, so many years ago, the city in which they had spent some of their honeymoon. The weather was much warmer here than in Geneva, the Mediterranean breezes at this time of the year keeping much of the night chill away and warming the day. From the back seat of the taxi he could see the shining dome of St Peter's inside the narrow confines of Vatican City. He was not enjoying the view.

They had agreed on the Baroque-style Giulio Cesare Hotel, Via Degli Scipione, where they had stayed before. It had been intimate then, on the Vatican side of the Tiber River. For a moment he remembered the walks they had taken, hand in hand, without any cares, through the Vatican City one day, to the Piazza del Popolo and the Palace of Justice another day. He had such memories of this city—the Coliseum, the ruins of the Forum and the Circus Maximus on the Palatine Hill. Those memories seemed such a long way away, almost as if they belonged to someone else.

By the time they reached the hotel, he had the first part of a plan ready. He watched Fatima as they stood in the elevator on the way up to their rooms. She had been very quiet on the aeroplane, caressing Joseph and trying unsuccessfully to sleep. She had shunned the food the solicitous stewardesses had offered.

In the room he knew the time had come to tell her what he had in mind. She wasn't going to like it—but he knew there was no real alternative.

"I want you to go to Australia and stay with your father." He was sure she would be safe with Miguel Santamaria. It was the one steadfast rock he could think of to cling to at this time.

She had put Joseph to sleep in a small cot in the master bedroom, and now faced him in the small living room. "Not without you," she said resolutely.

He shook his head. "My darling, I can't go with you. Not yet. I have no idea how safe we are here. Until I know we're safe, you must do as I ask."

"Why, Gerry?" There were tears in her eyes. "Why must I leave you?"

He moved to her, cradling her gently in his arms. "For Joseph's sake."

She sobbed and he felt the tears wet his shirt. She tried to argue and he spoke softly to her. She knew, and he knew she knew, that he was right. Santamaria's country estate north of Sydney was the safest place in the world for her and Joseph. If they came for him here, Gerry would stand a much better chance alone. It had been one of the conditions he had finally accepted on the aeroplane from Geneva. Whoever they were, they really wanted the number of the account. Having failed to get the money before it was banked, they had to have the number. If they caught him he would never be able to stand their tortures. He was not a brave man, except maybe to Fatima. The pain they would inflict would make him talk. And if he gave them the number he was sure of what they would do next. They would kill him. He shuddered.

Later, when she was quiet and had agreed to go, he called the airport. There was a Qantas flight that evening. He booked seats. There were only two things left to be done. He called Santamaria, told him little, only that Fatima would be arriving and she would tell him the rest.

Soon after the phone call, when she was in the shower he went to the cot where Joseph was sleeping. He found the small yellow rattle that was shaped like a duck. It had been with the baby all the time, fastened by a short cord pinned securely to the blanket. Carefully, so he wouldn't wake the baby, he unpinned the rattle and took it to the small desk by the window.

He had difficulty getting the rattle off its handle but the duck finally came loose. Inside was a small metal ball that produced the sound. At first he had thought of writing the number on a piece of paper and merely putting the paper inside the duck. But he realised that wouldn't work. It would stop the ball from bouncing around. The rattle wouldn't rattle and Fatima would try to fix it. She couldn't know the number. It would be too dangerous for her.

Staring down at the hard plastic, he tried to figure it out. He had to hurry. She was getting out of the shower. He ran his finger down the cord, swearing silently as he pricked his finger on the open pin. He sucked the spot of blood from the small puncture and an idea came to him. It was crude, but it would do.

Swiftly he took the pin, pushed its point inside the hard plastic and started scratching. After the first two numbers had been scratched on the inside of the rattle he held it up and looked inside. They were clearly readable. He finished the number and slipped the handle back on. By the time Fatima came into the room he had finished and was straightening Joseph's covers, the duck once again fastened to the blanket.

She stood in the doorway, one towel wrapped around her hair and another held in front of her.

He straightened up and looked at her, feeling the tenderness he had tried to push away during the past couple of hours. It wouldn't go. Instead it flooded him, bringing tears to his eyes. As if she could sense it, she dropped the towel from her body and remained very still, letting him feast his eyes on her nakedness. Then, after a long pause, she walked across the room to him, taking his trembling hands and lifting them to her neck and slowly lowering them across her damp skin.

Hours later he kissed her goodbye at the airport, fighting back his tears but knowing it was the only way. He took the baby in his arms, lifting him up so their eyes met. *For Joseph,* he said to himself, *this is all for Joseph.* The baby held the little yellow duck and pushed it out at him until it hit his nose. He kissed the baby warmly. Then he gave his son back to his wife and watched them disappear around the partition into the safety of the security area leading to the waiting lounges.

The paranoia was strong. As he walked through the busy terminal he kept imagining men watching him, eyes that met his and were then averted, eyes that seemed to stray from behind magazines and newspapers to seek him out. He concentrated on the next stage of his plan to try and focus his attention away from all those eyes. There was no way the men could have followed him here. What had happened in Geneva had occurred so quickly. Whoever had been chasing him wouldn't have had time to react. The only link was the passenger list at Cointrin. He had used his real name; he had to do that in order to use the red diplomatic passports. The next step in his plan would cut that link, sever the only connection between him and his pursuers.

He went into the terminal's coffee shop and sat down at the only empty table. Ordering coffee, he took out a railway schedule and started running his pen down the timetable. Finding what he wanted, he drew a line under the listing. He would go south to Naples, take a local flight to Cagliari on the island of Sardinia, wait for a day and then fly to Athens and on to Hong Kong. He would be close to home then. It would be easier to make contact, to try and fit the pieces of the puzzle together.

As the coffee arrived at his table, a girl bumped his elbow. He looked up. She was a teenager, complete with backpack. She smiled at him and excused herself. For a moment she looked around for a place to sit down. The tables were all occupied.

"May I sit here for a moment?" she asked timidly, her blonde hair washing around her head and partly covering her face.

He smiled. "Certainly."

"Thank you ever so much."

He liked the sound of her voice. "British?"

"Very much so," she answered. "You?"

"Filipino."

She nodded, lowering the backpack to the floor.

"Would you like a coffee?" he asked.

"I'd very much like a tea, but I have my own money."

"Save it for a rainy day." He signalled the waitress and ordered her tea.

47

She looked down at the open train timetable. "Taking a train ride?"

"To Naples," he said, and then realised his error. "I think." He folded the timetable and put it into his shirt pocket. He dismissed her query. His paranoia was getting the best of him. He was even suspicious of teenage girls.

She nodded and changed the subject. "Have you been in Italy long?"

"Just passing through. I've been here before though."

"It's my favourite city," she told him, "after Paris, I guess. There's so much history here, so much to see."

They talked about the sights of Rome for a few minutes until her tea arrived. She sipped it and smiled at him. Her face was young and so pale, he thought, and yet the eyes sparkled like the eyes of the woman he had just kissed goodbye. He looked at his watch. Time to go.

He stood up.

She made no attempt to rise. "Thanks for the tea. Have a safe journey," she said to him.

"You too." He walked away, leaving her at the table and paying at the cash register by the door. As he crossed the terminal he looked back. She was still sitting at the table, her teacup in her hand, her blonde hair hanging long and loose around her young face. For a brief instant he felt envious of her carefree spirit. If only he and Fatima could find that time of their lives again.

* * *

Rome's central railway station was east of the city's centre. The taxi ride had been expensive, the driver was ill-tempered and it had taken a long time to battle their way through the clogged streets. He got out in a piazza and entered the station. There were lines at every window and it took him some time to get his ticket. The journey was only a few hundred kilometres, but he paid the extra lire for a first-class sleeper. He wanted the privacy. Once aboard he pulled the curtains half shut and watched the crowds moving back and forth on the platform. Twice he thought he saw a flash of blonde hair that reminded him of the girl in the coffee shop. Both times he dismissed it all. He knew it was only his fears, but the knowledge didn't make it any easier.

He felt a sense of satisfaction as the train started to move. He was on his way. He looked at his watch. Fatima and Joseph would be safely high over the Mediterranean by now and in a few minutes he would be thundering along the line to the south. He lay back and closed his eyes, letting the rattle of the train lull him into a light doze.

He awoke some time later as the train pulled into a station. He had slept well. He felt rested and the paranoia had dwindled away. There was the luxury now of believing he might just make it through whatever lay ahead. Peering out into the dusk he read the station sign: Gaeta. They was well down the Italian coast. Hunger pains reminded him he hadn't eaten since the night before. He toyed with the idea of having a meal brought to his sleeper but the cramped room was becoming claustrophobic. He needed to get out. The train started rolling, pulling away from the station. He watched until they were clear of the small city, then rubbed his stomach. It was time to eat. He remembered a dining car three or four carriages forward, toward the engine.

Opening the door he started up the carriage corridor, stumbling as the train picked up speed. A few more paces and he was moving with the gentle sway of the floor. He opened the doors between the carriages. The next car was a standard coach, filled with adults and noisy children. He had made the right choice; the sleeper might be more expensive but it was also much quieter. He paused as a fat Italian woman backed into the aisle and opened a picnic hamper for her children. When she realised he was standing there, she apologised in a long torrent of busy Italian and let him pass.

He had trouble with the doors leading to the next coach. One of them stuck but he gave a push with his shoulder and it opened. He walked forward three or four paces, and froze. She was there. The girl with the blonde hair. The girl from the coffee shop. Before he could turn away she looked up and saw him. Her face was no longer smiling. It looked serious and surprised at the same time. She leaned across and spoke to a large man who sprang to his feet and turned swiftly toward him. A second man across the aisle was also on his feet. They were all looking at him, suddenly moving toward him.

Fear gripped him tightly. He swung around and ran down the corridor to the door. It didn't stick this time. He flung both doors wide and hurried down the length of the coach, passing the Italian woman and her children. The men entered the coach as he left the far end. They both had a hand under their jackets, up near their shoulders. He knew what they were holding.

Quickly he swung open the next doors and started down the sleeper corridor. For an instant he thought of the safety of his cramped room and then dismissed it. He would be trapped there if he entered. He could only keep moving.

They were closer now, trying to run without causing too much disruption. The next car was also a sleeper and Gerry gained a few moments as an old man left his cabin after he had passed. As he left the carriage he could hear the gunmen yelling at the man to get out of their way.

There was a large sign on the door of the next carriage. It was in three languages: French, Italian and English. No Admittance. Staff Only. He was trapped. He tried the handle. The door swung open. He raced through. Cargo. Boxes and crates, but there was nowhere to hide. He ran the length of the car and swung open the next door. There was nothing there—just a small iron platform and railing and the track flashing by below. He was at the end of the train.

The men entered. They slowed down, guns finally out. They knew they had him. There was nowhere for him to go. He turned and went out onto the platform, slamming the door shut. A ladder led to the roof and he swung onto it.

The train was winding through a narrow, rocky gorge. Off to the left was a massive rock wall, to the right a cliff and far below a river with white water that crashed against jagged rocks.

He almost slipped as the train veered around a corner. He gripped the rungs tightly and climbed. His hands caught the roof. As he swung his leg over, the door below opened and a gunman stepped out onto the platform. He had to get away. He was down on his stomach, sliding forward over the dirty roof. His muscles cramped as he waited for the bullet that would end it all. He was halfway along the roof.

His heart dropped as he stared ahead toward the distant engine. The second gunman had climbed up the ladder at the other end of the coach and was now scrambling onto the roof. He glanced behind. There was a man there too. They had cut him off, front and back. They had him.

He stood up, balancing precariously. The men

had put their guns away. They wanted him alive and the guns had only been a precaution in case he was armed. They had guessed right. And so had he. They wanted him alive because they wanted the number. Without the number they couldn't get at the money. But how had they known? The girl? Obviously the girl. He'd told her Naples. But this particular train? And then it was all clear. She had been looking down at the timetable. He had drawn a line under the time of the train to Naples. She had caught him.

The men were close now. Neither of them said a word. The train raced out onto a small bridge spanning a vast chasm where the river far below boiled and turned beneath the track. He would never be able to stand their torture, and they would kill him anyway. He moved toward the edge of the carriage. It was such a long way down. His heart ached for Fatima and Joseph. They would never know. *I love you two,* he said as he jumped, pushing himself away from the carriage, feeling no joy at having cheated the two men. It was almost over. The Tagalog words of his beloved Philippines came to his lips one last time as he smashed into the sharp rocks far below—*Mahal ko kayo.*

CHAPTER FIVE

It was all over in just seventy-eight hours ...

Chester and I kept slapping each other on the back, as if this had been our revolution. It wasn't, of course. It belonged to the smiling throngs who had burst into the streets. We were just caught up in it. It had been a long time since I had seen so much colour and warmth in the streets of the normally staid financial district of Makati. Exploding fireworks echoed between the modern buildings and a snowstorm of yellow confetti fell from the windows where workers peered out, singing and shouting. Ayala Avenue echoed with the braying of horns. There was too much traffic. No one was moving. No one wanted to move. They were savouring the moment. Along the sidewalks, vendors were doing a brisk business selling T-shirts. The most popular had big letters: C-O-R-Y. Chester pointed out a toddler swinging on the hip of a very young mother. On the back of the baby's T-shirt was the slogan: JUST LIBERATED.

"Wonder how they'll feel about all this tomorrow morning?" Chester yelled at me over the din.

I didn't bother answering. For all her charisma, Cory now faced serious economic and reform problems. It had to be worrying. Her battle was probably best summed up in something Bertrand

Russell once said: if one man offers you democracy and another offers you a bag of grain, at what stage of starvation will you prefer the grain to the vote? But that was for tomorrow. Today there was only rejoicing.

A couple of hours amid the noise and celebrating and we'd had enough. We both had stories to write and file. My place was as good as any, we agreed. It took us another couple of hours to get across the city through the crowds to my hotel. What taxis were operating were mostly being driven by Filipinos who had been hitting the bottle as part of the festivities. I joked with Chester about becoming a casualty after the revolution was over. He didn't even smile as he gripped the front seat to steady himself when the taxi swerved through a long line of street dancers.

* * *

It took us the rest of the night to wrap it up. We exchanged notes on what we had seen and what we knew. We used the phone to try and get through to clarify a few points. And we wrote, grinding it out, trying to capture on innocuous paper what it was like to be right in the middle of history, to be present at the end of one era and the joyous burden of a new birth. I had a feeling, and Chester agreed, that if Cory Aquino and her colleagues thought it was tough getting this far, then they had a rude awakening facing them in the first light of dawn on day one of their administration. It was going to be an uphill battle all the way.

When the stories had been put together, we did our own skirmishing with the international telephone operators to get an outside line to phone our reports through—Chester to New York and me to Melbourne. The disembodied voices on the other ends of the lines told us we'd done well and suggested we get some rest. Understatement, at least about the rest. We were both asleep within minutes of hanging up the phone. The television youngsters could head for the bar after filing their stories, but not us. We'd both learned a golden rule about this kind of news: rest when you can get it because the only thing certain about the course of a revolution is that, at best, it's all uncertain.

The next morning we split up to make our rounds, to try and put together the aftermath. The city was much quieter, the emotions played out, the glitter already starting to fade as everyone realised you can't eat principles.

Three days later things, at least from my point of view, were getting back to normal. Our biggest problem was journalists trying to beat up the story into something it wasn't. I'd seen it happen before. No revolution can seem complete without a lot of bodies and blood and the newshounds, at least some of them, were acting as if they'd been cheated. They wanted to see murder and mayhem where there wasn't any.

Chester and I were disgusted. But there wasn't much we could do except keep reassuring our touchy editors that what we were filing was the truth, no matter how somebody else's papers might be painting the scene.

We were back to breakfasting at our old haunt, Taza De Oro, a small cafe tucked away off Roxas Boulevard and facing across the main highway onto Manila Bay. It was an institution among Filipino journalists and a few of the foreign correspondents, a very unofficial, very relaxed journalists' club. I was halfway through chicken adobo and a third cup of coffee when Chester arrived.

He settled in and we exchanged what we had. It was meagre. Everywhere we turned was uncertainty. There was also a slight change in the way Chester and I were doing business. We didn't need to talk about it. It was understood. For the big story that was larger than both of us, we teamed up. But the big story was fading now. It was digging time now. Analysis and commentary, they sometimes call it. Feature time. Magazine-type stuff. Perhaps, if you were lucky, an exclusive. *Scoop,* they used to call it. That was something you did alone.

The conversation swung away from the news.

"Got a letter from Jade this morning," Chester said with a frown.

"Bad news?"

He laughed hollowly through his frown. "She wants me to write an article for an anthology she and some of her *comrades* are working on."

"What subject?"

"Can you believe it? The Downtrodden of Asia."

I chuckled. "That covers us correspondents. Lots of fertile ground there."

He shook his head, not prepared to be amused. "She reminds me of a couple of editors I've known. Preconceived position. She even had the audacity to provide a list of headings I could write to, like we were in some kind of political science class out here."

I baited him. "What are they?"

He took the letter from his pocket, turned to the second page and handed it to me. The script was flowing and well formed, almost delicate. It matched the more recent photographs of her, but certainly not the scrawny teenager I'd once met. I read the lines: "American interference in sovereign nations. Multinational rape of pastoral lands."

"Enough," Chester interrupted. "Don't remind me."

I folded the letter and handed it back to him. "I take it you're not going to write the piece."

He had a twinkle in his eye. "I've half a mind to write a piece for her. But when she read it she'd probably launch another demonstration in the streets, the time against her old man."

"She'll grow out of it."

"I keep telling myself that. But she's already twenty-five. Time for her to get married and have kids."

I was trying to find an appropriate retort when the black-and-white television set on the bar drew my attention. A routine news bulletin had been droning away, the words going in one ear and out the other. Television was behind the times as far as I was concerned. Headline stuff. No depth. But what drew my attention was a picture on the screen. It was Gerry Roa—the man Tony Sorrento had told me had carried one hell of a lot of money out of Manila for Marcos.

I'd already missed the first couple of paragraphs and I had to wave Chester silent to hear the rest.

" . . . Italian police tentatively identified the body from a diplomatic passport found on the corpse. No further details are available at this time."

The scene changed to Mindanao and the Moslem insurgency. That was a rehash of an old story. I looked down at my chicken. Italy? That didn't make a lot of sense.

Chester had seen me look this way before. "What you got, Julian?"

I hadn't told him about my conversation with Sorrento. There had been more than enough detail without introducing the Roa rumour. But I wasn't ready to cut Chester loose yet. We had an agreement and the Roa rumour had grown out of our partnership. "The picture on the television was of a guy close to Marcos named Gerry Roa."

"The steamship company boss?"

"The same. At Malacanang on Monday night, one of the servants I'd met before told me Marcos had sent Roa to Geneva with quite a few million American dollars, to be deposited in a bank account for the president."

He looked interested. "He wouldn't have been the first to carry money out."

"Eat your fish while I check something." I got up and went to the bar. Taza de Oro's manager was propped up on a stool beside the television. It was on Channel Nine. I knew the news editor there. The manager was used to guys like me. I put a few pesos on the bar and he replaced them with the telephone.

A few minutes later I was back at the table. Chester pushed his empty plate aside and looked at me expectantly.

"The Italian police picked up Roa's body, at least it's his according to the passport and a general description, from the bottom of a gorge halfway between Rome and Naples. Apparently he jumped from a train as it was going over a bridge."

"Suicide?"

I shrugged. "Doesn't make much sense to me. He was one of Marcos' inner circle. All he had to do was join Marcos in exile in Hawaii if he was so inclined."

"Or come back here, if he had nothing to hide," Chester added.

I agreed. "Exactly. So what's he doing smashed up on some rocks in Italy?"

"He's married, isn't he? Seems I remember something in the society pages about his wife having a baby recently."

I nodded. "That's right. I met her when they launched the line's new flagship. Nice lady."

We sat silent for a moment.

"You want we should work on it?" Chester finally asked.

He was giving me an out. "I don't think we have much yet, but I'll make a deal with you."

He was instantly suspicious. "What deal?"

I looked serious. "Two things. I'll work on the Roa angle for a day or so and share it with you, while you keep tabs on Cory and her mob."

"Deal," he acknowledged. "You said two things. What's the second?"

I got up from my seat. "You pay for breakfast." I headed for the door.

CHAPTER SIX

The Australian voice on the telephone was very angry, a kind of controlled anger that sounded even more ominous for its lack of raving. "I'm extremely disappointed in the failure of your efforts. We were counting very much on adding that money to our coffers."

The American voice was bland and defensive. "We almost had him, but then he went and killed himself."

"I told you very clearly to get the money before it was deposited. Instead, you allow him to hand it over to the bank and then you let him lead you a merry chase to Rome. I don't pay you to fail."

The American responded carefully. "I'm sorry. I won't fail you again. I already have a candidate picked out for the new assignment."

"You'd better succeed this time," the Australian threatened, the anger still ripe and patently understated. He didn't wait for an answer before hanging up.

The American stood rigidly beside the large window in his hotel room, still holding the telephone. His knuckles were white and stretched. His hand shook slightly as he finally relaxed enough to replace the handset. A migraine was beginning from some deep, dark recess in the back of his head. He fought back a sense of depression and stared blankly out at the morning frost lying heavy and white across the trees and lawns of Washington's Arlington National Cemetery.

* * *

The noisy street march was one of those innumerable demonstrations largely ignored by average Americans, even more ignored by the politicians to whom it was directed, and taken seriously only by the demonstrators, the media— mostly television because of the chance of getting pictures of confrontation—and the police charged with the unenviable responsibility of getting the marchers off the street with a minimum of violence before their antics and placards held up the traffic and created jams in the homeward-bound lines abandoning Washington for weekend retreats.

This particular demonstration was not much different from the others. A dozen men and women blocked an intersection with placards and chants decrying the current Administration's policies on Nicaragua, El Salvador and Central America in general. There were television news crews filming for the nightly bulletin and the cameras were working their way toward one particularly pretty woman, standing in the middle of the ragged oval formed by the marchers. She had a megaphone and was counting the cadences for their chants.

"What do we want?" she yelled.

"America out!" the crowd chanted loudly, making up for their lack of numbers by shouting enthusiastically.

"Out of where?" she asked them through the megaphone that made her voice sound almost tinny.

"Out of Nic-ar-agua!" they answered her, accenting the last syllable.

"When do we want it?" she exhorted them.

"Now!" they answered her.

A television reporter turned to face his camera, microphone to his mouth, the woman in the background and the marchers crowded around him. He nodded at the cameraman.

"Any time you want to start," the skinny man handling the camera yelled at him above the roar of the chants in the background.

"This is Paul Donnelly reporting from Pennsylvania Avenue. To my left is the White House and behind me is Dr Jade Price and her followers who have this week been highly visible in their demonstrations against the White House policy of aiding the Contras in their continuing campaign against the Sandinista government in Nicaragua."

He turned toward the woman.

She was ready, lowering her megaphone and smiling as she waited for the questions. She'd done this before.

"Dr Price, do you have any indication that anyone in the White House is listening to the message you and your followers have been trying to get across?"

Her voice was much softer, almost lyrical, without the megaphone. "They're listening. That's one of the things they're paid to do. To listen to the people. They'll hear what we have to say."

"But will they really do anything about it?" the reporter asked.

The woman smiled. "Our message is the right one. They'll have to listen. The United States has no right to be involved in the sovereign affairs of another country. Nicaraguans want the Sandinistas to rule."

The reporter had the quotes he wanted. He tried

to interrupt but Dr Jade Price was not finished.

"The United States is causing incredible heartache for the Nicaraguan people. Money they need for health and to feed their people has to be used to arm the country against the American-backed mercenaries coming in from Honduras . . ."

The reporter elbowed her gently away from the microphone and turned back to the camera. "From near the White House, Paul Donnelly, NTV News."

The cameraman lowered his camera.

Jade grinned at him. "One of these days you'll give me a chance to finish my speech."

Donnelly laughed. "Not much chance of that, honey. All our viewers want from you is a oneliner. Anything more than that bores them."

"You guys would have cut the Gettysburg Address after the first line," she said.

"Probably after two or three lines. Lincoln wasn't talking about a place nobody gives a shit about."

Jade shrugged and looked unhappy. She knew he was almost right. Nicaragua didn't really make it as one of the burning issues of the time. If only she could make everyone realise the suffering of the Nicaraguan people. She sighed. Perhaps it was her medical training. She knew about malnutrition. She looked around at the marchers and the people passing on the sidewalk. They weren't suffering enough to care about people who were.

The reporter had moved away, helping the cameraman load the equipment into the station wagon.

Her followers were waiting for her signal to start chanting again but she was tired. "Okay, people, that's enough for today. We meet again tomorrow at ten am, front steps of the Pentagon."

They nodded and drifted away. She watched them go.

The voice that sounded nearby was quiet but demanding. "Dr Jade Price?"

She turned. He was tall and thin, and wore a black overcoat that looked expensive. His face was filled with tight, sharp lines that softened only around the smile and the inquisitive eyes. "Yes."

He reached out his hand and she shook it. There was strength in the fingers. "My name is Arnold Alberts, and I was wondering if I could have a few minutes of your time."

She searched his face. He looked like a reporter, like her father. "I'm tired, Mr Alberts. If you want an interview, perhaps tomorrow . . ."

He laughed pleasantly, interrupting her. "I'm not looking for a newspaper story, Dr Price. Something far more important than that."

She tilted her head, her curiosity obvious.

"I'm interested," he continued, "in knowing whether you would like to do something somewhat more realistic about the cause you so doggedly pursue—about really helping the Nicaraguan people."

"This is pretty real," she answered defensively.

"Granted, if you want fifteen seconds on television and sore feet." He paused. "What I have in mind is something a little more lasting."

She was interested, largely because of the mystery and a little, she admitted selfishly, because he was ruggedly handsome and well spoken. "What is it you're proposing that's so lasting, Mr Alberts?"

"How would you like to lead a medical team into Nicaragua, backed up with money and all the medical supplies you could dream of?"

She said nothing for a minute, shocked at the magnitude of his question. It wasn't very often that people stopped her in the street with offers like he'd just made.

"Just think what you could do for your suffering peasants with that kind of help," he added.

She nodded toward the White House. "The men over there don't look kindly on that sort of assistance."

"Forget them. We don't do it from here. I may sound American, but my boss works out of Australia. His name is William Carson. He's very rich and he likes to use his wealth for good causes. He's decided medical aid to the Nicaraguans is a good cause and he thinks you would make an excellent leader for the medical team he wants to put together."

Her uncertainty showed. "Why me?"

He grinned at her. "Because you care and because you're a medical doctor. Most doctors are too busy trying to make money to have much of a social conscience these days. You interested?"

Jade nodded. "I'm interested."

Alberts took a card out of his pocket and handed it to her. I'm staying at the Sheraton National out in Arlington. Think about it. Call me if you'd like to discuss it further." He turned abruptly and walked away to a waiting limousine.

She looked at the card. It had his name and some Sydney, Australia phone and telex numbers. Across the top of the card in block letters was the name THE DECEMBER FOUNDATION. The name would be easy enough to check, she thought as she looked up and watched the long, white limousine carrying the mysterious Mr Alberts drive away. The fancy vehicle was tangible evidence that Alberts might actually be real. She wasn't foolish enough to take what he had told her at face value. Over at the *Washington Post* there was an editor who knew her father well. She'd called on him before to ask little favours, mostly to allow her into the newspaper's vast library. If the December Foundation was worth knowing about, the *Post* would have a file on it. She hoped there was a file—perhaps, she thought vividly, this was the something more she felt she needed to do about this cause she felt so deeply about.

CHAPTER SEVEN

Arnold Alberts watched from his hotel window high in the building as Dr Jade Price left the hotel and entered a taxi for the ride back into the capital. He was smiling. He had done well. He looked at his watch. It was ten o'clock the next morning in Sydney. He moved across the room to the bar, fixed himself a drink, then crossed to the table and the telephone. He dialled the long ISD number and waited while it rang. It was a private number. Only he and Kasilov had access to it. He frowned and felt the stomach acids trying to reach up into his mouth. Kasilov! He even hated the sound of the Russian's name.

The telephone was ringing. He let his competitor's image drift away and concentrated on the ringing phone. It was picked up. There was a moment's pause while the electronic scramblers took hold of the signal and mixed it up enough to prevent eavesdropping.

"Go ahead," the voice said.

As he took a breath, he thought Carson sounded tired. "Alberts here, Mr Carson. The woman is in. We have our medical doctor. Her name is Jade Price."

"Have you checked out her credentials and background?"

"Yes sir. Credentials are perfect. Walter Reed Hospital for training. Top scores right across the board."

"Connections?"

He hated hiding anything from the man in Sydney. The risks were very high. He was doing it now. But it was only a small thing. So what if her father was a reporter? The two didn't appear to be very close anyway. "No problems there."

"Sounds okay, then. When can I meet her?"

"I'll bring her to Sydney next week. Wednesday your time." Alberts said.

"That'll do just fine."

They hung up.

Alberts disconnected the scrambler box disguised as a small clock radio, crossed to the bed and lay down. He stared at the ceiling and thought of the woman who had just left. She was very pretty. He closed his eyes and recalled the small waist, the perfect flare of her hips and her long legs. For an instant he wondered what it would be like to be with a woman like that, to be wanted by a woman like Jade Price, to run his hands across her fine skin, across those breasts. He dismissed the thought almost as quickly as it had appeared. It was dangerous to think like that. He must never allow himself to contemplate such things. He reined in the galloping heartbeat that had already started thumping hard to match the furious sexual fantasy he was now attempting to turn off.

Arnold Alberts was not what he appeared to be, had never really been as normal as some of his closest friends had believed he was. He accepted that. He knew it, understood it, and took immense pride in the double, sometimes triple, identities that his work forced him to adopt. He had mastered those skills of moving in and out of multiple personalities when he had been with the CIA. Now he was out of the government service, away from those public service ranks and meagre salaries. He was out where the real money was.

He did, indeed, work for William Carson. But Carson's humanitarian aid organisation was, like him, not really what it seemed either. It was, to those few who knew, a front for a very sophisticated international arms dealership. He laughed out loud as he thought about the way he had labelled it. That description was totally inadequate. Carson also provided the men and the training to go with the weapons, from the simplest infantry rifle through the most complex hi-tech equipment. Some of what he sold was so secret that the buyers hadn't even known it existed until Carson briefed them. This was no used car lot. He bought and sold the best and the newest killing machines available and he provided guaranteed training and after-sales service—to anyone who wanted it.

It was all available for a high price, to whomever could afford it regardless of race, creed or political persuasion. It was an extremely profitable global arms and dirty tricks operation. And Arnold Alberts was one of two deputies who ran the network of contacts and put together the deals under Carson's ever-watchful and demanding control. The second deputy was the Russian, Vladimir Kasilov. Kasilov! He conjured up an image of the burly ex-KGB man and winced painfully.

Alberts wanted this new mission, the Nicaraguan deal, to go well because Carson had made a big thing about Kasilov's most recent success—organising and executing a terrorist raid in Athens that had killed more than sixty innocent civilians in a flurry of machinegun fire and exploding grenades. Someone had paid a huge bill for that show. For all his hatred of the Russian, Alberts had to give him grudging credit. Kasilov engineered the whole attack in such a way that the world's press credited the infamous Carlos the Jackal with the act, even though Carlos had never left his villa in the Libyan capital, Tripoli, during the whole time the mission was being planned and carried out. Carson had let Alberts know that Kasilov had done well. The unspoken threat was obvious to the American.

Carson was not too pleased with Alberts. It was Carson who had ordered Alberts to track down Gerry Roa and relieve him of Marcos' $50 million. Carson had done some work for Marcos back in the early 1970s, when the president declared martial law in the Philippines—mostly training right-wing murder squads that Marcos used to keep down dissidents opposed to his iron-fisted rule. One of the killers Carson had trained for Marcos was also put on the Carson payroll to report to the Australian anything that might be useful for the international network. He had reported to Carson that Roa was being dispatched with the $50 million. Another Carson contact—a Filipino air force officer at Clark Air Base—had provided the time and destination of Roa's flight. Alberts had been ordered to intercept Roa and the $50 million.

And Alberts had failed. He had been clumsy and slow and for the first time he had failed dismally. Failure was not acceptable to Carson and redemption must come quickly, Alberts knew. This time it would be very different. There would be success. He would show Carson.

Dr Jade Price was the last cog to be fitted into the machinery Alberts had welded into place for guaranteeing delivery of the major arms shipment to Nicaragua. It had been Kasilov's job to get the weapons into Australia and the Russian had done that efficiently. It was Alberts' job to deliver them to Nicaragua. A shipment of medical supplies had a nice touch of credibility if it was accompanied by a medical doctor with a known record of sympathy for the suffering Nicaraguans to whom the medical supplies had been consigned. Jade Price would be shown just enough of the medicines and hospital equipment—a few crates and a bogus manifest—to keep her happy and unsuspecting of how she was being used.

CHAPTER EIGHT

My research into Gerry Roa started the way most
routine journalism is usually carried out—asking
lots of questions and reading what had already
been written. In the case of what had been written
before, I was wary. 'Don't believe everything you
read' may sound like curious advice coming from
someone allegedly responsible for writing the
news, but I'd been in this business too long not
to be suspicious of alleged facts on the printed
page. So the files provided only a framework for
the questions that had to be asked.

The first thing I wanted was the focus of the
story. Did Gerry Roa carry millions of US dollars
out of the Philippines and, if so, did he commit
suicide? And where was the money now?

As I rode in the taxi towards the corporate offices
of the Roa Steamship Company, I thought the first
premise was that he had not committed suicide
at all—which meant his death was an accident
or murder. I didn't yet know a lot about Roa, but
the one time I had met him, he hadn't seemed
like the kind of man to go strolling on the roof
of a speeding train crossing a bridge over a deep
ravine in central Italy. There was no mistake about
his having been on the roof of the train. The
engineer and his assistant had been able to see

the last car on the train as the track curved across the ravine. They had clearly seen the man fall from the roof. I had that much tied down. The Naples police sergeant wasn't crash-hot with his English, but we managed to work our way through the official report during half an hour on the telephone. I even made him go over a key part of the report twice just to make sure I was hearing him right. There had been, he told me, *three* men on the roof of the train—and only one of them had jumped.

When I asked the Italian cop if the police had questioned the other men, he told me no one knew who they were. He guessed the two might have been trying to talk the would-be suicide out of jumping. That sounded suspicious to me. Why would the two good samaritans disappear rather than talk to the police?

The cop didn't have an answer for that question—in fact, he didn't have anything to add that wasn't in the report. Gerry Roa had jumped from the train or, the cop was prepared to concede, he might have fallen. But, to his Italian mind, both actions were the same. The Filipino had clearly gone up to the roof in order to jump. The cop turned the tables on me quite easily. If the Filipino hadn't intended to jump, the sergeant asked, why in the name of Caesar's ghost was he up on the roof?

To bring in the issue of the millions of American dollars that had supposedly left Manila with Roa would have cluttered up the sergeant's neatly closed mind, so I kept it to myself and ended the conversation. The report had made no mention of the money.

By the time the taxi let me off at the Makati headquarters of the Roa Steamship Company, I had two theories to prove: first, that Gerry Roa hadn't jumped from that train willingly, and secondly, the two mystery men on the roof with him were after the money. By the time the elevator had taken me from the ground floor to the eighth-floor offices of the steamship company, I'd added part of a third theory. Roa had been running from someone or something at the time of his death. Proof was still needed, but it fit. The Italian cop had made no comment about Roa's wife and son, there was no Roa luggage, only a diplomatic passport found on the body. Rich men like Roa who had flown to Geneva would have had little reason to be on a train between Rome and Naples without luggage. There were holes in my theories, but the man I was about to see could either plug them or split them even wider.

Luckily for me, he was prepared to talk. A lot of people were talking now that Marcos was out and Aquino was in, especially when talking helped shift a major part of the responsibility for past misdeeds to a dead man who could no longer defend himself. The morality of such a stance was not something I was going to let interfere at this point. I had too many questions to ask the chubby little vice-president of the company who ushered me into his opulent office with a solemnity that had me believing he really cared about what had happened to his boss.

The politics aside, the vice-president made a couple of contributions to my theories. Roa was a deeply religious man who would never have contemplated suicide. It was *too* great a sin. That bolstered my confidence. He had no idea who might have been pursuing Roa. When I suggested Marcos, he shook his head. He agreed he hated the former president, even more so now that the dictator had fled the country, but *if* Roa had been depositing money in Geneva for Marcos, there would have been no advantage for the embattled leader to order the killing of Roa. I agreed with that thought.

We kept talking, but about the only item of interest was the profile I was developing around the personal life of Gerry Roa. It wasn't evidence as solid as you'd need for a court case but Roa had everything to live for—a beautiful and devoted wife, a son he obviously wanted to protect, and a company of which the new government just might return full ownership to Roa. The vice-president of the line was very guarded about that possibility, but sources close to Aquino were already talking about restoring some of the assets the old regime had corruptly seized from their original owners. Roa Steamships, the chubby little man admitted, fell into that category. So with all this going for him, I asked myself as I left the building, why was Gerry Roa lying dead on a slab in Naples?

* * *

Two hours later I'd tracked down one of the men Marcos had left behind—a man who didn't want to be tracked down by anyone, at least not until after he was sure about his own place in the new order of things. Why would he see me? I guess he'd learned to trust me. Rafael Lorenzo was a senior official of the Philippine National Bank. He'd been a source—both identified and unidentified— on many occasions, and he'd always found that what he had to say to me was reported more or less accurately.

I had three places to look for Rafael. The first was his office and there wasn't much chance of his being there. I wasn't sure about his home in one of Manila's posh suburbs but after the tenth ring, I gave up and put the telephone back on the cradle. I went to my diary, paged back a couple of months and found it. Rafael kept a flat in Malate, along with a beautiful mistress younger than his daughter.

Rafael had nothing much to add, except that the money had really existed and the amount was at least $50 million American dollars. He also told me Roa had used an official VIP jet, part of the president's flight maintained by the Philippine Air Force at Clark. I thanked Rafael, wished him well, admired once again the beauty of his young girlfriend and left for the air base. I held the image of the young Filipina for as long as possible. It was a pleasant thought.

At Clark I knew I was in trouble from the moment I started. I was kept waiting in the gatehouse for an hour. That had never happened before. It was, at least nominally, a Filipino base under the command of a Filipino Air Force general, just as Subic was a huge US Navy base, ostensibly commanded by a Filipino. But everything else was American.

Finally, as I fumed impatiently in the gatehouse, an American turned up who could help me. At least that's what she was there for. Cindy Ross was a lieutenant, a public relations officer. She had answered my questions in the past but when she entered the room this time, she looked unhappy and tense. She made an apology for the delay— an excuse that sounded hollow and reeked of post-coup politics. Cory Aquino was supported by some factions who were clearly anti-American. The Yanks were nervous and it showed, even as far down the ladder as this fresh-faced young lieutenant. I wondered if she'd get around to admitting it. Usually we went to her office, but this time she steered me to an empty office in a temporary building only a few paces from the gatehouse.

She turned to me as soon as the door was closed.

There was no air-conditioning and the place was a sweat box. "What can I do for you, Julian?" she asked without enthusiasm, sweat already staining her tan uniform shirt.

I grinned, not sure what had changed, except a revolution at the palace, since the last time I'd been at the base. According to the textbook the revolution shouldn't have affected the America military base. Strange how textbook theories about foreign relations and reality seldom bear much resemblance. "Not much, Cindy. A couple of pieces of information."

She looked suspicious. "What information? Nobody here is talking about anything."

"No trade secrets. My interest is strictly historical." I paused. "But before I ask, let's put it all off the record for a moment."

She nodded her assent. We'd been through similar exercises in the past. She knew that when I said it was off the record, I meant it. She sighed. "I'm only a simple lieutenant, Julian. If you think *I'm* uptight, you should see the captains and the admirals."

"That only explains what I can already see." I waited.

She wiped a line of sweat off her lightly creased forehead. "Officially we now back Aquino but Marcos was the man who could hold this country together in the face of the communists," she said carefully. "As well, we're not sure Aquino will last. She's in power because of the military and as long as she can keep the military under control she holds on, but we don't know for how long."

Paranoia, I thought. The symbol of superpower foreign policy. Simple paranoia. "Marcos bled this country dry," I argued.

She shrugged. "Sure he did, but there are some things we can overlook. That's one of them.

Strategy, good strategy in this part of the world is what we're talking about. Not civil liberties and land reform."

"Maybe your policies are part of the problem," I countered argumentatively.

"We've got strong communist activity in more than fifty of the seventy-odd provinces in this country. Christ, Julian, a week ago one of our security patrols over at Subic found a New People's Army squad inside the outer perimeter fence within mortar range of one of our ammo dumps." She stopped suddenly, realising she'd given away one of those secrets I'd like most to hear.

I groaned, then smiled at her concern. "Come on, kid. Relax. We said off the record and I meant it."

She relaxed but was obviously not prepared to continue the discussion. "You said you wanted some historical information. What is it?"

"I'd like you to confirm an aircraft movement that might have taken place a few days ago."

"Sounds simple enough."

"I hope so. I believe one of Marcos' VIP fleet flew out of here a day or so before Marcos himself left. The plane went to Geneva and it carried a businessman named Gerry Roa, his wife Fatima and infant son. All I want is confirmation, and I'd also like to know where the plane went after Geneva."

The lieutenant thought about it for a moment. "What's it all about?" she asked.

"Routine. I'm just trying to tie down where some of Marcos' court are." This was not the time to complicate the request with everything else I had.

Cindy crossed the bare office and sat down behind a desk on which a telephone was the only item. She dialled an internal extension, made a few comments and then hung up. She turned to me. "Five minutes, while they ask some questions at operations."

We talked through the minutes. Cindy was in her second year at Clark. She was used to keeping reporters happy. It came down to recognising that most of us were just doing a job, not trying to topple governments or dig up embarrassing state secrets.

The phone rang loudly in the empty room.

Cindy picked it up, listened while someone said something and then looked at me sharply. "Leave it with me," she said. She put the phone down, unsmiling. "Straightforward request for information?" she asked me in a way that suggested she didn't believe me any more.

I kept my mouth shut. Something had stirred someone somewhere.

The lieutenant frowned. "There's a Filipino officer on his way over here to talk to you."

"That's all?" I asked.

"That's all I can say, Julian. We just have to wait until their man gets here."

"You staying?"

She shrugged. "It's their base."

I would have laughed had I not been worried. No one really believed that line. This was an American base, no matter what the imagery suggested. We were both silent for a minute. I was about to open the topic from a new angle when the door opened and a Filipino Air Force captain walked in. Cindy tensed as if she recognised the guy and didn't particularly like him.

He introduced himself, then turned and politely asked Lieutenant Ross to leave. She left quickly without saying anything to me; as she had said, it was their base. *Keep it simple, Castle,* the little voices were telling me somewhere just to the left and behind my eyes.

As the door closed, the captain pulled out a pack of cigarettes, took one for himself and offered me one. I declined, wondering if I was going to get answers or be faced with an interrogation. I guessed interrogation.

"Mr Castle, I understand you want information about a VIP flight out of Clark?"

"That's right."

"Why do you want this information?"

"I'm writing a story and I've been told the flight took place and I just want confirmation."

He took a long drag on his cigarette. "You're interested in Gerry Roa?"

I nodded.

"Mr Roa's dead."

"I know."

"Do you know where his wife is?"

It was an odd question, simple enough, but too odd to be answered in any other way. "No."

He studied me, trying to determine whether or not I was telling the truth. "Do you know why Mr Roa might have flown out of here in a VIP plane?"

"I believe he was a courier for Mr Marcos."

"And what do you believe he was carrying for the former president?"

I bluffed. "A message? Money? I'm not sure."

He smiled. "Mr Roa did fly out of here; his destination was Geneva and we believe he was carrying money to be deposited in a Swiss bank account—probably an account for Marcos."

I was surprised at how much the captain was telling me. He had decided to talk. I wondered why. "Did he make the deposit before he died?" I asked.

"We have no way of knowing. Swiss banking officials are very quiet about such things." He paused, then continued, "You can help us, Mr

80

Castle. We'd like to know. And if you could tell us, we'd make it worth your while."

So that was it. They didn't know how much I knew and they were prepared to offer something to find out.

"What happened in Geneva?" I asked.

The captain wasn't sure. I could tell from the way he answered. "Someone got killed . . ."

"Who?" I interrupted.

He shrugged. "No one knows. There was no identification on the body and so far no one has made any claims on it. It's a mystery."

"What's the connection with Roa?" I continued.

"Immediately after the shooting, he and his family disappeared. They left their suitcases in their hotel. They never turned up to take the flight back here. The plane came back empty."

I thought about that. Something had spooked Roa. He'd started running and whoever was after him had caught him on top of a train in Italy.

The captain intruded on my thoughts. "I'm assuming, Mr. Castle, you'd find it within the scope of your profession to tell me what you find out about all this?"

I smiled. "I've no problem with that, Captain."

He didn't return the smile. "Preferably before you publish the story and tell the whole world." It wasn't a question.

I turned slowly toward the door. "I'll do the best I can for you."

He nodded, making no move to stop me from leaving or to accompany me.

Outside the office I walked swiftly towards the guardhouse and through the gate. There was a taxi rank half a block away, out of sight of the temporary office where the captain had entertained me.

"Julian!"

I turned around at the sound of her voice.

Cindy Ross looked worried. She came up close to me. "A word of warning, friend. The captain *isn't* a captain—at least, not in this air force."

I searched her face. What was she telling me?

She swept on. "I'm not sure what he is, but he has clearance from the highest level at Philippine defence HQ. If he wants to play general, he's got somebody's authority and backing to do it."

"Why are you telling me this?"

She faltered a little. "Because we're trying to run a clean show here and guys like that are dirtying it up. It's only a warning. What you do with it is your own business."

"On or off the record?"

"I don't give a shit! Take care, Julian." She turned and walked swiftly away.

* * *

I took a taxi back to my hotel. Chester Price was in the bar, and we exchanged notes. I had nowhere near the kind of facts that would make a coherent story but we both agreed I was on to something worthwhile enough for me to continue digging. Chester had been busy covering the news. He briefed me, turned over enough notes for me to write my report for Melbourne and then we went back to the Gerry Roa mystery. We travelled over all the ground once again and Chester found the focus.

"It seems to me that Fatima is the key to all this. With Gerry dead, she's the only one who has the most complete version of what happened."

I agreed. "She was with him in Geneva. She wasn't with him on that Italian train."

He nodded. "Give me a couple of hours. I know a couple of guys who can ask questions that might give us an answer to where she went."

We separated. Chester went off to his office and I went up to my room to phone through the news he'd put together. It wasn't exactly the way our editors would like to see us operating but when the right reporters teamed up this way, like Chester and me, it worked.

It didn't take long to file and then I lay down on the bed. I had more calls to make but Chester's contacts might help fill in a few gaps, so I decided to hold off until he got back.

* * *

I was in the shower when I heard the noise in the other room. Chester was back more quickly than I had expected. I called out to him but there was no answer. That didn't make any sense. I turned off the water and listened. There was obviously someone in the next room. I heard a drawer shut and another one slide open. Chester wouldn't be going through my dresser drawers! There were no clothes in the bathroom, just a big towel which I wrapped around my waist.

With what I thought was a certain amount of care I opened the door a crack. Whoever it was knew what he was doing. The contents of the dresser drawers were already on the floor and a small man in a shirt that looked like a reject from a Waikiki beachside stall was throwing books down from a bookcase as he searched for something. He looked much smaller than I, and I stepped out boldly.

"Just what do you think you're . . ."

That was as far as I got. A piece of metal was pushed hard against the back of my skull and I knew exactly what it was long before the ugly voice spoke.

"Not one move, Castle."

I stood perfectly still. The small man didn't even

look up from where he was literally tearing the place apart. These guys had done this kind of thing before. The ease with which the gunman had slid in behind me as I came through the doorway suggested this was no mere mugging. I managed to find my voice.

"Rather than tear the place apart, why don't you just tell me what it is you're looking for?"

The man with the ugly voice stepped around where I could see him. "We're not looking for anything, so you can't help us." He was an American in green army fatigue pants and a black T-shirt. "Put your clothes on," he ordered.

He was holding a big gun with a huge silencer screwed on the end. He could blow me apart and all they might hear in the hallway was the sound of my body hitting the floor.

"We going somewhere?" I asked, moving toward my pants and shirt lying on the lounge.

"Keep quiet or I'll blow you away right now. I can always dress you after you're dead."

I shut my mouth and pulled on my pants. That line didn't make much sense. Why dress me after shooting me? It started to make more sense as I watched the man in the gaudy shirt take out one of my suitcases, throw it open on the floor and toss into it the few valuables in the room—a camera, my watch and wallet from the table, a small clock. So it *was* a mugging. But the guy with the gun had said they weren't looking for anything. And why dress me? An ordinary mugger wouldn't bother. Logic was never one of my strong points but it didn't take long for the evidence to fall into place—and I felt cold and very alone with the conclusion.

This was no ordinary mugging. This was going to be a murder made to look almost like an accident. I had stumbled into my room and disturbed a thief, who panicked and shot me. That's why they were dressing me. Simple. Case closed. No simple thief would rob the room with me in the shower. There were too many other rooms in this hotel where the occupants were away for the day.

I didn't like my chances because the whole time the small man kept messing up the place and filling the suitcase, the big guy with the gun never took his eyes off me. I dressed slowly, running through the few options.

"I guess you're not going to tell me what this is all about?" I asked.

The gunman grinned. "We're just the hired help, just following orders."

I nodded. "No way I can talk or buy my way out of it?"

"You wouldn't have the words or the money, Castle."

The small man was closing the suitcase.

I needed desperately to find some more time and I had precious little to negotiate with. "We could talk millions of dollars!" I blurted out.

There was the slightest flicker of hesitation but the gun stayed up. "Reporters don't have that kind of loot," he said sarcastically.

"Let him talk," flowered shirt said. "We got nothing to lose but thirty seconds."

The gunman remained unconvinced, moving away from me toward the door. It was clear he didn't think I had anything to offer and all he wanted to do was pull the trigger and clear out. He was too far away for me to stand any chance of reaching him.

The small guy moved in close to me. We made a strange pair. He hardly reached my shoulder in height but he was doing the ordering. "Tell us about the millions."

"It's Marcos' money and it was smuggled out

of the country." I wanted to string it out.

"And you know where it is, right?"

"Right!"

"And you'll take us to it, right?"

I lied. "Right!"

"Let me take a wild guess," he sneered. "It's in a numbered account in Geneva and the deposit was made by a man named Roa. Am I close?"

My heart was banging away inside my chest. We'd made it past the thirty seconds but I didn't have much time left. They knew all about it. "Yes."

The small guy turned around and started away. "You got nothing to bargain with," he said. Then he motioned to the gunman by the door. "Shoot him!"

I watched the gun come up.

"I know the number of the account," I blurted out desperately.

The small man's hand shot out to signal a stay of execution, then he spun around and faced me.

"I know the number," I repeated, forcing a calmness that wasn't there into my voice.

We stared at each other for a moment, his eyes narrowed and a slight grin twisted the corners of his mouth. "Nice try. But you don't know the number."

Thirty seconds had become ninety seconds and I was frantically trying to find more words when there was a knock on the door. "Come in," I shouted, reaching forward and grabbing the little guy at the same time. I pulled him close to me, crouching, trying to hide behind him.

The door swung open. Everyone was off guard, scrambling to react.

Chester was in the doorway.

"Watch the gun!" I yelled.

There was a dull click and a mirror by my

shoulder exploded, sending splinters showering across the floor.

Chester was fast. The gunman was by the door. They grappled, the .45-calibre pistol locked in Chester's grip as he twisted the gunman's arm up and away from my direction.

I lost sight of them as the small guy butted an elbow hard into my stomach, caught his foot behind my ankle and threw me neatly over his shoulder. I hit the floor hard and he was on me with his boots. No rules here. I took two blows on the face before twisting out of the way. I backed away from him as he swung a lamp at me. It caught my shoulder and slammed me sprawling across a coffee table. As I went down I heard another muffled click and a scream. Someone had been shot!

The gun clattered and slid across the floor, midway between the small guy and me. I rolled toward it as he dived forward. He was going to get there first. My foot lashed out, caught the barrel and the gun rattled across the floor and slid far under a tall bookcase. No one was going to get it out from under there in any kind of hurry.

The small man paused for only a moment then ducked away toward his partner, who was wrapped up in Chester's bear hug. Blood was pouring down the black T-shirt from the gunman's shoulder.

One solid kick in Chester's ribs, delivered by the guy in the Waikiki shirt, was enough to break the hold. Chester stumbled and sank to his knees, clutching his side. The two men dashed out of the room through the open door.

I was weak, mostly from having been so close to death. That kind of thing takes the stuffing out of anyone. I didn't even bother getting to my feet. Rolling over twice I reached the bookcase.

With a book I fished out the gun, clicked on the safety catch and with the gun in my lap, sat up and rested against the bookcase.

"You okay?" Chester asked as he hobbled over, shut the door and locked it.

"I'm okay. You?"

"Black and blue and bloody stiff, but in one piece. He shot himself. Couldn't see which way it was pointed and took a punt. He lost." Chester paused for breath. "We're getting too old for this, Julian. Some friends you got." He eased himself down to the floor and we sat there looking at each other.

I filled him in about the fake mugging. "And they knew about Roa and the money. My guess is they didn't like me asking questions for some reason. If you hadn't come along they were going to kill me." I shook for a moment as it started to sink in just how close I'd come to dying. "Thanks, Chester," I said softly.

He grinned. "It'll cost you dinner tonight."

"Done!" I knew he'd find a way to get even for my having left him the bill for breakfast at Taza de Oro.

We were still sitting on the floor.

"I found out why Fatima Roa wasn't on the train," Chester said.

"Why?"

"Because she and her son flew out of Rome under her own name and passport."

"To where?"

"Sydney."

I nodded. "That makes a lot of sense, Chester. Her father lives on a property north of Sydney."

"After what happened here, I'd say we've got a problem." Chester said.

"What's that?"

"If I can find out she went to Sydney, anyone

88

else who's got an interest could find out too."

"You're right, but we might have a small advantage. I know she has a father there and I know roughly where he lives. It might take the competition a little time to put it all together."

"So, what's next?"

"I go to Australia to see her."

"Your paper's not going to like that."

I shrugged and started getting to my feet. I hurt all over, especially my head and neck. The small guy had kicked hard. "Someone tried to kill me. It may not be a story but until I find out all the whys and hows, they might just try again."

Chester was on his feet, still rubbing his ribs. "I'll cover for you here in return for a favour."

"Name it."

"My daughter's in Sydney. I got a message this morning. She's taken a job with some human aid group called the December Foundation that sends medical supplies into Third World countries. See her for me, Julian. Make sure she's got her head screwed on the right way around."

"I've heard of the foundation. They've had good publicity for some of their aid projects."

"Jade says she's involved in medical relief mission going to the Sandinistas in Nicaragua."

I shrugged. "People bleed no matter what the politics. And Jade's a doctor."

"So you'll see her for me?"

The last thing I felt like doing was arguing leftist politics with Jade Price, but her old man was concerned about his offspring and he'd just saved my life. "Sure I'll see her." I wandered into the bathroom. It seemed like an eternity since I'd stepped out of that shower. In the mirror my face stared back at me and winced. The bruises were already forming and the left eye was going to be very black for a few days.

Chester stood in the doorway. "When you going?"

"This afternoon, if I can get the connecting flight through Singapore."

"Great way of getting out of buying me dinner."

"Raincheck, mate." I splashed cold water on my sweaty face.

PART TWO

THINGS
BEST LEFT
UNSAID

CHAPTER NINE

William Carson was sixty-five years old, and on some days he felt every one of those years. But this was not one of those days. Today he was excited. He had felt the sweeping elation that gripped him now on many occasions. It came from that frozen moment when other men might feel fear—that intense moment when the climax of some massive activity loomed directly in front of him. Not the successful resolution—that was merely an anti-climax—but the ultimate moment of truth when there was still a chance of failure. It was then he felt excited. Afterwards, when other men might rejoice in victory, he had always felt drained. His interest would flag and he would already be thinking of the next mission. On this day the climax was breaking before him and he was on a high. The next hour would tell the difference. There was still a chance of failure.

He walked down the corridor alone. At the end of the long hall, high up in the windowless North Sydney office tower, was a plain door. It looked no different from any one of the dozen doors that opened onto the length of the corridor. But he knew the difference. Pausing, with his hand on the doorknob, he squared his shoulders and entered.

Inside there was tension among the half dozen men who sat is front of a vast array of electronic gadgetry. The walls were covered with high panels on which were displayed maps with coloured lights and arrows. This was William Carson's war room, where he played out the destinies of companies and countries, of presidents, prime ministers and pretenders to great numbers of thrones. Right now William Carson's soldiers were in central Africa, in a large country rich in gold and silver deposits. He moved close to one of his aides and looked up at the glowing status boards.

The aide spoke quickly, betraying his tension. "They've taken the central barracks, two of the radio stations, the television station and they're inside the presidential compound."

Carson shook his head impatiently. "I can read the bloody board."

The aide fell silent.

Carson let his eyes run across the detailed electronic map of the country's capital. The detail was exact. Every building was displayed, the streets, the positions of the government troops, the palace. His men's positions were in blue and the tiny transmitters each man wore sent a coded identity message to a larger transmitter recently installed outside the capital. The identity signals were beamed up to a satellite hovering above the equator and then relayed to the large dish antenna on top of the Sydney tower. As his men moved, so moved the blue dots on the electronic display. It was the ultimate in tactical war games—except that this wasn't a game.

From a speaker on the wall came a voice, authoritative and urgent. "We're inside the presidential compound. Minor resistance." There was the sound of small arms fire in the background.

Carson recognised the voice. It was his colonel, a veteran of the Falklands War, cashiered from Her Majesty's military for excessive brutality against Argentine POWs being held in prisoner pens in Port Stanley, and chosen by Carson precisely because the colonel had shown such cruelty. Carson had listened to the voice many times. The colonel might be in command on the day but Carson had selected him as he had chosen all of his senior commanders. He had been there for their training on the small island off the coast of northern Queensland, away from the prying eyes, away from the foolish politicians in Canberra who had made it a crime to train mercenaries in *his* Australia.

"They're through the main doors now," the colonel reported. "I'm going inside the palace." There was a loud explosion that sounded slightly tinny and almost unrealistic as it was relayed through the transmitters.

"Grenade," Carson said to no one in particular. For a moment he wished he was there with them. In the beginning he had gone along, but that was a long time ago. To do it now was just wishful thinking. He was too old for this kind of thing. It was *his* plan, though. That gave him great satisfaction.

Most of the blue dots were coming together inside the palace. One of the aides flicked a switch and the main display showed a floor plan of the palace. Ground floor first. The blue dots were heading for a staircase leading to the upper floor. The display switched to the next floor. The president's office and residence were on this floor, in the west wing. The blue dots moved toward it.

An aide turned to Carson. "We have Shuhati on the radio, sir."

Carson grimaced. Shuhati was in a helicopter heading toward the capital. He was paying the bills for this day and all those that had gone before, in preparation for his takeover of the country. Probably shining his buttons and straightening that stupid cap with all the gold braid, Carson thought. He nodded at the radio operator and then picked up the microphone. The scrambler system was very advanced. No one, anywhere, would be able to unscramble their conversation. "Carson here."

"This is Shuhati. Do they have him yet?"

"Not yet, Mr President, but any moment now."

The deep tones of the African's voice were demanding. "Remember, I want him alive. He must stand trial."

"If it's possible, we'll take him alive."

"Are you sure he's still in the palace?"

"I'm sure. We've had every exit under surveillance since noon. He's still inside."

"How long before I can go in?"

"Just a moment, Mr President." Carson turned to his aide. "How far away from the palace is Shuhati?"

The aide consulted one of the electronic maps on a video screen. "Twenty minutes."

Carson checked the blue dots. They were entering the living quarters. "You can go in now, Mr President. Your escort will be waiting when you land."

I'm on my way." Shuhati's voice reeked of satisfaction, as if he had personally engineered the coup rather than just paying for it.

Carson nodded at the radio operator, who flicked a switch cutting the helicopter off from the war room.

The colonel's voice came over the loudspeaker. "We have the president. I repeat, we have President Munthaw. He's alive and scared shitless, but alive."

Carson pressed the button on the microphone. "Very good, Colonel. You have about fifteen minutes until Shuhati arrives."

"Yes, sir. Understood. We've got it all under control. When everyone wakes up here tomorrow, they'll be greeted by Shuhati's ugly face on their television screens."

Carson took a breath and then spoke. "Slight change of plans, Colonel. I want you to execute Munthaw. Right now."

Everyone in the war room was watching him.

The colonel's voice betrayed his curiosity. "Execute him? I thought . . ."

Carson interrupted. "Kill him, Colonel. Now!"

"Yes, sir," came the voice.

"And when Shuhati gets there, tell him it was unavoidable. Tell him Munthaw tried to shoot it out."

"Yes, sir."

Already he could feel the lack of interest seeping through. It was over. Shuhati would deliver the gold and silver concessions to the international consortium that had financed the coup. Carson would be paid his fees and one corrupt regime would replace another. A good night's work, financially worthwhile, was finished. He turned to leave and then stopped. The men in the room were still looking at him. He knew he didn't need to explain his reasons to them, but he had the time.

"Munthaw had to die," he said to them. "There's no percentage in allowing him to live, to return perhaps to fight another day. No victory is complete unless it is secure. No victory is complete unless the victors can go on, go forward. If Munthaw lives, Shuhati will waste valuable time putting him on trial, dredging up history. Always move forward, not backwards—that's victory."

He held his grin back. His men were nodding, accepting what he had to say. He started toward the door, motioning to a large man standing nearby. "Kasilov, give me half an hour and then come to my office. There's work to be done. We have a new mission to plan."

* * *

He needed some time alone. He looked around the room that served as his office and command post and paused on some of the many mementos of past campaigns. There was a small sign on his desk that summed up his philosophy: "The Meek Shall Not Inherit Anything!"

Carson was an eccentric who believed he could rule the world far better than anyone else. In the absence of any mechanism that would give him that grand power, he had taken to playing the game of power broker to those who were rich enough to buy his particular brand of power politics. His weaponry and advice had been bought far and wide and he had influenced the successful outcome to many coups and revolutions for, he reflected on the immense time span, more than twenty years.

He had a book prominently displayed on the boardroom table that occupied one side of his office. It was a history of guerrilla warfare, coups and revolutions from 1946 to 1986. He loved to page slowly through it and dwell on the fact that, quite unknown to anyone out there in the big, comfortable world, he was represented in more than sixty per cent of the conflicts.

In Lebanon alone, with the shifting allegiances of the many factions—most of whom he was arming—he had ended up with military advisers who actually directed actions against each other. And he had been well paid by both sides.

He had remained, quite deliberately and with great success, a secret, shadowy figure operating just far enough outside the searching queries of at least a dozen intelligence agencies from both East and West to allow his long-acknowledged cover of humanitarian and philanthropist to cloak all his activities.

He operated through deputies, the usefulness of any given lieutenant directly related to that assistant's lifespan. And some of those lieutenants had found themselves with very limited lifespans.

His staff was multiculturalism personified but he doubted the Canberra mandarins who had advocated a multicultural Australia had in mind any model that approached his. His key personnel came from at least a dozen countries and almost all of them had been recruited out of government service—from the CIA in Washington, from the KGB in Moscow, MI-6 in London, DGSE in Paris, Mossad in Jerusalem and the BND in West Germany. He even had a couple of Australians from ASIO.

There was a knock on the door.

"Come in," Carson said.

The door opened and Kasilov entered. He filled a room quickly, his impressive bulk seeming to reach out to each wall no matter what the size of the room. Even in Carson's huge office Kasilov loomed above the furniture. Where other men might quake in the presence of the Russian, Carson was unaware of the man's overwhelming presence. He knew the ex-KGB man was dangerous but it was that constant threat that Carson had harnessed. Kasilov was the organisation's best debt collector.

"Have a seat, Vladimir," he said easily, having already noticed Kasilov's sour expression. "Problem?" None of his lieutenants liked reporting complications.

"A temporary one, sir," The Russian spoke excellent English. He had been well trained at the KGB's favourite school, Patrice Lumumba University in Moscow. "Two of my people failed to take out Julian Castle."

"Your people in the clear?"

"Yes. I used cutouts. They'd been briefed about Roa and the money in case they saw or heard anything they could report, but there was nothing. The cutouts isolated them from us. But in any case, it wasn't needed because they got away clean."

The phone rang. Carson picked it up, listened for a moment then gave the handset to Kasilov.

The Russian listened for a few seconds, asked a question and replaced the handset on its cradle. "Castle is on his way to Sydney. He flew out of Manila a couple of hours ago."

Carson was silent for a moment. "He might be coming back because your people scared him. Or maybe his newspaper recalled him."

Kasilov shook his head. "We can rule out the newspaper. We checked that out. His editor doesn't know he's on his way back. He thinks Castle is still in Manila."

Carson nodded. "Then he's running scared, or he's coming here for some other reason."

"There's still the question of Roa's wife," the Russian said. "Our Italian contacts say she came to Sydney with her kid, but the trail ends at the airport. She arrived here but where she is now is unknown."

"Let's put everything you've got into finding her. Borrow some manpower if you need it. And put some of your people onto Castle. Leave him alone for the time being. Just follow him. Let's see what he's doing here before we make any new decisions on his future."

Kasilov smiled. "If he gives us Fatima Roa we might yet be able to get our hands on the Marcos money."

Carson said nothing. Kasilov would enjoy succeeding where Alberts had failed. Carson was still angry at Alberts for screwing up the collection of the $50 million. He needed that money. But if Kasilov could finish the job, good on him. Both of his key lieutenants had their strengths. Alberts seemed to be doing quite well on the Nicaraguan assignment. He changed the subject.

"Have you checked the shipment for Nicaragua?"

Kasilov nodded. "Yes. It's all there, ready for loading aboard the ship."

"The ship arrives tomorrow night?"

"Exactly. We should have it all aboard within twenty-four hours. How's your doctor?"

Carson smiled. "She'll do just fine. We had a long chat and she's completely committed to the cause. She's got the qualifications and she'll pass scrutiny."

They spoke for a few more minutes, then Kasilov left the office to continue his search for Fatima Roa. Carson crossed his thick beige carpet to a well-stocked bar in the corner, ignoring the dark woman who sat behind the white desk at the far end of the long room. She had been there for so many years he took her for granted. She was busy reading through a pile of reports, seemingly oblivious of the conversation that had gone on between Carson and the Russian. He poured some vodka into a glass and added orange juice.

CHAPTER TEN

I'd flown into Sydney many times and nothing much had changed at the international airline terminal. Everything was fine for aeroplanes, but those planes carried people, and the airport arrival area was always crowded, far too small and understaffed. Whoever was running this place could learn a thing or two from the management of Changi airport in Singapore.

I was tired and sore, and perhaps because of the bruises on my neck and face I had the distinct feeling everyone who was supposed to serve me was keeping a distance. By the time I'd unpacked my bag for a curious customs agent who seemed to think I was capable of transporting half the contraband of Asia in one small carry-all, I wanted nothing more than a shower, a can of cold beer and a few hours of peace and quiet.

The last thing I wanted was to hear an announcement over the public address system requesting Julian Castle to make himself known at the Qantas information counter. I never made it to the counter. A hand touched my arm and I turned to look into the pale green eyes of Jade Price, Chester's little girl. Except she wasn't a little girl any more, not even the scrawny teenager I recalled from that summer in Hong Kong, and even prettier than the pictures Chester had produced from his wallet.

Her face twisted into a frown at the sight of the bruises. "Dad said you'd been in a fight but he didn't say you'd come off so badly. I hope the other guy looks worse than you."

"He doesn't," I said simply. "What are you doing here?" I was tired and it came out sullen and almost angry.

"Dad asked me to come." She paused, a certain arrogance tightening the soft angles of her face. "I can leave if you prefer."

"Sorry. It's been a bad forty-eight hours and I just wasn't ready for you."

The hard lines melted. "Hey, Julian, I'm the doctor. Remember? I prescribe rest and good food and I know just the place for it."

She took my arm and steered me toward the exit. "And where might that be?" I asked.

"The organisation I work for has a flat for me in Coogee, near the beach. Let's go there. I'm a pretty fair cook and there's a guest room."

"I don't want to cause you any trouble."

She laughed, the sound light and young. "I'm only in Sydney for another couple of days anyway, then I'm off to Nicaragua and you're on your own."

"Your Dad told me," I said.

She grimaced. "With a suitable commentary, I assume."

It was my turn to laugh. "No comment."

"I guessed that much."

We had crossed to the car park. There was a brand new Honda Prelude waiting for her. It was bright red.

"They're paying you well or the bank still owns it," I said as I got into the passenger side.

"Company car," she grinned. "I have to give it back when I ship out."

She drove well.

Coogee had changed since the last time I'd seen it. At one time it had been an 'in' address. Now it looked cluttered and almost decaying, like parts of Manila. The only saving grace was the nearness of the sea, sparkling and deep blue. The flat she was staying in was utilitarian and comfortable.

She brought me coffee and sat down nearby. "Dad said you were here on a story?"

I explained the Roa connection to Australia. She listened carefully, nodding from time to time. When I finished she took a sip of coffee.

"Can I come with you?"

"No way."

"I can help."

"How?"

"Do you know Fatima Roa?" she asked.

"I met her once. She probably won't remember."

"And you want her to open up to you?"

I nodded.

"Then take me along. I'm a woman and a doctor. She's a woman with a baby. She might talk to me before she'll talk to you."

Jade was making sense. I didn't like it very much but she had a point and I had a feeling—my reporter's gut once again—that I was working against some kind of undefined deadline. Getting Fatima to talk was important.

* * *

Carson was sitting at his desk when the phone rang. It was Kasilov.

"Fatima Roa's father lives on a property near Gosford," the Russian reported. "Name's Santamaria."

"Good work, Vladimir," Carson said. "You'd better get up there right away. Handle it yourself with a few men you can trust. If she's there and if she knows anything about the money, I want that information."

"I'll look after it, sir."

"Where's Castle?"

Kasilov took his time answering. "My men lost him in traffic. Some woman picked him up at the airport and my men followed him as long as they could."

Carson was unhappy. "You'd better get up to Gosford right now," he said coldly.

"I'm on my way," the Russian said.

Carson put down the telephone slowly. If Fatima Roa knew anything, Kasilov would come back with the information. He looked down the length of his long office toward where the dark woman was still seated at her desk. She was peering intently into a computer terminal. He admired the strength in the lines of her face silently, without being obvious. The new thought came to him suddenly. He hoped Fatima Roa knew something and he hoped she spoke up quickly, before Kasilov became angry. She was already dead, merely because he had ordered Kasilov to go to her. But the manner of her death would be so much less painful if she just told the Russian what he wanted to know.

The dark woman rose from her desk and left the room. She made no noise, no gesture of farewell, in fact she totally ignored him. As the door swung shut behind her, Carson felt strangely alone in his big office. It was a new sensation and he didn't like it.

* * *

Santamaria had done quite well for himself. He had a big property, a horse stud and an entrance that made the place almost a replica of JR's Southfork. A long rambling driveway wound down into a valley where the main buildings were set well out of sight from the highway. It was idyllic, with a stream meandering through a nearby meadow. We stood by the car on the edge of the highway looking down into the valley. We could see some of the property. I wished we could see the main house. There was something wrong but I didn't have the slightest idea what it was. Just another feeling.

"We're going to walk in. We're not taking the car," I announced to Jade.

She looked at me curiously. "Isn't that going to look a little strange?"

"No doubt when we first get there, but your father made an astute observation when he said that if he could find out where Fatima Roa was, so could whoever was chasing her husband. And if everything is okay when we get down there, our explanation for being there will justify our taking precautions and approaching as quietly as possible."

Her stare suggested I was playing out some scene from a spy thriller.

I shrugged. What the hell! She had invited herself along in the first place. "Let's go," I said shortly.

We stayed on the fringe of the long lane for the first few minutes, walking quickly and listening carefully. Jade kept close. The bush was heavy right up to the edge of the lane and I kept one eye on it, picking places we could hide quickly if someone came along. I was rapidly convincing myself that someone would appear. The attack in my hotel room had shaken loose large parts of my confidence.

Shortly after we lost sight of the highway behind us the bush thinned out. Workers had done a fine job of landscape gardening on a grand scale. The bush formed a perfect screen that gave way to manicured trees around which the ground had been painstakingly cleared and a hardy grass introduced.

The main house loomed in the centre of an array of smaller buildings and beyond the living compound were stables and what looked like kilometres of white fencing. Handsome horses stood in many of the paddocks.

Everything seemed in order. There were a couple of four-wheel drive Land-Rovers in the curved driveway with two older Mercedes and a newer BMW. Nothing particularly suspicious there. I shook my head and Jade stirred beside me.

"What's wrong?" she asked quietly.

"Nothing. Absolutely nothing." I paused and kept looking. I knew I could be listening to demons who were trying to fool me. They'd done that before. But those little voices had also been right more often than they'd been wrong and ever since that attack in my hotel room, those same voices had been working overtime with their cryptic warnings.

"What are we going to do?" Jade asked.

We had to do something. Standing out there in the bushes wasn't getting us any closer to what we'd come for. The lane was on our left, curving through a large empty paddock before passing the front door of the mansion. To our right were trees and a long stable. The stable would provide us with some cover. I pointed to it. "We'll cut across there and have a look."

"What are we looking for?"

I shrugged. "If we don't see or hear anything suspicious, we'll go back and get the car and go in like normal people." I'd change the plan a bit. Maybe just walking in out of the bushes would be harder to explain than I had originally thought. Too much looked normal.

She grinned and spoke softly. "You call on people this way very often?"

I ignored the sarcasm, preferring her grin over her words and set off fast and low. We kept as many trees as possible between us and the house. It was easy going. The grass was clear of vines and sticks and I could afford to keep both eyes on the house and other buildings. The mere fact I had seen no one added to my concern. There should have been at least a worker or two around. Santamaria didn't run this big a place on his own. And at least five vehicles were in the driveway, with another two pickup trucks parked near the long stable.

We made it to the corner of the stable. I peered around the corner. Two long blocks faced each other with at least twenty horse stalls in each. The alley between the blocks was covered with some kind of artificial turf, well tended.

There was still no sign of anyone, although the soft sounds of resting horses filled the alley. At least some of the stalls were occupied.

I signalled Jade to stay in close and started moving down the long alley. It was spooky. The whole scene was just too deserted.

Jade gasped loudly and grabbed my arm tightly at the same time. I turned to her. Her face was stiff and scared. She pointed at the ground ahead, in front of a stall a few paces away. A pool of fresh blood had formed just outside the stall door, a red stream slowly dripping from the gap under the wooden door. I walked forward, not sure what to expect but fearing the worst, and reverently thankful for those little voices.

There was a lot of blood. Cautiously I looked over the chest-high door. Three bodies, one obviously a teenage boy and two men, were sprawled on the floor inside. It was an ugly scene.

A thick track of blood led from each body, the tracks joining together under the door.

I opened the stall door and went inside. Kneeling down, I touched the neck of one of the men. The skin was still warm. There was no pulse.

Jade was down on her knees beside me, pale and fighting back the need to vomit. She reached over and rolled the body of the teenager. The wounds were all in the chest. Someone had shot him with a machinegun, stitching him from just above the right hip all the way up to the left shoulder.

Jade turned and was quietly sick. Her shoulders were shaking. She knew the danger that was all too real now and she was working hard to keep her retching quiet. I felt what she felt but I'd been through it all before. The shock would come later for me. Right now all my senses were concentrated on trying to figure out where the machinegun was that had done all this, and who was holding it.

"I want you to get out of here," I whispered to her.

She shook her head sickly, her white face crumpled and fearful. "Let's both get out of here," she managed to say.

"I've got to see what's going on," I said.

"Then I'm staying with you."

I stared at her. There was a lot of her father in her. As I turned toward the stall door I wished her father was with me now.

We went forward along the alley much more slowly, very cautiously. I was less jumpy now I knew I'd called it right. At the end of the stable I looked around the corner. There were enough sheds between us and the mansion to give us some cover. I checked out each of the house's windows; no sign of anyone. We moved quickly across the small open area and passed the rear of the buildings. Close to the house I stopped. We needed a way to get inside. The front and rear doors were less than appropriate.

The place looked as if it had a basement and some steps led to a low door that was slightly ajar. I pointed at it and we ran, low and fast, across the gravel driveway. The crunch of our feet sounded very loud. Jade was right behind me as I went down the steps, bumping into me as I paused for a moment by the door. The room was dimly lit inside from light through a single small window at ground level. It was a big storage room with steps leading to an inside door on the far side of the room.

I went into the room, quickly pointing at some paint cans that would have made a loud racket if we had knocked them over. There was still no sound upstairs. I almost expected that; the mansion was very solidly built. If the doors were as well made, the sound of voices wouldn't carry very far.

The stairs leading up to the inside door were made of thick planks. There were no squeaks or creaks as we climbed up to the door. I put my ear to the wood. I could hear nothing from the other side. I wanted to believe that whoever had killed the three men had gone, but my little voices overruled me. The three cars and two Land Rovers suggested otherwise. There were just too many vehicles outside. It hadn't been so obvious when I'd first seen them. Now it was.

I tried the doorknob. It turned easily. I pushed. It opened a fraction and then hit an obstacle. There were voices, loud and urgent, somewhere off down the hallway. They were men's voices but that was all I could make out. The words were muffled by the distance. Looking down, I could see part of what was blocking the door from opening—a man's legs. I could only see the legs and the shoes and they were not moving. They were expensive shoes. Putting my shoulder against the door, I held my breath and shoved. The body moved, sliding a little. There was more blood on the floor at the top of the landing. Four bodies. Whoever had done all this was playing for keeps, just like the guys in my hotel room in Manila. Once again I wished Jade was somewhere else—anywhere else but here. She could see past me through the widening gap as I moved the door and the body enough for us to squeeze through.

She took the sight of the new body better than the first three. That's something I've learned: unless you know the guy sprawled out in the pool of blood, you get more and more detached as the number of corpses increases. Vietnam had produced more than my quota of dead for this lifetime. From her reaction in the stall, those three were Jade's first dead, apart from bodies she might have come across in the clinical surrounds of medical school. She handled the fourth very well.

My guess was that the man lying in the hallway was Santamaria. About the right age, good-looking, aristocratic bearing even in death, expensive leisure clothes.

I looked up the hall quickly. There was a new voice in the middle of the drone of masculine voices. I couldn't make out the words but it was feminine, frightened feminine—and pleading.

Reaching back, I took Jade's hand and we started down the corridor. There was a sense of urgency now. If Fatima was still alive, she was one of the few left in this house who knew what was really going on.

The voices were louder. We were getting close. Two hallways came together at a ninety-degree angle and there was a double door leading off into a huge lounge room, what might be called a great hall. The double doors were almost closed and I couldn't see who was inside but the words were clear now—demanding, intimidating and angry. If Fatima Roa didn't provide the answers her interrogators wanted, she was dead. And I knew that if she gave them the answers—if she had the answers—she'd also be dead.

I looked around desperately. Inside the room, about on a level with a second or third storey was a kind of gallery, like a choir loft in a church. There had to be another way up there. I spun around and went further down the corridor. There were stairs off to the right. They were narrow and steep but they obviously went exactly where I needed to go.

Just as I turned to climb, Jade grabbed my arm and whispered, "A guard!"

At the end of the hall were frosted glass doors that led to an outside veranda. A man had moved onto the veranda and was reaching for the door handle.

I pulled Jade roughly out of the corridor and started quickly up the stairs, wondering how many more guards had been posted around the mansion and the grounds. It was getting more dangerous all the time. I would have given anything for a weapon, any weapon. It was a despicable fallacy that journalists were non-combatants. Whoever made that rule up had never left the newsroom.

We came out of the stairs at the rear of the upper-floor gallery that ran around all four walls of the hall below. Lying down, we eased forward so we could see the entire room below while maintaining adequate cover. The room was sumptuous and finely decorated. Everything looked just right and very expensive. But it was the tableau being played out around the frail-looking woman tied to a chair in the centre of the room that commanded our attention. I heard Jade's involuntary moan of dismay at the sight of Fatima Roa's badly battered face.

The three men had been at it for some time. The blood that had poured from her nose and mouth had already caked and dried on the skin of her chest and on her breasts where they had ripped her blouse away. Her head hung down, the dark hair wet with sweat. She was slowly shaking her head. She was past crying.

The three men—two had sub-machineguns, the leader's hands were empty—were all cut from much the same cloth. The leader was even bigger than the other two, and *they* were big brutes. He was doing all the talking. His English had a decided accent: east European was my considered opinion, maybe Russian. But whoever had taught him to speak my language had done well. His voice carried up to where we were hidden.

"Simple numbers. That's all we want. You give them to me and we let you go. You'd like that, wouldn't you?"

The woman didn't seem to hear. She was still shaking her head.

The gesture angered the man. He lashed out with a big hand and the blow swung her head around so I could see the entire bludgeoned face. I hardly recognised the beautiful model who had graced so many magazine covers and who had smiled at me so warmly on that ocean cruise. The anger welled up in my throat.

The man leaned over her, leering down at her as if he was going to open his huge mouth and bite her head off. Instead, he raised a grubby hand and let a finger wander through the blood on one of her breasts. He rammed his fist hard into the soft skin and the woman's head arched back in pain.

"You want me to stop, don't you?" he yelled.

113

Her eyes were wide with pain. This time she nodded, fast, wanting to agree with anything he demanded.

"What are the numbers of the bank account?" he demanded harshly.

Gerry Roa's bank account in Geneva! They didn't have the numbers yet. Gerry hadn't talked or they wouldn't be here.

"I don't know," she screamed. "I've told you over and over again. I don't know the numbers."

The man gave one last twist of his strong fingers, wound deeply into the skin of her soft breast, holding them there through her agonised screaming and finally stepped back away from her.

"She doesn't know," he said to his gunmen. "I really believe she doesn't know." He reached into his jacket pocket and pulled out a small-calibre pistol. With a swift movement he took a pace forward. One hand went into her hair, yanking it back, the other hand thrust the barrel of the gun into her mouth.

She struggled against the chair but there was nothing she could do.

"One last chance, bitch. The number or you die." He cocked the pistol with his thumb.

I started to my knees but Jade grabbed at me. I pushed her away. I had to do something.

It was too late. Fatima was shaking her head wildly. He pulled the trigger, the gun went off, the noise reverberating through the room. The head jerked and bounced loosely on her shoulders as he released her. He put his big foot on the chair and slowly toppled it over then reached down and cleaned the barrel on her soiled dress.

If ever I got the chance, I promised myself as the echo from the gunshot continued to bounce around my head, I'd make him eat that gun.

Someday . . . somewhere . . .   My attention was drawn back to the scene below.

The three men were leaving. They did it quickly.

We stayed where we were until we heard one of the vehicles start up and head off down the driveway.

We moved slowly, still cautious, still both caught up in the horrific scene that had unfolded before us. I was thankful for the need not to speak. What could I tell Jade if she started asking questions? I knew the questions would come. I just hoped they would be delayed long enough for me to pull myself together. It was quiet downstairs. We moved into the great hall, as if pulled by some force toward the body of Fatima. Without thinking, I bent down and lifted the corpse and the chair upright. There was blood everywhere. The ropes that bound her wrists behind her back were tight and I struggled with them until they came loose.

Jade tried to help, easing the woman out of the chair and lying her body out on the floor as if she was just asleep. There were tears in Jade's eyes.

I had to get us out of there. Things had to be done. The police should be called. There was a story here. For the first time that day I remembered I was supposed to be a reporter, and just as quickly I forgot it. Nothing here could be written about, at least not yet.

"What are we going to do?" Jade finally asked as we stood together looking down at the dead woman.

"We're going to get the hell out of here," I said quietly.

Just then there was a cry from some room nearby. A baby's cry.

Jade had already started to move toward it.

"Slow down," I said, not sure. "Fatima had a baby son named Joseph."

The sound of the baby crying was louder now. "Let's find him, Julian. We can't leave him here."

We went out of the big room and stood for a moment at the junction of the hallways. The cry came again, off to the left. We hurried down the corridor. There were doors on both sides. Jade opened one, looked inside and then came out, moving on to the next door.

I picked one on the other side. The baby's crying was louder now. It was the right door. I went in, Jade right behind. Young Joseph was lying in a cot, wrapped in a blanket.

Jade picked him up and made soft noises. The baby continued to cry for a moment, then settled down in her arms, restless and perhaps not sure of all the strangers, but more contented than when he was alone. Jade smiled down at the baby, then up at me. "I bet he needs to be changed."

I looked around. There were all kinds of baby things around the room. There was a box of nappies beside a changing table. "Let's do it quickly and get all of us out of here," I said.

She carried the baby across the room and started to change him. A rattle dangled by a string attached to the blanket. It was a little yellow duck and it rattled as it swung back and forth. I picked up the duck and held it over the baby. He grabbed for it and I let go. The last of the Roa family, I thought, and the feeling of guilt was strong. If we had just been a little earlier . . .

"Find a bag or something and put as many of the baby things in that you can find," Jade said to me. "Bottles, nipples, nappies, everything."

There was a small carry-all on the counter nearby. It was already half filled with baby stuff and I added as much as the bag would carry. By the time I was finished, Jade was fastening a pair of pants on the kid.

We made our way out through the back. I wasn't following any plan. For a moment I considered using one of the vehicles in the driveway, but the little voices in my head counselled caution. Instead we moved as quickly as possible down the side of the long driveway, me first, constantly listening for approaching cars and watching for places to dive for cover if anything or anyone approached. But we had a clear run and were soon back to where we had parked the car. Jade and the baby climbed in and I started the engine and drove out onto the highway. A few minutes later we were on the expressway heading for Sydney.

Jade kept herself busy with the baby until he was asleep in her arms.

"I think I know someone who will look after him until we get all this sorted out," I told her.

"How are you going to sort this out?" Jade countered sharply.

I glanced at her and she relented a bit. "I mean, there are dead bodies all over the place back there and the murderers are still out there. We should go straight to the police."

"We will. But let's get the baby settled first."

She nodded and we drove on in silence.

It didn't take long to pass the Hawkesbury River and then slow for the tollgates. In Hornsby I stopped at a pay phone and looked up the number of a journalist on the *Daily Telegraph*. I phoned his home. There was no answer. I called the newspaper. He and his family were overseas, I was told. I looked up two more numbers and called them. There was no answer at either place.

When I got back in the car, Jade had guessed what had happened. "Let's take him to my flat. We can work it out from there."

I nodded and started down the Pacific Highway toward the city. We had to go across the bridge and through the city in order to get to Jade's flat in the eastern suburbs.

As we approached North Sydney, Jade turned to me. "Turn right at the next intersection. I want to get something from my office before we go to the flat."

I shrugged. It wouldn't take long. I was too preoccupied with my own thoughts to even ask her what she was going to pick up. I made the turn and she pointed out the glass and metal skyscraper that housed the December Foundation. I didn't know much about it, except that it ran a lot of aid programs around the world. There was a mess of busy traffic and pedestrians around. North Sydney was almost as busy as Sydney's central business district across the bridge. But for the first time I could remember in all my trips to Sydney, there was actually a parking place available only a few paces from the ornate entrance to the building. Long rows of concrete steps led up to a patio that fronted it.

Jade started to get out of the car, then stopped. "Come with me, Julian, please."

She was still a little shaky. I got out of the car, taking the keys but not locking the doors. We were only going to be a minute.

She was carrying Joseph and we started walking up the long stairs. We went through the sliding glass doors into a massive lobby. There were five elevators and a sixth off to one side. It had a sign on it: PRIVATE.

We were standing by the first elevator when farther down the wall the one with the sign opened its shiny doors. Three men stepped out. Jade and I both recognised them at the same time and froze. They were the three men who had killed Fatima. It was a crazy conclusion but it was a fact. I looked around. What could I do? Jade was staring at them and backing away from the elevators. The distance between us was opening quickly.

The men didn't see me at first but one of them saw Jade. He pointed and his words were clear across the short distance between us. "That woman picked up Castle at the airport."

There was no time to try to make sense of what had been said. I spun around. "Run!" I yelled to her.

We sprinted out the glass doors and down the steps toward the car. My hand was in my pocket fumbling for the keys. Thank God I hadn't locked the doors. Jade got to her side first. I swung around the front and wrenched the driver's door open.

The three men were running after us. One of them had a gun half out of a shoulder holster and the big guy, the leader, was reaching over, pushing the man's arm back under his jacket. There were too many people on the footpath. They were in the way.

The engine caught the first time and I pulled out into the traffic without even looking to see if anyone was coming. There was a squeal of brakes as someone tried to miss us. He made it.

I looked in the mirror. The men were piling into the Mercedes that was parked nearby. As I swung around the first corner, they pulled away from the kerb. I gunned the engine and sent the car speeding down a steep hill. There was a sign at the bottom of the hill pointing toward the Harbour Bridge. I followed the arrow. At the next corner there were traffic lights. I prayed they would stay green but they went amber when I was still half a block away. In the mirror the Mercedes careened into view. I pushed the accelerator all the way to the floor and the Honda responded, surging forward. The light went red when we were still two car lengths away. Out of the corner of my eye I saw a bus edge forward. I twisted the wheel and we swung around his front bumper, clipping the side of it. Horns honked and I fought the wheel to gain control. We shot to the other side, bounced off the concrete wall back into the lane.

There was no time to look at Jade but I could almost feel her cringing as we took the final turn onto the bridge approach on two wheels. The light should have saved us. I slowed down and took a moment to look in the mirror. The Mercedes was right there, right behind us and gaining. He'd followed us through the red light. I floored the accelerator again and the car leaped forward. Twisting the wheel, I worked back and forth through the traffic. Now there was a truck and another bus in the two lanes ahead. I honked the horn and aimed for the narrow slot between them. Unless one of them moved we didn't stand a chance. My fender struck the rear of the truck and the driver pulled over quickly, blasting his horn at us as he lost control and turned almost sideways in the lane behind us. I caught sight of the Mercedes as it ploughed into the truck, swinging it all the way around.

The Mercedes lost speed during the collision and looked for a moment as if it had damaged one of its wheels. But it still kept coming, just slower.

We raced across the bridge. Where were all the cops when you needed them? I would gladly have surrendered to the police at this point. As we crested the middle of the rise in the bridge and started down the city side, I could see the tollgates ahead. I had a choice of about six to get through but there were cars in every one of the gates. Someone had to move soon, I thought. I gripped the wheel tightly, ready to spin it and send the car through the first empty gate. They'd have to get their toll out of me some other day, I told myself, wanting to laugh at the absurdity of the thought. There wasn't going to be another day unless one of those cars moved. I had no time to look in the mirror.

I was angling to the left when a car moved away on the far right. I swung the wheel and we cut a steep angle across the approaches to the booths. Cars honked their horns. Two slammed on brakes and slewed to a stop. We were almost there. I swung the wheel to the right and the Honda blasted through the narrow hole. The toll collector's startled face flashed by. More choices. I could pick the expressway, York Street or the George Street turn. I picked George Street. It would be filled with cars but it would be easier to get lost in its traffic.

The speed was too fast and the corner too sharp and we half slid into the oncoming lane before I was able to gain control. Down the hill we swept. The light was green but there were pedestrians. I slammed my hand on the horn and everyone jumped back. I braked hard and turned the car right onto George and then left into Hunter Street.

I took time to look in the mirror. There was no sign of the Mercedes. A plan was starting to come together. I turned right into one of the city streets. I couldn't remember the name but I remembered the car park halfway up it. I slowed down, ignoring a couple of pedestrians who were pointing at the obvious damage to the Honda's body. The Mercedes was still not in sight.

I swung into the parking lot, opened my window and took out the little card the metal box offered and then drove inside. There weren't many parking slots but the ones marked for disabled drivers were empty. I parked there.

"Let's go," I said.

"Where?"

"Come on." There wasn't any time to answer questions.

I led the way through the parking lot. On the other side the street was one-way toward the direction we'd come from. There wasn't much chance the Mercedes would be there.

The hotel I wanted was only a block away and we walked there quickly. The baby was still asleep. It was astounding, but he'd slept through it all.

By the time we arrived in the lobby of the hotel my plan had been thought through. What I needed was some time. This was what I was about to buy. I put Jade and Joseph in a corner of the lobby and then checked in, using my credit card to overcome the lack of baggage. The clerk was bored by it all, put the card through his machine and handed me a key. I asked where I could rent a car. He pointed to a table in the far corner.

A few minutes later I went back to Jade carrying two keys—one to the room we weren't going to use, and one to a new car we were going to escape in.

Half an hour later we were sitting on the beach at Bondi, ignoring the surf and sand and trying to sort it all out.

"Why don't we go to my flat?" Jade asked as she rocked Joseph back and forth.

It was a good question. My little voices had already given me the answer but now I had to convince her. "Because of two facts that just don't seem related to one another. First, the men who chased us were the men who killed Fatima Roa and, presumably, all the others at Santamaria's."

"But they didn't see us there, Julian."

"Didn't you hear what one of them said on the steps? Something about the girl at the airport and he mentioned my name."

"I don't understand?"

"Neither do I, but we've got a link between me and you, between Fatima and her killers and between all that and the December Foundation."

She leaned back on the sand, letting the baby slide gently down beside her. He was awake now, making quiet noises. "That's ridiculous. What would killers be doing in the foundation?"

"You've never seen any of those men at the foundation?"

"Never. The idea's ludicrous. The foundation's record of humanitarian good works is exemplary. Carson would never have men like that around. He's a great man."

She made sense but the doubts still nagged me. "Anybody else in that building?"

She shook her head. "Not that I know of. The foundation occupies the whole building."

I couldn't see the connection but it had to be there. Three killers coming out of the building. They had named me. They had only referred to Jade as *that woman*.

"Carson's a great man," she repeated. "He cares about people."

I nodded. I wished I knew more about her benefactor. Assuming Carson was involved, the only connection I could see was the Roa money. That made sense. But it was thin because the money was adequate motivation for all kinds of people to do evil deeds. Millions of dollars could turn a lot of people.

It was getting dark. I had a baby I hadn't counted on and someone after me, after all of us now. And Jade was defending the only man who seemed to have any kind of motive—weak as it was—for any of this.

She turned to me. "There's one thing, though," she started, before pausing as if she didn't want to believe it.

123

"What's that?"

"The elevator, the one marked Private."

I remembered. "What about it?"

She was pale. "It's Carson's personal elevator. Only he and his private staff ever use it. It goes to the top of the building, to the personal floors he occupies. It doesn't even have exits on the lower floors."

I nodded. It was all the link I needed.

CHAPTER ELEVEN

We left the beach as the sun set. Jade changed the baby in the back seat while I bought some milk and conned a nearby takeaway operator into warming the baby's bottle. All the time I kept mulling over the possibilities. Jade and Carson. Carson and the killers. That didn't work. Carson and Jade. Jade and Castle. Castle and Carson. Castle and Roa. Castle and the killers in Manila. Castle and the killers in Sydney. I shook my head.

The warm bottle was passed across the counter and I carried it back to the car. Jade started feeding the baby. For the time being the baby was good for her. It helped her set aside the trauma of what she'd been through that day.

"When are you supposed to be leaving?" I asked her.

"Couple of days."

"What happens between now and then—from the foundation's point of view?"

She shrugged. "Loading the medical supplies aboard the ship."

"Do you know when that's happening?"

"Tomorrow, I think."

"You've seen the supplies?"

"Sure. I checked them off on the master list."

"All of them?"

She grinned. "Certainly not. The manifest is thick, Julian. Thirty or forty crates."

"So, tell me about your checking."

"I went down to the warehouse, checked the first couple of pages. It was all first-rate stuff. Medicine. Medical gear. Carson doesn't scrimp."

I still didn't have anything. I kept probing. "Why were you recruited?"

"I'm a doctor. They needed a doctor to take the medical supplies into Nicaragua and then to supervise the operation inside the country."

"And your political beliefs probably helped."

She bristled a bit. "I believe what Carson believes—that the peasants in Nicaragua are getting a raw deal because of the interference in their sovereign affairs by the American government."

I nodded, then changed tack. "Let's go over what you said earlier. The foundation's building. You've been through all of it?"

She shook her head. "Not all of it. Like I told you. Some of the floors, the upper ones, are off limits."

"Off limits?"

"That's right."

"Why?"

"How would I know? I had a job to do and it was all going quite smoothly, until you came along."

"Sorry about that," I said, a little too sarcastically.

She looked at me kindly. "Sorry I said that."

"Don't be, because it brings us full circle again. I'm trying to track down a Filipino named Roa who carried $50 million to Geneva. He was killed in Italy. In Manila someone tried to kill me. I come to Sydney after Fatima Roa and someone kills her,

126

then someone coming out of your office tries to kill both you and me."

"And you think Carson's involved?"

"Off the cuff, and with little evidence to support it, the answer is still yes."

"And I say you're wrong. Carson wouldn't be in it."

"You're overlooking that private elevator." I paused. There was one way we could go to clear up part of the mystery. "Are you prepared to help me do something to try and prove you're right about Carson?"

She pulled the empty bottle out of the baby's mouth. "Sure. What do you want to do?"

"I want to get into that warehouse and look around."

"Why?"

"Because I don't know where else to start."

She was quiet for a minute. "I'll help you, but I know you're wrong."

I started the car and drove across the city toward the harbour and the docks where she said the warehouse was located. We stopped once while I tried to call the telephone numbers so we could find a temporary home for Joseph. I had no luck.

We agreed she and Joseph would wait in the car and we'd park two blocks away. I didn't like leaving her but there weren't a lot of choices.

I left the car under a street light and walked slowly back toward the warehouse she had pointed out. I went right past the huge building that backed onto one of the wharves. There was no one in sight and no cars or trucks on the street. The whole scene was deserted, as well it might have been at this time of night.

The warehouse was in darkness. It loomed like a large monolith and it had an air about it in the night's gloom that encouraged a sense of fear.

There was a large flashlight in a tool kit in the trunk of the car. The light was going to be needed. The only windows were so high on the two-storey walls that there was little chance of light getting inside from the street.

The chain link fence provided no real barrier. I climbed over it where it touched the wall of the building, dropping down on the concrete driveway inside. A small metal plate attached to the fence named a local security firm that patrolled the area but I knew what that meant—not much more than a folded business card stuck in the front door. All that was needed was a piece of tape to hold it in place so the security man driving past in his car would see it was still there, apparently undisturbed. I wasn't going in the front door anyway.

I moved quickly down the long wall. There were a number of loading docks, but each door was firmly locked. At the end of the wall the warehouse backed out onto a dock and beyond the dock lay the harbour. For at least a block in both directions the dock was deserted. There was a truck and some lights and men some distance away but they appeared to be busy and I planned nothing that would attract them. I walked the length of the back wall and turned down the far side of the building. It was even darker there, and narrow. It was a sheer drop from roof to ground and the alley was too tight a fit for trucks to turn around.

Peering through the darkness I finally saw what I wanted, an old-fashioned fire escape with its bottom rungs swung up just slightly out of reach. It angled back and forth up the wall, the stairs steep, to the roof. At one point it cut neatly across a window. The roof or the window looked like my best way in. There was nothing at ground level.

An old packing crate at the end of the alley was

128

empty and easy to move. It provided the height for me to reach the metal ladder and pull it down to where I could step onto the bottom rung. It creaked and groaned in the night, the sound echoing off the walls of the neighbouring building. The bottom of the ladder was on some kind of spring and it swung back up behind me with a loud clang. I clambered up as far as the window, mindful of the noise my feet were making.

The window was dirty and hadn't been opened in years. There were thick cobwebs around its corners. I shone the flashlight inside. A lot of the light was lost in the dirty glass but there was enough to show piles of crates on what appeared to be the second floor. The floor only ran around the inside few metres of the vast storehouse and I could see over the edge into the vast darkness of the main part of the building. There was no give in the window when I tried to push it up or sideways, but the drop inside was not far. With the window open I could get in and out without too much trouble.

I continued climbing until I was over the lip of the roof. It was dirty and covered with a thick coating of gravel and bird shit. I crunched across to the front of the building and looked down into the street. I could just see the car in the distance; it appeared lonely and small. I turned away, determined to get on with it quickly. The sooner we could be away from here the better.

Access from inside the building out onto the roof was through a small boxlike structure on the alley side. There were also a few skylights, but I discounted these. The flashlight revealed a long drop down into the darkness. No one was going in or out that way, unless they'd spent a few months mastering the tricks of the SAS. The roof access door had no visible handle or lock and it was well secured from the inside. That left the window on the fire escape.

As I walked back across the roof I picked up a robust piece of plank. A quick check of the rear of the building showed the same scene along the wharf. There was no one nearby that I could see. With the wood tucked under my arm I went over the edge of the roof and back to the window. I shrugged out of my jacket, wrapped the wood inside it and thrust it against the glass. Nothing happened. It was stronger than I thought. I swung much harder, right at the bottom corner.

The glass shattered, the sound bouncing around the alley. I held my breath. There were no other sounds, no alarms. Carefully I knocked out the rest of the glass, taking care that it all fell inside. Then I shook the jacket, put it on and stuck my head in. The drop was less than my height. With the flashlight I noted where the glass shards lay and then eased through the frame and dropped inside. My legs took the shock and for a minute I just stayed in the crouched position and listened.

The old building had its own sounds. It creaked and groaned with age and the pressures of night damp and day heat. Finally it was time to move. The flashlight revealed crates all around the vast cavern on the second storey. There was a set of steps a few metres away and I went down them quickly. The crates where I came in were covered with a thick layer of dust. My guess was they'd been there long before Julian Castle and Jade Price had become involved in any of this.

On the ground floor the front half of the warehouse was one large room. Jade had told me that it was here she had been shown the cases of medical supplies. I swung the light around. The cases she described were easy to spot. They had bright red crosses on them. I circled the pile.

Nothing seemed out of place. She'd checked the front row of cases, so I ignored them. At the back of the pile I knocked gently on a crate with the light. The sound was dull and heavy. On a nearby table was a crowbar. I picked it up and felt along one of the cases until I found a board that was slightly loose. Inserting the end I pried out the wood just far enough to let me shine the light inside. There were bundles of white cloth and around each bundle an identifying wrapper listed the size and shape of the bandages within. Using the end of the crowbar I carefully tapped the board back into place.

I did a quick count of the pile. Four high, four wide, four deep. In a block. That was sixty-four crates. Jade had said about forty. There was a discrepancy, but one easily explained, I thought. Still, I pondered the number. There was a small stepladder nearby. I moved it against the pile, climbed to the top and shone the light across the crates. The boxes were all identical. I tapped the flashlight against the top box I was leaning against. It rang with the same solid sound I had heard on the crate I had opened. Reaching across I hit one of the inside boxes. It had a different sound. I tapped it again. It sounded hollow. I climbed up on the pile and laid the light in a position where it lit the hollow-sounding box. The crowbar quickly lifted away the wooden top. I picked up the light and shone it inside. Nothing. It was empty. It didn't tell me much but it did suggest something strange was going on. Why put empty boxes in a pile and surround them with filled boxes? I tapped three more tops. The same empty echo sounded.

I climbed back down. I still had no idea what I was looking for. Picking my way through various crates, some open and some closed, I went into

the back half of the warehouse. It was compart-
mented off into rooms. Most had solid walls but
one looked like an office. There was a desk and
chair, some filing cabinets and the walls were part
glass. The door was open. I went in and rifled
through the papers on the desk. Routine stuff. The
filing cabinets were all unlocked. I pulled out
drawers at random. Again, it was all paperwork
that revealed nothing suspicious.

I wandered back out into the big room and
walked past the doors to the other storerooms. A
couple of the largest rooms had locks on them,
the rest had doors that swung open at the touch.
There was nothing of interest in any of them.
Examining the big padlocks on the locked rooms
I knew there was no way I was going to get past
them—with a few hours and the right equipment,
maybe. But I didn't have the time or the gear.

I went into a room next door to one of the locked
vaults and shone the light on a wall that both
rooms seemed to share. It was just planking.
Sturdy, no doubt, but with just enough cracks
between the boards to let me get the crowbar in.
I paused for a moment. There was a chance this
was going to show. A crate could be sealed up
again with little evidence to show the tampering.
The wall was another story. But I'd come this
far and those little voices in the back of my head
were clamouring loudly to see what was beyond
the wooden wall. I stuck the crowbar through and
leaned against it. The plank splintered, protested
loudly with a squeal of sliding nails and then came
loose. The light showed another board on the other
side of the two-by-four frame. I needed more room
to move. I wrenched out three more boards and
then attacked the first board that made up the
inside wall of the locked room.

It proved more difficult. Something was packed

132

almost against the wall but slowly, and with what seemed like a tremendous amount of sweat, I was able to slide it sideways. As the board slid away, the side of a wooden crate came into view with just enough writing and symbols to show it was identical to the crates in the big pile I had just checked. As I worked at removing more boards I tried to guess the possibilities. Could be the medical drugs that went with the shipment. Logical to keep them under lock. That still didn't account for the empty boxes seemingly hidden inside the pile.

Finally I'd removed enough of the boards to squeeze through but the crates were in the way. Higher up, though, there was enough room to squeeze between the top crate and the roof. I went out into the main room and carried the stepladder inside. Very faintly through the thick walls I could hear a couple of cars driving past. They seemed to be going very slowly, but the sounds of the engines drifted away as they passed on down the street. The crowbar went into my belt and I climbed the ladder, cursing as I banged an elbow against the rough edge of the wall's frame. Hell of a way to make a living, I thought wryly.

I squeezed over the top of the crate and brought the light to bear. The room was full. There was only the narrowest of passages down the centre of the large room and another passage that led to a door obviously leading into the next room that, on the outside, also had a padlock. The door facing me was closed but there was no sign of a lock.

Swinging off the crates, I lowered myself down to the floor. I'd check these crates next. First I wanted to try the door. It opened easily and swung away from me into the dark. I brought up the flashlight. Bingo! My little voices cheered as I gasped at what lay beyond.

I'd seen military equipment before, in military camps and in the mountains with guerrillas and most of all in Vietnam, and the scene in front of me was up there with the best of them. Racks of M-16s from America, AK-47s from Russia, mortars of various sizes, small artillery guns. Boxes marked with stencils defining different types of ammunition and, on the first swing of the light, at least four different types of grenades. Claymores. Plastic explosives. Enough to start a large-scale war. I corrected my assessment: enough to start a lot, one hell of a lot, of little wars. I shone a light into an open crate boasting red medical crosses on the outside. There were a couple of dozen semi-automatic pistols, brand new and professionally packed in gun grease.

I'd seen more than enough but I just had to be sure. I walked back into the first locked room and jimmied open one of the sealed medical crates. Well-packed M-60 heavy machine guns. Sonofabitch!

It was a good plan. I had to give Carson that. Jade Price as doctor and protester against the militant aspirations of her government would make the perfect foil. Who'd question her credentials? Even she believed it. I smiled as I thought about the stout defence she'd launch against anyone who suggested there was anything in these crates but medical supplies. And if they pushed, she'd open a few of the crates—the ones outside, and the curious would be satisfied. Bandages and splints, medicine and syringes. I toyed for only a moment with the question of how widespread this arms racket really was. The December Foundation was active throughout the Third World and in many of the hottest spots on the globe.

That was the key, of course. I didn't know much

about Carson's activities but it dawned on me that I couldn't think of one of the December Foundation's sites of activity that didn't involve the opportunity to arm someone. Aid to the Third World! Some aid!

The little voices heard the sound before I was aware of it. Perhaps the voices had lost interest in this armoury faster than me. But I was ready for the second burst of sound. It was an electric motor, followed quickly by the noise of a large metal door rising. I had visitors and they weren't sneaking around. They were coming right in the front door.

I remained perfectly still. I was in trouble but there was just a chance they wouldn't know I was in here. The broken window couldn't be seen from the main floor area. I was locked in. If they stayed out of the room where I'd pried loose the boards, they might do whatever they came for and then leave. Who worked long hours at this time of the night?

I listened carefully. The motor stopped, then started again. The door was closing.

There was some talking and a lot of feet moving around.

"Castle!" someone shouted.

That was the last thing I expected—wanted—to hear. How the hell?

"We know you're in here and we're going to find you, so you'd better come out right now and save us the trouble," the voice said. It sounded such a reasonable request. There was no anger in the voice, just determination.

I moved to one of the rifle racks. I had no idea how to run an AK-47 but the M-16 was different. I'd played with one of them before. I carried it over to a box of ammunition, slipped the clasps off the lid and opened it up. The bullets were in special loaders. I had the magazine out quickly, pressed two clips of bullets into it and then clicked it back into the rifle. I hadn't done it often but it went more or less smoothly.

"Castle! Time's almost up."

I didn't understand that threat. I gently pulled on the mechanism and put a bullet into the breech. It wasn't the best answer but I couldn't think of a better one just now.

"Castle, I've got no more patience. Come out or I kill the woman and the baby."

My fingers tightened on the rifle.

"Julian! They've . . ."

Jade's voice was cut off. It sounded like someone had thrown a hand over her mouth.

"You heard that, Castle. We shoot the kid, then we start with the lady. You save both of them if you come out now. Time's counting down."

I looked down at the M-16. I wasn't a soldier. I was a reporter. I'd gladly have traded this gun for any typewriter right now. My fingers released the magazine and I tossed it on top of a crate, then walked up to the door and thumped the butt against it a couple of times. Then I tossed the rifle away.

Feet ran to the door. "Hands on the head, Castle. Stand back."

Someone put a key in the lock. A few seconds later the door slid back and I stood there, as they'd called it, hands on the head. The lights were on and I blinked at the vicious glare. As I focused, my eyes caught Jade and Joseph. They were standing between two men, both with handguns. Jade looked miserable.

My attention went to the three men standing off to one side watching me. The one on the right was the guy who had killed Fatima. I didn't know the guy on the left. The man in the centre was distinguished-looking, shorter than the other two, with greying hair and a three-piece suit. He stepped forward.

"Mr Castle. That was a very smart move. My name's Carson. William Carson. You've broken into one of my warehouses and I don't like that."

I didn't have many lines left. "Maybe we'd better call the cops and get me arrested for breaking and entering."

Carson didn't laugh. He didn't even smile. "Unfortunately, Mr Castle, you and Miss Price seem to have a habit of screwing up things that are very important to me. In fact, you've done it twice lately."

"Roa's money?" It wasn't even a guess.

"Exactly. And now I have to decide how to save my investment and what to do with you two," he looked toward Jade and Joseph, "you three." He turned away quickly. "Tie them up and lock them away for a while. And get their car off the street."

There were half a dozen gunmen besides Carson and his two deputies. They pushed me over next to Jade.

"I'm sorry, Julian. They just came up to the car and smashed the window and grabbed us."

I nodded at her and tried to grin but one of the men pinned my arms behind me and started tying them. The cords bit painfully into the skin.

Another gunman grabbed Jade.

"The baby?" she said painfully.

The man saw the problem. "Mr Carson?"

Carson stopped walking away and turned back. "What about the baby?"

Carson shrugged. "Leave Dr Price untied but double the guard on her and if anything happens, shoot her. Don't think twice. Just shoot her." He started to turn away, then reconsidered. "And separate them. Put Mr Castle in another room. I don't want them to talk to each other."

I watched him walk away. He was very dangerous. He was too collected and calm, too completely in control of what was going on. Men like that believed in themselves past the point of showing any weakness. Rough hands spun me around. I couldn't see Jade. I was pushed forward toward one of the unlocked rooms. Already my hands were aching from the tight ropes.

CHAPTER TWELVE

Carson stood in the middle of the warehouse office with his back to his two lieutenants. Kasilov and Alberts were both silent. Carson knew why: they'd both screwed up and they knew the penalty for that. But he knew something they didn't. He couldn't afford to dispense with their services just yet. Soon! No doubt about that. But not just yet. There was too much to salvage in order to keep this operation from floundering further. A lot of his money was tied up. Ortega's Sandinista government was paying a lot of money for the successful completion of this arms delivery. In fact, a lot of the money had already been paid in advance. He could sell some of the weapons elsewhere if he had to abandon the mission, but never in such quantities as he could to the Sandinistas. Nicaragua's military had been hardpressed ever since Washington had started aiding their enemies the Contras. Managua needed what Carson had agreed to deliver.

He turned back to them. His cold fury was well under control but he let just enough of it seep through to the surface to make them realise they were very close to the chop. "You both screwed up ... both of you should be staring down the barrel of a gun. How many times have I told you

there is no prize for second place in this business?"
It was like lecturing two errant schoolboys. They
both had their eyes on the floor. For a moment
he was disgusted. Both these men had been senior
people in their respective intelligence agencies.
Alberts' CIA career had included some of the more
covert operations—Allende's and Diem's
executions. Kasilov had babysat Carlos the Jackal
through so many terrorist operations that the
Russian could pull off a job anywhere and make
it look like Carlos was the author.

"Jade Price and Castle. Of all the combinations.
A direct link between Roa's millions and the
Nicaraguan operation. Jesus!" He paused for an
instant, then stepped closer to Alberts and lowered
his voice to make it sound even more ominous.
"You checked out Jade Price. You must have
missed something."

Alberts shrank a bit. He was visibly thinking,
the furrowed brow suggesting he was running
through the combinations of information he had
turned up about Jade Price. It didn't take him long;
his expression betrayed the seriousness of the
oversight.

"Well?" Carson asked. "What was it?"

"Her father is a correspondent for a New York
newspaper. He's based in Hong Kong."

"You didn't tell me that," Carson accused him.

Alberts shrugged. "It didn't seem important at
the time. We recruited her in Washington. The
operation was Australia–Nicaragua. I just couldn't
see how it would interfere."

Carson shook his head, less able to control his
anger now. "We have policies in this company,
just like in any business. We don't do business
with anyone with connections to the press—and
most assuredly not to the American press."

Alberts said nothing. He had no defence.

"And Castle's based in Manila. There's a bloody revolution going on in Manila. It doesn't take much to see that a Hong Kong-based reporter might find himself in Manila where the goddamn story is." He let his words sting. "Castle and Jade Price's father probably know each other—and they sucked us right in, knowingly or not."

Kasilov had said nothing, letting Alberts take the heat. It was his turn now as Carson swung to him.

"And you, you stupid giant, can't even recognise the girl at the airport as one of our key cutouts for the Managua mission?"

"I just didn't recognise her," he said lamely.

"There's files in your office covering the mission. It didn't end with your getting the weapons into Australia. Didn't you read the briefing papers and look at her picture?"

"No, sir. I only read my part."

Carson shook his head. These two were well past the point of the chop. He had already picked out their successors. He couldn't afford having failures around. In past years lieutenants who had failed on far less important missions than this had been given the chop without any chance of reprieve. He turned away from them and looked out the glass windows of the office. The pile of medical crates brought his attention back to the most pressing issue. How could he salvage this mission? He needed Jade Price to accompany the shipment. How could he use her now that she knew the truth?

Kasilov and Alberts said nothing.

"Bring the doctor in here," he ordered.

Alberts left the room.

As soon as he was gone, Kasilov cleared his throat and spoke. "None of this would have happened if Alberts had done his job in Geneva."

Carson waved his hand harshly. He didn't want

to hear Kasilov try to shift the blame. The Russian was equally guilty and there was no way he could get out from under that responsibility. If he had taken out Castle when he was supposed to, the problem wouldn't exist.

Alberts returned with the woman. She was still carrying the baby. The kid, Carson noted, was covered with a blanket and there was a rattle in the shape of a yellow duck pinned to the cloth. He tried to put together a plan while he watched her shift the weight of the baby in her arms.

She stared at him with a defiant look that suggested that she had mastered some of her fears. He had seen that look a few times before, a look that had turned from defiance to surprise as he had ordered the defiant one's death. He could do that now with so little difficulty. Alberts, Kasilov, Price and Castle—and the baby, too, for that matter. Nicely wrapping up part of his problems. There were men outside the office, waiting around the warehouse for his signal. They would gladly handle the executions in order to move up in Carson's hierarchy.

"You won't get away with this," she told him.

He smiled. "Won't get away with what, doctor? It seems to me that I'm the one with all the points here. You hardly seem in a position to tell me what I will or won't get away with."

His words made no impact on her. "You can kill us and it still won't get your damn bombs and guns into Nicaragua—I assume that's what it's all about."

"Is that what you assume?" he asked, stalling for time. Something she had said triggered a response inside his mind. He was good at this type of thing. Crisis management.

She nodded at Kasilov. "I saw him kill a woman earlier today . . ."

Carson was startled. He looked at Kasilov who was just as surprised. "You saw what?"

She hesitated, as if not sure whether she should proceed.

"You were in the house?" Carson asked.

She nodded. "I was there. I saw your man's handiwork. Five dead bodies. Some humanitarians you have around you."

The utter negligence of it all, he thought angrily. Suddenly the plan was there, unfolding before him and he knew exactly why Kasilov was being spared—at least for the moment. "So you saw Kasilov kill a woman?"

She said nothing.

"And no doubt torture her as well?" He wanted it all out now.

She remained quiet.

"And I assume the woman suffered at the hands of Kasilov? He is a highly skilled killer, doctor. Trained by the KGB, the best in the world at that sort of thing. Utterly brutal. He's worked with some of the world's most infamous terrorists. I assume you've heard of Carlos the Jackal?"

Jade nodded, her face curious and frightened.

Carson was ready now. "Do you think you could stand that kind of torture, doctor? Or your friend, Mr Castle? Or that baby?"

Most of the defiance had melted away. Her arms tightened around the child.

"You know damn well what Kasilov can do," he said, nodding at the Russian. "Alberts here is just as capable. Although somewhat less physically imposing than Kasilov, I think Alberts' forms of torture would be somewhat more technical—electric currents, cigarette burns, that kind of thing. Certainly no less painful."

She shivered.

He hardened his voice and stepped close to her.

143

"And that is exactly what is going to happen to you, to Castle and the baby if you don't do exactly as I say."

"I won't do what you ..."

He stiffened. Time to crush that last resistance, he concluded. He kept his eyes fixed on her pale green eyes. "Kasilov!" he ordered, without turning. "Kill the baby!"

Kasilov stepped forward and Jade backed away from him. Her face had completely lost all signs of its former defiance. There was nothing there now but fear. Carson watched, saying nothing. The Russian was close. He reached forward to rip the baby out of her arms.

"Okay!" she screamed. "I'll do what you want."

Kasilov paused and looked toward Carson, who nodded at him. He fell back to where Alberts had remained motionless.

"Good girl," Carson said happily. "And lucky baby." He paused while the words sunk in. "So you'll do exactly what I want?"

She nodded, trembling.

"You'll carry on with the mission we have laid down as if nothing has happened. You'll escort the supplies to Nicaragua. You'll say whatever words are necessary to anyone who asks, and in return you and Castle and the baby just might live."

"Might live?" she said in a quiet voice.

"That's the operative phrase. But don't think you have any negotiating power. You don't. You can die now. Maybe you can die later, or maybe you can live. The final decision is based on how well you do. Do you understand?"

"I understand," she mumbled.

"And just to make sure it all goes smoothly, your Mr Castle and the baby will go with you to Nicaragua on the ship. Kasilov and Alberts will go along too."

She said nothing and he was finished with her for the time being. He turned to Alberts and Kasilov. "Find a drug that will keep Castle out of action. Fill him full of it tonight and keep him that way until you get to Nicaragua. Get the ship in here, loaded and out to sea as fast as possible."

The men nodded, realising they were being given another chance.

"Get her secured. Fix Castle and then come back to headquarters. We've got some planning to do," Carson ordered. He walked quickly out of the room and down the long room past the pile of crates with the medical crosses on them. He looked at the stencilled name of the December Foundation neatly painted on each of the crates. He had pulled their asses out of the fire one more time. He was very pleased with the way he had handled it.

* * *

High in the North Sydney tower, Carson sat behind the shiny black top of his desk. The forty-year-old dark-skinned woman who had served as one of his principal assistants for almost two decades entered the office with a cup of coffee. She was absolutely devoted to him, living, along with a couple of other private staffers, in an apartment on one of the upper floors. It was hard to find staff so devoted. He watched Consuela cross the room. She still looked as good to him as she had done twenty years ago when he lifted her out of the Congo during some of the fiercest fighting there. She had been a teacher and had become, like so many blacks and whites, a refugee, displaced by government and rebel troops who took no pity on civilians as they waged their bitter civil war.

She put the coffee down in front of him, her black hand and arm almost lost against the ebony finish of the desk. He had first used her as an interpreter, then later for the relief of his masculine needs. She had asked nothing in return and he had often wondered if she gave herself to him so willingly because she liked him, or because it meant she had become his property and thus fell under his protection. It was probably the latter, he had concluded. She would have been taken by the soldiers, one way or the other, anyway. She had too much beauty to be ignored and left alone very long.

When his contract expired in the Congo, he'd lifted his men and Consuelo away from the butchered land. He had kept her with him in all his travels, had sent her to university to learn more language skills, had even sent her to Switzerland to a finishing school. She was polished quickly and became his right arm—an excellent ambassador for his company, often at his side at the annual Monaco socials and at the Chilean dictator's birthday parties, or sitting nearby during the most secret of negotiations with the power brokers he had to deal with.

They still slept together occasionally, when he needed such company. She was always willing when he summoned her to his Vaucluse mansion. He was sure it was just another duty she performed faultlessly for him. She made no demands. He watched her as she crossed to her smaller white marble desk at the far end of the large office. He admired her body in the colourful kaftan she often wore around the building. She might be twenty years older than the first time he had taken her but her body was almost the same, firm and lithe and able to please him effortlessly.

He picked up his coffee cup, followed her across the room and stood by her desk.

She looked up at him, expectantly.

"I have a mission for you."

She smiled, her teeth white against the coal-black skin.

"I want you to go with Alberts and Kasilov to keep an eye on things. Dr Price and the baby are the only insurance I have. Castle is an unknown quantity. I don't know if she would go through with all this for him. But she will for the baby. I need you there to keep the men in place. They musn't tamper with Dr Price."

She knew his plan. He had briefed her as soon as he had returned from the warehouse. She had been asleep in her suite but had dressed quickly and gone to his office when he summoned her. She was used to such interruptions to her sleep. "And when the shipment is safely ashore?" she asked.

He shrugged. "Kasilov and Alberts get the chop. Colonel Radcliffe-Jones will handle that, as well as the execution of Price, Castle and the baby."

Her eyes flickered briefly at the finality of the sentence passed on the baby. But she said nothing.

He had seen the eye movement but he knew she would carry out her instructions and the colonel would be there to do the actual killing. He knew that if he asked Consuelo to pull the trigger, she would do it herself, but he would never ask her to do *that*. He softened, realising the enormity of what had just passed through his mind. He spoke softly to her. "Why don't you call the house and have the chef cook up your favourite meal? We'll have a quiet time together."

She smiled and nodded slightly.

He turned away as a voice on an intercom announced the arrival of Kasilov and Alberts. His face hardened as he thought through what he was going to tell them. It was all a sham. He only needed them for a few more days to get the arms shipment

147

across the Pacific Ocean and into Nicaragua, then the colonel could do his job and give the former CIA man and KGB man what they deserved right now—the chop.

He was behind his desk when they entered. They crossed the room quickly, as if wanting to please him. He let them stand stiffly in front of his desk, taking away their accustomed privilege of sitting on one of the plush chairs near his desk. He regarded them with suspicion, fighting back the urge to open his desk drawer and lift out the pearl-handled Colt Commander and chop them down right then and there.

CHAPTER THIRTEEN

Jade Price missed baby Joseph as soon as she woke up in the small room where they had held her since separating her from Julian. The baby had been in the second folding army cot the gunmen had given her. She looked around, knowing protest would be useless. There were no windows in the room, and her watch had been taken. She had no way of telling if it was day or night. They had brought in two cots and some military blankets and told her to get some sleep. She had made up a bed for Joseph, carefully rolling up blankets and putting them around the edge of the cot so he wouldn't fall out. Then she had made up a bed for herself.

It had taken her a long time to settle down. She had accused herself over and over for being such a damn fool. Why hadn't she seen some evidence of what was going on around her? Was she so blinded by her own self-interest? She could find no answers that would provide her with an explanation to ease her doubts about herself.

She thought of Julian and wondered where they had taken him. His safety, and that of Joseph, now rested on her shoulders. She hated having that responsibility, knowing there was so little she could do to help them. And as she went over what had to be done, she realised that, no matter what,

Carson would have to kill all three of them at some point. Even if she cooperated totally, there was no way Carson and that big man, Kasilov, could let them live to tell what they knew.

Where was Joseph? She'd had the baby in her arms for only a few hours, but she had grown quite fond of him. He was a warm little bundle, wrapped in his blanket with the little yellow duck rattle swinging on the end of its string when it wasn't clutched in his eager little hand. Where had they taken him, and why?

The door suddenly opened and a gunman brought in a cup of coffee and some toast. He put them on the end of the cot without saying anything.

"Where's the baby?" she asked, trying to keep the urgency out of her voice, making the question as undemanding as possible.

"He's being fed."

"Who's feeding him?"

"Don't worry about it. He's in good hands." The gunman turned and left the room, shutting the door behind him and turning the key in the lock in such a way that she shivered as metal scratched on metal.

The coffee and toast signalled her hunger. She realised how long it must have been since she had eaten. She bit into the toast. It was warm. The coffee was hot and she had to blow on it for a few minutes before she could drink it. Who was feeding Joseph? Certainly not one of the toughs she had seen when they had wrenched her out of the car and used her as bait to force Julian to surrender.

Later, as she was holding the warm cup and making the final drops of the warm liquid last as long as possible, the key sounded in the lock again and the door swung open. She looked up expectantly, wanting to see what was happening—

and knowing she was safe, at least for the time being. She was surprised as the woman entered.

The woman was black, not black American or black Australian but black African. She was tall and stood erect, even weighed down with Joseph on her hip. In her hand she was holding the carry-all they had filled with the things Joseph would need. They must have retrieved it from the car. Jade searched the woman's face. Her face was beautiful and, although no longer young, she had fine features and eyes that drew Jade's gaze.

"My name is Consuelo," she said in perfect English. "I will be going with you to Nicaragua."

Jade stayed seated on the cot. "You fed Joseph?"

Consuelo smiled, her thick lips curling away from white teeth. "I did. And he ate well, too." She looked at the small plate on which a few crumbs of toast remained. "Which is more than it appears you did. Would you like some more?"

Jade shook her head. "No."

The black woman walked across the small room and handed her the baby. "You might like to keep him with you for a while. It will help me make preparations for the trip."

"How's Julian?"

She smiled again. "Sleeping like a baby. They filled him full of a sleeping drug, and they plan on keeping him that way."

"That's too dangerous," she said with alarm.

"Only to him. It's far more dangerous to us all to have him fit and trying to find a way out."

"But the drugs could kill him if not administered in proper doses, and that dosage will have to change as his system gets more exposed to it."

She shrugged. "Okay. You're the doctor. After we get to sea and only then, I'll let you have a look at the dosage. You keep him under safely and I'll be happy."

Jade felt Joseph tugging at her finger. She put the rattle in his grasp and looked back up at the woman. "What's going to happen?"

"From your point of view, not very much. You stay here for a couple of hours, then we transfer you to the ship. That won't be a problem because it's tied up right out front. You stay locked up until we are out to sea and then I'll see that you get to Mr Castle and that you and the baby get some air."

Jade listened, not interrupting.

"But remember, doctor, you hold in your actions the safety of both Castle and this baby."

Jade asked the question quickly, needing an answer. "How can you work for them, for these killers?"

Consuelo paused and smiled. "It's easy. Someday I might tell you about it." She turned and walked out of the room. The door swung shut behind her and the key turned loudly in the lock.

She was puzzled. The woman had spoken well, was dignified and talked as if she had a certain amount of authority. She was going to let Jade see Julian, even administer whatever drug they were using to keep him unconscious. Jade shook her head and rubbed the baby's tummy absently with the back of her hand.

Joseph was dry and had eaten well; his little tummy was full. He was still wearing the same clothes he had been dressed in when they found him in that house. He looked up at her and the small face crumpled and he started to cry.

Jade put him over her shoulder and cradled him close to her. "Take it easy, little man. It can't get much worse." She held back the tears that suddenly formed in the corners of her eyes. The baby was missing his mother; and she was suddenly, for the first time in many years, really missing her father.

A couple of hours later they came for her. The key ground noisily in the lock and the door opened. Two gunmen motioned and told her to move. She gathered up Joseph from where she had finally settled him down on the cot, picked up his carry-all and went with the men out of the room.

Both men had their guns out of sight, though each had a hand in the pocket of his jacket. The warehouse was much busier now. There was a light streaming through the open doors along the side wall and opening out onto the street. There were dockworkers running forklift trucks. Most of the pile of medical supplies was gone. She wondered how much of the other rooms—those with the guns—were going aboard the ship. For a moment she caught sight of Consuelo talking with Alberts. Jade wasn't as scared of Alberts as she was of Kasilov. But then she knew what Kasilov could do. She wondered how far Alberts would go. For that matter, she speculated, how far would Consuelo go?

The men steered her wordlessly across the warehouse floor. There was no sign of Julian, but a number of rooms had big locks on them. She wanted to ask where he was but she knew there would be no answer. They walked through the door, out into the pungent sea air and the bright sunshine. To the right she saw the Harbour Bridge, and she squinted in the bright sunlight. There were cars on the bridge: normal people going about normal routines. They didn't even know she was there. No one knew. Only Julian, and he was powerless to do anything.

The freighter towards which they were walking looked no different from the half-dozen others she could see moored around the dock area. She spotted the name high on the superstructure that rose boxlike in the middle of the long hull. *December Star*.

Huge cranes on the ship were lifting crates aboard, fore and aft of the cabin area. Workers were everywhere. All she had to do was yell out, to run toward them. Even if she made it—and that was highly doubtful, given those hands in those jacket pockets—they would still have Julian. She also realised that Carson was smart enough to have some kind of plausible cover story ready. The December Foundation was too well organised to be brought down by the frantic ravings of one woman running down a dock carrying a baby, pursued by two gunmen.

A ship's officer stood at the bottom of the gangway. The gunmen nodded at him.

"This the doctor?" the officer asked.

The gunmen nodded again.

The officer turned and waved at a sailor at the top of the gangway. The sailor waved back. "He'll show you where to put her. It's quite secure."

Jade's momentary hope was dashed. Even the officer knew she was a prisoner. The *December Star* was a willing part of the conspiracy.

The sailor—South American, she guessed—led them through a seemingly endless maze of corridors deep into the ship. There was even less relief inside the ship, she knew. If she managed to escape from her cabin, she would never be able to find her way out.

The sailor finally stopped in front of a narrow door. "This is it," he said. He opened the door and stood back for her to enter.

As she stepped inside, she was surprised to see a very comfortable stateroom. There was a single bed and a baby's cot. There was even a nappy-changing stand in the corner, and a bottle warmer sat on a shelf beside a small sink. There was an unopened box of baby formula and a small fridge. She crossed the room and opened the fridge. There was fresh milk inside.

The two gunmen stood by the door. The sailor followed her inside. "My name is Hector. Doctor, I understand your situation and I'm part of Mr Carson's team. He asked me to make sure you understood that."

She nodded.

"Beyond that, I'm here to assist you in any way you want."

She put Joseph in the cot and then turned to Hector. "Consistent, of course, with being part of Carson's team," she said.

He ignored the sarcasm. "Of course. You will find all your belongings in the drawers and hanging in the wardrobe. I brought everything over from the flat. I think I got everything." He smiled.

She thawed a little. "Thank you, Hector."

He tipped his head slightly. "Now, I must get back to my post. If you want anything, just press that buzzer." He indicated the button just below the light switch and left the room without looking back.

She heard a key turn in the lock.

* * *

I couldn't put it all together. It didn't add up at all. There had been intense pain and then the pain had passed. Chester Price was there, dressed in his dirty fatigues and carrying the rifle he had picked up from the dead Marine. I wanted to tell him to put it down, that we were reporters not troops. But I kept my mouth shut because I was carrying the dead officer's pistol in my hand. There was something wrong with my left arm. It was hanging uselessly by my side. I could remember a corpsman sticking a needle into it, but I couldn't find any wound that would account for its numbness. I was dizzy. I could remember getting sick all over the ground as the first surge of whatever they shot into me took effect. God, it was strong stuff.

I looked around. There was jungle everywhere and bodies, lots of bodies. What remained of our helicopter, burned out and still smouldering, was lying on its side half in and half out of the stream. Overhead the canopy of trees was so complete there was only the dimness of dusk down where we were. I looked at my watch. It was just after noon.

"The doctor's still alive," I heard Chester say. I turned and crawled on my belly across the muddy ground between us.

I looked down at the mess. There was a cavity in the doctor's chest about the size of a fist and it was sucking air. Lung wound. Not much chance of getting him out alive. The face was dirty and feminine in its youth. The eyes were emerald green. No, more like jade. For an instant, I tried to remember whatever it was that was provoked by that combination of colour and youthful feminine looks. But if there was anything, it was gone before I could call it forward.

There was the nervous sound of isolated gunfire nearby. We ducked almost involuntarily, afraid of even the sound of the rifles.

"How many made it?" I asked.

Chester shook his head. "Not many."

The doctor groaned, reached out for me with stiff fingers. The green eyes pleaded, went wide and then the whole body sagged and the hand fell away. Chester reached forward and laid his fingers across the sightless eyes. The gasping sound in the chest wound stopped.

"One less now," I said simply.

"What we going to do?" Chester asked, his fingers nervous on the M-16.

I was still having trouble thinking. We shouldn't even be here, I thought. We should be back in the Continental Hotel drinking that pungent brew that passed as Vietnamese beer. Hell, we shouldn't even be there. The war was over. A long time ago. I shook my head. The notion was foolish. The war couldn't be over. Here I was sitting in the middle of the goddamn jungle surrounded by a lot of dead and very few living, if you discounted whoever was on the other side of the stream trying to blow my head off.

The whole scene seemed to be getting clearer. The dizzy feeling was beginning to melt away. I started to get to my feet but a hand on my shoulder held me down. It wasn't Chester. He was crouched right in front of me. The pain came again as someone jabbed a needle in my arm. Hands gripped me tightly. I couldn't move. I couldn't even turn to see who it was. Then the hands let go. The dizzy feeling swept me up and the jungle started to sway back and forth in front of me. I looked around to see what idiot had robbed me of my senses just when I needed them most. No one was there. I looked down at my arm to see if I was dreaming. I wasn't. There was a big red welt where the needle had gone in and a small bubble of blood formed over the puncture wound. Troppo wasn't the word for it. I was going mad!

"Let's go," Chester said.

I followed him as he started heading for the bush behind us. It was getting darker and darker. I fought to keep up with him, but the dusk was turning to midnight black. My watch stared up accusingly when I looked down at it. Twelve-thirty in the afternoon . . .

* * *

Consuelo kept her word. Six hours later the lock clicked open and the African woman came into the stateroom and asked after Joseph. She stood by the cot and stared down at the baby, called Hector into the room and ordered him to watch the baby. He nodded his acceptance of her order and settled down in a chair with a paperback novel.

Together Jade and Consuelo went through the corridors and onto the deck. The ship was well out to sea. Jade looked off to the west and the land that was just barely sticking up above the far horizon. She felt terribly homesick, even though that land was not her home. Before she could sink further into depression, the black woman spoke.

"You are free to come and go from your cabin as you like, doctor, bearing in mind that you are a prisoner and that any action I or Kasilov or Alberts deem as antagonistic to our mission will, at the least, result in your being locked up and, more likely, the death of Castle or Joseph."

It sounded so cold. "Just like that?"

Consuelo nodded. "Exactly. Make no mistake. I, we, have a mission to perform and that takes priority over everything else."

"Will you let me see Julian, as you promised?"

"Certainly. Right now if you like."

Jade nodded and Consuelo led her back into the ship's superstructure. She couldn't tell exactly where they were going but she knew she had to start learning her way around. If they were going to stand any chance, she would have to start it all happening.

There were no guards at the door and the key was hanging on a hook nearby. Consuelo took it down and unlocked the heavy door. Inside, the room had been stripped. There was nothing there except a cot on which Julian was lying, moving uneasily. He wasn't tied down or restrained in any way.

"As you can see," Consuelo said, "he's helpless under our sedation and that's the way it must remain."

Jade knelt down beside him. His shirt had been ripped across one arm to make the skin more accessible and there were angry red welts where the needle had been thrust into the arm. Jade grimaced. "Whoever gave him the shots didn't have any idea how to go about it, did he?"

"That's why I said you could take over."

"Where's the medication?"

Consuelo took her back out into the corridor and opened a metal box near the door.

"You'll administer two things. The medication to keep him out and the drip that'll provide him with what he needs to survive. The drip's straightforward."

Jade nodded. She'd seen the clear liquid bottle by the bed. It would keep him alive. She looked into the box. There were two cartons and a handful of syringes inside. There was no antiseptic or bandages. Jade picked up the carton and read it.

"This is very powerful stuff," she said. "Too powerful for sustained usage."

Consuelo shrugged. "That's what we're using. The only freedom you've got is to vary the dosage a bit if you like. But I want Castle out all the time. The alternative is to tie him down. And I don't think you'd like that."

Jade agreed. After a couple of days pumping this stuff into him, it would take a long time for his system to overcome the effects. It wasn't like a hangover that would pass quickly. If she was going to do something, it would have to be almost immediately. She went back into the room and started examining him. She checked his eyeballs

159

and reflexes, at least as well as she could with him sprawled on the cot. Consuelo stood and watched, holding a notebook in her hand.

"This is the log of the injections," she said. "Every six hours. He's due for another now."

She looked at the log, then took a vial of the drug out of the carton. She inserted the syringe into the bottle and squeezed enough out to make sure there was no air bubble. As she slid the needle into Julian's arm, she heard him mutter. She couldn't make it all out but there was some reference to Chester and a map. She knew he was dreaming. It was one of the effects of the drug. The 'Chester' he mentioned was undoubtedly her father. She said nothing to the black woman, who watched carefully as she pulled out the syringe. She dropped the empty needle into the waste basket outside the door but pocketed the small bottle, talking as she did so, and waiting until Consuelo was busy locking the door.

They walked back together through the corridors. She noted every turn, every reference that might be helpful in the future. She felt better, knowing she was finally doing something positive.

"How about some lunch?" Consuelo asked pleasantly.

"I'd like that. I'm hungry." she said.

They walked down more corridors, then entered what was obviously the officers' mess. She shrank back a bit when she saw Kasilov and Alberts and carefully placed herself at the far side of the table well away from them. But Kasilov was ignoring her, talking instead in Russian to the officer who had been at the bottom of the gangway when they had come aboard. It was Alberts who was looking at her now, staring at her, making small talk around her and to her. She felt uneasy under his gaze, as if she could feel him trying to undress

160

her. She tried to steer the conversation back to Consuelo, but the African was more withdrawn now, as if she wanted to share nothing with Alberts and Kasilov.

The two women ate slowly, Jade matching Consuelo. For some reason she felt safer with her nearby. The men ate more quickly and then left the room.

After they had left, Consuelo's spirits rose and Jade felt better.

"I saw Kasilov kill a woman," Jade said simply.

"That's what he does best."

"Alberts made Carson sound so believable," she tried. "I was really convinced he was doing something important."

"Don't feel too bad about it. He's fooled a large part of the world over the years." She paused and then added, "And don't judge him on thugs like Kasilov. Men like Kasilov are needed in the business Carson is involved in, but mostly it's just a business."

"Some business."

"He buys from people who want to sell and he sells to others who want to buy. It's as simple as that. And, like a good businessman, he provides services for those who buy from him. He tries to keep his customers happy."

Jade almost laughed. Consuelo was making Carson sound like a candidate for an award from a better business bureau or the chamber of commerce.

"He's helped a lot of people over the years. There is a humanitarian aid side to the foundation as well," Consuelo told her.

"Just as a cover for what really goes on, though."

"Sure. But even that aid helps. If this mission hadn't come apart because of your friend Castle, you would have gone into Nicaragua with your medical supplies. Not as many supplies as you would have liked, but you could have saved a lot of peasants with what you had, and with your medical skills."

"More than his weapons kill?"

"That's where you are wrong. Weapons don't kill anyone. It's men who kill. No rifle ever shot a man without another man pulling the trigger."

Jade changed the subject. "How'd you get mixed up in all this?'"

Consuelo pushed her empty plate away and sat back in the chair. "Before your time, there was a civil war in the Belgium Congo, Zaire now."

"I've read the history books."

The African ignored her. "I was a teacher then. At least as much as it took to become a teacher. I could read and write and the government paid me a stipend to teach at a little school near Elizabethville."

Jade nodded, about to ask another question, but Consuelo was finished, at least for the time being. The African got up from behind the table.

"I'll take you back to your room. You'd get lost otherwise."

Jade followed her. They were both silent. Again Jade noted each passageway. She thought she was getting the place mapped out in her mind.

When Hector left and the door closed behind her she listened carefully. No key turned in the lock. She waited, then tried the door handle. It turned easily. She opened it and looked into the corridor. No one was there. At least she could come and go. She closed the door again and examined it. There was no way of locking it from the inside. That bothered her. She thought of Kasilov and Alberts, particularly the way Alberts had been looking at her. But there was nothing much she could do about it.

162

She checked Joseph. The baby was asleep, the little yellow duck firmly in his grasp.

Crossing to the sink she took the empty drug bottle from her pocket and looked at the seal. She needed to get the top off; this would take a nail file and some time. She was able to pry the seal in such a way that it finally came off. She filled the bottle with water from the tap and replaced the seal, carefully pushing down the edges with the back of the file. When she was finished she examined her handiwork. It would pass scrutiny, she thought. There was nothing she could do about the small puncture where the needle had entered the top. She turned the bottle upside down and shook it. Nothing leaked out. She put the bottle back into her pocket. She had to get Julian back from wherever the drug had carried him. That was only part of it, of course, she knew. But she wasn't going to get any kind of a plan together without him, she concluded.

* * *

I was drifting away from my body. I'd read about how it happens to some people sometimes. They would let their souls drift upwards, leaving the body below, watching the earthly skin and bones like some kind of ghost floating free. I could see Julian Castle lying, resting, in the mud. He was propped against some kind of large vine.

He was hallucinating now. Two women came in and out of his nightmares, gliding out of the jungle as he tried to get some rest. One was a tall black and the other a sweet-faced white girl. He could never quite hear their names. They never went near Chester, who had become very quiet as the fatigue set in. Then the women would drift away. The terrible pain in his arm had gone away now but he would feel dizzy after their visits. He

163

looked forward to seeing them. They were his only link with some other place and time, but he hated the dizzy feeling and the overwhelming need to be physically sick after they had finished with him and had left.

"Let's go," Chester said after they had rested awhile.

Time to come back together, I thought, *body and soul*. I willed myself down to where Julian was stirring in the mud. It seemed all so simple, a simple merging of body and spirit. There had been so little pain while I was separated from that body. Now the pain was back again, and I didn't like it. I wanted to tell Chester to go on without me, to leave me there where I could float free again and leave all that suffering. But I couldn't let Chester down. He'd saved my life once in a hotel room where a guy in some kind of flowered shirt wanted to kill me. I couldn't quite remember how it went. Strange that I couldn't remember. It seemed like it had only just happened. But Chester was already on his feet and moving. I had to stay with him.

I struggled to my feet and followed him as he lurched on up the hill. It still seemed very dark under the trees . . .

CHAPTER FOURTEEN

Jade Price was always locked in her room when they put in at some island on the long voyage across the Pacific. She couldn't tell exactly what was happening but had the impression that some crates were always unloaded and more were loaded. During one dinner in the officers' mess, she had been told that stops were to be made on the journey, including one stop in South America where she would be questioned by a customs officer. They said nothing else to her about it and for a few moments she had entertained the hope she would be able to tell someone about their predicament. But then she went back to her room and cuddled little Joseph, and she knew she would do exactly what they ordered.

The first time she was able to give Julian water instead of the drug was when Hector had started deputising for Consuelo during the regular injections. She had been nervous and had to concentrate to keep the needle from shaking. But Hector had been busy playing with the baby. She'd purposely taken Joseph to Julian's room. Hector was forming a bond with the child and Joseph kept his attention away from what she was doing. She had not only completed the injection and thrown the bottle in the waste basket, but was able to take five more bottles away with her from the box outside the door.

Later, she had opened each of the seals and drained the bottles into the sink before filling them with water and resealing each one. The next time she went back to his room she replaced the water-filled bottles in the carton and took more out. Within a few days she had replaced the top two cartons with water.

Now her problem was more difficult. She had to find some way to let Julian know what was happening. But not too soon. If he was slipping in and out of the drugged state, he might babble the wrong words to someone in the room. And if he suddenly woke up and found himself in the stateroom, he was sure to say something to the first person who entered.

She also had another problem. Alberts was starting to close in on her. At least that was the way it felt. Kasilov pointedly ignored her, but Alberts was starting to turn up whenever she appeared for a meal, as if he was hovering nearby waiting for her. From time to time, he knocked on her stateroom door to ask if she needed anything. She thought of saying something to Consuelo but held off, realising that this might cause even more problems. Alberts was nowhere as big and powerful as the Russian, but Jade wasn't prepared to make an outright accusation that would antagonise him. She tried to keep her words to a minimum in his presence and pointedly resisted any move he made to enter her cabin.

Julian's awakening remained her most serious problem. There had to be a solution. She started spending time on the ship's bridge. The captain and the officers ignored her. All Carson's men, they had obviously been briefed about her presence. She came and went as she liked and her casual questions were answered as long as the queries kept to general subjects. These men were doing their jobs. They were, in the main, she recognised, just professional seamen. One afternoon, as she climbed down the ladder, Consuelo called her over to the railing.

"How's the baby?" the African asked.

"Just fine."

"And your Mr Castle?"

This was the opening she was waiting for. "He's not doing as well. The drug has a debilitating effect and his lying on that cot is causing trouble for his muscles."

Consuelo said nothing. Julian Castle was a means to an end only.

"I'd like to exercise him," Jade said carefully.

"How do you do that? He's out like a light."

Jade held her breath. Had she said something wrong? "Sure he is, but the muscles can be worked if I move his arms and legs a bit each day."

Consuelo looked out across the featureless sea.

Jade pushed. "He's part of the deal, Consuelo. If I do what you ask, then you don't kill him or Joseph. Right?"

She nodded.

"Then let me exercise him. Lock me in there with him for a while each day, if you like. Just let me help him stay alive."

"It isn't that necessary," Consuelo said.

Jade turned toward her, moving closer. "It is if you want my cooperation," she said quietly, already worried about the impact of the sentence.

Consuelo cocked her head slightly and fixed her with an icy stare. "You're not exactly in the strongest position to issue threats."

She could back away, she knew. "I'm not asking much. Let me exercise him and I'll continue to help you."

The dark eyes squinted angrily. "I could dump him overboard right now and you'd still help. Don't forget the baby."

"And I could give up right now, too, and let you kill us all, but it wouldn't help you get your guns through."

Consuelo said nothing for a long time. Then she smiled. "You should be working for Carson."

"Not on your life," Jade said.

"And that's exactly what it is, doctor. Your life!" She paused, letting the thought sink in. "You can exercise your Mr Castle all you want behind locked doors and with one of our people standing out in the corridor. And if one thing is ever out of place, over the side he goes. Do you understand?"

It was definitely time to back off. She had what she needed. "Yes," she answered simply, adding, "And thank you."

The black woman suddenly grinned. "You really should be working for Carson."

Jade walked away, quietly triumphant. Now, if only she could get Julian to respond more quickly. The exercise would help, not only in getting him back on his feet but in breaking down the residue of the drug still active in his system.

One of Kasilov's men locked her into the cabin with Julian that night. She said she wanted two hours and he nodded. The men on the ship had broken into three groups: those who followed Kasilov, those who followed Alberts and the ship's crew. Jade noticed that they all followed Consuelo's orders.

She crossed to Julian's bedside and sat down beside him, lifting one of his arms and beginning to move it rhythmically, up and down by his side, then across his chest and back again. She repeated the motion. Over and over again.

"Come on, Julian, come back to me," she said

quietly to him, repeating the line over and over.

"Come on, Chester, don't give up on me," the man on the bed muttered.

* * *

Chester wasn't making much sense and he was beginning to sound like an old woman. He was tired. I was tired! But that wasn't going to help get us up onto the plateau. There was fresh shooting off to the west, at least I thought it was west. So I eased us toward the east. Our map showed a decreasing gap between the contour lines. At one point they were almost printed one over the next. The closer the lines, the steeper the hill. It would be very steep, but at least the steepness might mean less chance of running into the enemy.

I was feeling much better. The pain in my head had gone, the dizzy spells had stopped and I had no doubt that with a little help I was going to make it. But Chester was the only one there to help, and he was having enough trouble making it on his own.

The black woman who had drifted into my nightmares had stopped turning up, but the white girl was still coming. In fact she seemed to be there right now. She was far more real than usual. She was doing something I couldn't quite define. Her lips were moving. I concentrated, trying to hear what she was saying, trying to feel where she was touching me. It was somewhere on my arm. The muscles there were relaxing and tightening, on and off. If only she would work on my legs. That's where the cramps were. If she would just work on my legs I knew I could make it up those cliffs, out onto the plateau and home.

I tried telling her, whispering the words over again. *Work on my legs. Work on my legs.* Some expression washed over her face. She let go of my arm and started on my left leg. It felt much better. Then she moved to my right leg. What she did went on for a long time. I could move. It was all coming together.

I started to climb the cliffs. Chester was somewhere behind me. But there was no time to look back. If I lost him and got to the top, I would still have time to tell them he was there. They wouldn't go without him. The rocks felt hard and secure as I stepped on them, dragging myself up hand after hand. I was really going to make it.

Then the woman left, just floated away and I could do nothing more. The cramps returned and I collapsed on a rock ledge. I could see out across the valley now. I stared back over the edge. Chester was far below, but he was still coming. I tried to get some sleep, wedged into a crevice. I couldn't go on until my legs were stronger.

I woke up with the woman back by my side. She was talking again. I could hear her now. 'Come on, Julian, come back to me,' she was saying. Some little angel, maybe, I thought. I was back on my feet, climbing, as soon as she started working on my legs. *Keep going, girl*, I said, *keep going. Work on those legs. Give me the strength.*

The cliff was steeper now but I was making good progress. The plateau lip was not too far away. There was more gunfire now. It seemed to be coming from further around the hill, but higher up this time. Our people were into something vicious over there. Helicopter gunships were making sorties. They flashed past me, rotors beating up a storm. I could hear their heavy machineguns pounding away. Twice A6 Skyraiders went roaring by overhead and around a corner of the plateau out of sight. I heard the sickening *whoosh* of napalm and shivered. Ungodly stuff to dump on people—*any* people.

I'd lost sight of Chester but I knew we could come back and get him as soon as I found help. And there was lots of help up on the plateau. I was almost there. The lip was right ahead. I slowed down a bit. I didn't want some nervous sentry shooting me up, thinking I was the enemy.

Then I was over the edge, spreadeagled on the ground, lying there puffing. My angel was still working on my legs. I wanted to reach out and give her a big kiss but I couldn't because all my attention was focused on the bedlam ahead. The headquarters was there all right, but it was under attack. Two helicopters were burning, a third and a fourth frantically loading up troops. Rotors were flashing in the sunlight and machineguns mounted in the doors were laying down a murderous field of fire on the far edge of the plateau.

I started to my feet, then fell quickly as I spotted the black pyjamas and the silly little helmets of the enemy. They were moving toward the headquarters. It struck me almost as if a rotor blade had come loose and swung across the gap and hit me. The last of the troops on the plateau were pulling out. They were getting into the helicopters. The first of the two remaining choppers lifted away. There was only one man left to get into the other chopper. He was limping badly as he tried to climb in. He took a burst of fire in the back and fell across the skid. The chopper revved its engines and lifted away, the body going with it for a few feet, then falling limply back to the ground. It made no sound when it hit, just a puff of dust that went up around it and then disappeared in the wash of the chopper's blades.

I was on my feet running toward where the chopper had been, yelling. A hand was over my mouth. The enemy was running toward me.

171

Someone was smoothering me. The black woman was there, with one of those stupid helmets on. She had this great AK-47 up, aimed at me. I could see it in her eyes. She was going to shoot. There was a red flame spitting from the barrel. I braced myself to feel the bullets rip into my body and closed my eyes, waiting, waiting . . .

* * *

Jade tried desperately to keep her hand over his mouth. He was coming out of it but he was trying to yell. She wondered what devils he was wrestling with.

"Quiet, Julian. Quiet," she said, over and over again.

His eyes flicked open, went wide and then closed again. She could see he was fighting some tremendous battle deep inside. The eyes opened once more and found a focus on her face. He was moving his mouth under her hand, asking questions. She could almost make out the words as they vibrated through her palm. His arm came up and his fingers clutched at her arm like talons, as if he was afraid she was going to leave him.

"Can you hear me, Julian?" she asked him.

There was no answer. She lowered her face toward him. He pushed his head back into the pillow. There was fear on his face. "Easy, Julian," she said to him. "Can you hear me now?"

There was a slight nod of the head.

"Listen carefully. We're in great danger right now. Great danger. Do you understand?"

There was another little nod.

"I'm going to take my hand away. Lie perfectly still. Say nothing. Say nothing, Julian. Do you understand?"

Another nod.

She lifted her fingers away.

172

He opened his mouth and she quickly laid a finger across his lips. "Say nothing," she repeated.

He closed his mouth.

"Just nod that you understand what I'm telling you."

He nodded.

"We're on Carson's ship, taking weapons to Nicaragua. Do you remember Carson?"

He nodded.

"They had you drugged. They still think you're drugged, but I've been replacing the dosage with water. You're well out of it now but they mustn't know. Do you understand?"

He nodded and the lips formed a silent word. "Yes."

There was a knock on the door. "Time's up, doctor," the guard said.

She needed more time but she knew it would look wrong if she tried to break the routine she had been going through up to now. "Lie perfectly still. Close your eyes. Stay that way until I get back."

He nodded and mouthed silently. "Okay."

She got up and left the room. The guard walked with her down the corridor and then went in another direction. She hurried back to her cabin, let Hector go and lay down on her bed. It had worked. They were a long way from safety, but they had made it past the first hurdle.

She tried to sleep, but it was fitful. She couldn't wait to get back to Julian but she also realised that she had to maintain the strict routine she had established as the ship made its way across the Pacific. She was surrounded by clever enemies, she had come to realise. They would pick up on anything out of the ordinary. Their security depended on their ability to detect changes in patterns, no matter how subtle.

She played with the baby, recognising how much she had come to depend on the youngster for relief from the dangers all around her. In idle moments, she wondered about Joseph's future. There had been no time to think about it before. She could see the weakness of the thought immediately. The odds were still very much against the three of them having a future.

Six hours later she returned to Julian's room. Hector was back with the baby. A guard was posted as usual outside the door while she was inside. But she also watched carefully as he opened the door. There was still no attempt to use the key that was hanging nearby. The door remained unlocked; they believed Julian was under the influence of the drug. From the box she took a syringe and a bottle of water. She had now been able to replace all the drugs with water.

The guard watched while she gave the injection then went back into the corridor, closing the door behind him when she started exercising Julian's legs. Julian had obviously understood what she was trying to do. He lay very still and kept his eyes closed until she started working on him.

"He's outside. Talk very softly," she said quietly.

He opened his eyes and looked up at her. His eyes were clear. That was a good sign, she knew.

"Fill me in," Julian said.

She told him everything she could think of. While she talked she kept exercising his legs and arms. She was scared, knowing that if the guard caught them talking it would all be over. When she was finished, she watched him thinking.

"You did just fine, Jade," he told her.

"What are we going to do?"

"First of all, we've got to find out if I can walk. Go over to the door and lean against it. That'll give us a moment if anyone tries to come in."

She did as he said.

When she was against the door, she watched him struggle with his dormant muscles. The massages she had given helped, but he was still having trouble. With one hand he held the intravenous drip stuck in his arm. He almost fell to the floor, saving himself by falling back on the bed. She could see how much he was trying. Sweat formed on his forehead as he finally stood up beside the bed. He took a tentative step. It was a weak move but he managed to stay up. He took another step, then turned around and walked another pace in the other direction, staying close to the bed. He lifted his arms and swung them around, breathing deeply. As his strength came back he did some deep knee bends. But it was all he could manage.

She left the door and went to his side.

"I need some solid food," he said, "and you'll need to show me how to take this drip out and how to put it back in. I can't move much attached to that bottle."

She nodded. "What else?"

He grinned. "How's Joseph?"

"He's just fine. He's got a babysitter when I'm in here."

There was silence for a long moment. "We need to find out a few things . . ."

"I can do that," she interrupted.

"Good. First, we need to know where we are and, if possible, exactly where we're going. Most important is some idea of the time schedule we're faced with. How long have we got to put together a plan?"

"I don't know exactly where we're going but I think we have a couple of stops before Nicaragua. We've got to be most of the way across now."

He nodded. "We also need some idea of the competition aboard the ship. You told me Kasilov and Alberts are here. Also this woman Consuelo. A few of their gunmen. What about the crew?"

"Just professional sailors, I think," she said. "Most of the security seems to be being handled by Carson's lieutenants and their men."

"Can you draw me a diagram of the ship?"

"Sure. One of the engineers took me on a tour. And he's always prepared to answer my questions. I think he likes my legs."

He grinned. "Good. I need to know where the weapons are being stored and how I get from here to there."

She was surprised and worried. "You can't shoot it out with them, Julian."

"I have no intention of shooting anyone if I can help it. What I want is to find some way to disable the ship, maybe cause some kind of commotion long enough for us to get over the side."

Joseph was the first though that entered her mind. "What about the baby?"

"He goes with us. You make sure you know where there are three lifejackets and you figure out how to make one tight enough to keep the baby afloat without him slipping through. And see if you can pick up any money. We're going to need it when we get to shore."

They continued talking for a few minutes more. She wasn't sure if he had a plan, but the words sounded strong. Then she left and started immediately gathering together the items he had requested.

The food was no problem. She had access to the galley where the baby's meals were sometimes prepared. On almost every trip to see Julian, she was able to take him some food. She taught him how to take the drip out of his arm and she stood by the door while he exercised. Before long, he was almost fit.

She had even less trouble finding out exactly where they were and where they were going. Everyone was now accustomed to seeing her on the bridge. The navigation alcove was open to anyone there and she watched, showing enthusiasm as the young navigator plotted his courses. She asked questions and he gave her the answers. The ship was now one day out of Buenaventura on the Colombian coast of South America. But while the navigator could tell her where they were and where they were going, including a later stop in the small Costa Rican port of Quepos, before entering Nicaragua's waters, he couldn't tell her why they were making the stops. Or wouldn't tell her, she thought as she left the bridge.

She and Julian went over the diagrams she'd drawn for him. It was her guess—and it was only a guess because she couldn't appear to be interested—that the weapons were in both the forward and aft holds. She had walked along the decks. Heavy, wide hatches covered the holds, she told him. But there were smaller hatches that would allow a man access to the ladders leading down inside the holds. She had one more important piece of information. On the bridge she had seen a damage control panel. It showed all the waterproof doors and main bulkheads and it had a large display area of lights, red and green.

"There are green lights on the panel. They look as though they're located between each hold," she told him, feeling she might have the key to how they could move inside the holds without being seen from the deck. "My guess is that they are doors, or hatches, and the green light means they are open or, at the least, not tightly secured."

"There is another possibility," he said.

"What?"

"That they're some kind of alarm system in case anyone penetrates the holds."

She looked glum.

He grinned at her. "I don't know for sure, but let's assume you're right in the absence of any more evidence. So once I'm in the hold, I should be able to move from one to the next."

"That's my guess."

They both stared down at the diagrams.

She had to ask. "When, Julian?"

He pondered the thought. "I'm going to have a first look tonight. It's got to be tonight because tomorrow afternoon you say we put into Buenaventura."

"I should go with you," she said.

"No way. That just doubles the risk. You can be much more helpful by going up onto the bridge and talking to as many of the watch crew as possible. Every set of eyes you can keep away from the deck the safer I'll be."

"I can do that," she said. "When?"

"You normally give me my last shot for the night about eleven. I've noticed very little traffic past this door from midnight on, so I'll plan to start then."

She looked at her watch. "I've got to go. I've been in here with you too long."

Without warning, he reached forward and took her in his arms. She was surprised. In another time and place, it would have happened a lot sooner, she said to herself as they looked at each other and grinned. He kissed her quickly, then released her. For a moment she thought of protesting against the briefness of it all, and then she held back. There would be time to start again soon, she concluded. At least, she hoped, there would be time—despite all the odds lined up against them.

There was a momentary panic at the eleven o'clock injection. Consuelo appeared with the guard. She stepped inside and looked down on Jade, who was kneeling and filling the bottle.

"Your patient looks remarkably well," the African said.

Jade fought to keep the fear from her face. She tried to look grateful. "It was your letting me work his muscles that helped keep the skin tone up," she explained.

Consuelo nodded. "Just remember your part, doctor, and he might even be allowed to stay healthy."

"I remember my part—not that I've had much to do so far."

"You start earning your passage tomorrow," she said.

"What do I do?"

"I'll brief you fully in the morning."

She wanted desperately to say something to Julian but the woman's continued presence made it impossible. Jade looked down at his closed eyes and steady breathing and silently wished him well, a hidden prayer. It had been a long time since she had prayed, she suddenly thought. She rose to her feet and walked towards the door. Consuelo turned and went out ahead of her, saying nothing and walking swiftly up the corridor. Jade walked more slowly, pausing for a moment at the end of the hall and looking back. The guard had shut the door and walked off in the other direction. He had not locked the door to Julian's cabin.

She looked at her watch as she turned the doorknob of her cabin. She would give him ten minutes and then she would go up to the bridge. She had been there before at night, almost hiding herself in one corner of the red-lit steel and glass enclosure. The red lights helped night vision. She walked into her room.

When she had left, Hector had been sitting in the corner reading yet another of his seemingly unlimited supply of raunchy paperbacks. Now Alberts was sitting there, staring across the room at her. She hesitated, not sure what to say. She had steered well clear of Alberts, rejecting his offers of companionship. There was something about the man, something very different from the fears she felt in the presence of Kasilov, that scared her just as much as the Russian did.

"Where's Hector?" she finally asked.

"I sent him away because I wanted to talk to you."

She sat down on a chair, as far away from him as she could get without going back out into the corridor. "What do you want to talk to me about?"

"About *us*," Alberts said slowly, grinning.

"Us?" She didn't understand.

His words were quietly slurred, as if he had been drinking too much. "There has to be an *us*," he explained. "If there isn't, you are going to die."

She started to shake her head, but he continued.

"If there's an us, I can talk Carson into letting you and me go off on our own away from everyone else here. I can convince him to let you live."

She was fighting for control. This was crazy talk. She tried to think of anything she had ever said to him that would have let him leap to any conclusion like this. There was nothing. "They'll let us live if I do what they want."

"*Bullshit!*" Alberts said explosively, getting to his feet but not moving. "They'll use you and Castle and the baby and then they'll kill you."

He was saying what she had always really believed. "I can't accept that. I must do what they say, for the baby . . ."

180

He interrupted strongly. "I'm the only hope you have." He moved towards her.

The menace was overwhelming. She got to her feet quickly, looking toward the door but realising he had already thought of that and had angled in a direction where he could cut her off. "What do you want?" she said loudly.

"I want you. I've always wanted you, right from the first time we met in Washington." He reached out for her and she darted away to the other side of the room.

She was standing beside the small cot where Joseph was sleeping. She reached down and picked up the baby, as if the infant would defend her.

For a moment it worked. Alberts stopped advancing and held back. "You like babies, don't you?" he asked, his voice low and reasonable. "I've watched you with that one. You're very good with babies. I can give you lots of babies and you can be very happy."

He was crazy! She couldn't argue with a crazy man. Somehow she had to get to the other side of the room, to the buzzer button under the light switch. She walked towards the switch, which meant walking towards him. She tried reasoning with him. "Look, Arnold, it's late. I'm tired."

"Then let's go to bed," he said with a wicked smile, taking a step forward.

She shook her head. She was holding the baby tightly. Joseph was squirming in her arms.

Alberts lunged at her and caught her arm. She slapped at him with her free hand, hitting the side of his face just under his ear. He looked back at her, shocked. Then he slapped back, hard, hitting her arm and dislodging the baby and the blanket. She stumbled and fell to her knee. The buzzer was only an arm's length away but the baby was holding her off balance. She lowered Joseph the rest of the way to the floor as Alberts grabbed at her again. She swung around him and he grabbed the front of her shirt and pulled hard. The material ripped away from her chest and shoulder. She lashed out with her foot, hitting him in the shin. He backhanded her and she was hurled exactly where she needed to go, smashing up against the wall almost on top of the buzzer. She pressed it hard, holding her finger against the button.

Alberts saw what she had done and grabbed her arm, wrenching her away from the wall and back into the room. She fell over a small coffee table in the middle of the stateroom.

There was a howl from Joseph at exactly the same time as Alberts stepped on the little yellow duck rattle. There was the sound of plastic being crushed, followed by a snap as the tough material splintered.

Jade hardly noticed the large pieces of yellow plastic. She was hurting from the blows and from falling across the table. She was also worried about Joseph—and Julian. He was expecting her to play her part on the bridge.

Alberts launched himself across the gap between them, pinning her to the floor, fumbling with the rest of the shirt that now hung, ripped and open, from her shoulders. She strained to throw him off but he was too strong.

There were sounds in the hallway. She could hear voices nearby.

She screamed. "Help me! Help me someone!"

Albert's face was above hers. He was oblivious of everything except her body.

She couldn't see the door. But she heard it burst open. There was only a brief pause and then a gunshot rang out.

Alberts' expression registered shock, then disbelief, then he rolled off her as if in slow motion. He lay crumpled on the floor beside her.

Jade focused, shaking and pulling her shirt around her naked breasts and chest. Consuelo was standing in the doorway, the gun in her hand falling back to her side. Two guards pushed past her into the room and stood waiting for instructions.

"Get him out of here," Consuelo ordered.

The men picked Alberts up and unceremoniously dragged him out of the cabin.

"He was going to die anyway. He was a foul-up all along the way," Consuelo said, as if explaining.

Jade said nothing, lifting herself up and sitting on the bed. She watched as Consuelo leaned over and started to pick up the crying baby. The African reached down beside the blanket and picked up two of the larger pieces of the broken yellow duck. She knew what it was.

As Jade controlled her shaking, she watched Consuelo examine the yellow plastic closely.

"What do you know about this?" she asked Jade, walking over to her with the plastic and the baby. She held the plastic up so Jade could clearly see the numbers scratched on what had been the inside of the rattle.

"I have no idea," she said, honestly.

Consuelo gave her the baby and then studied the numbers again. "I've seen numbers like this before. Not the same numbers but the same kind of series. Three numbers, a gap, two numbers, a gap, then more numbers."

Jade shook her head. She didn't know what the woman was talking about. She was gently massaging the sore spots where she had been struck.

"How about the Roa bank account?" Consuelo asked, smiling.

She remembered. Jade knew the shock of what she had just heard had shown on her face. Fifty million. The Geneva bank account number. That's what had set so much of all this in motion in the first place.

"So maybe Alberts solved the puzzle after all—at least in his own clumsy way. Roa didn't give the number to his wife. That's why Kasilov couldn't get it out of her. It was written inside this duck and Roa didn't have time to tell anyone where the number was before he died . . ." She paused, then seemed to remember who she was talking to. "You get some sleep."

Jade had recovered. The number was important, but so was what Julian was doing right now. "I'd really feel better with some air. I'd like to go up on the bridge for awhile."

Consuelo shrugged. "Suit yourself. I'll get Hector for you."

"No," she said, looking at the cot where Joseph had quickly settled down to sleep. "I won't be gone long and I think he'll stay asleep."

"As I said, suit yourself." Consuelo left the room, clutching the hard yellow plastic.

Jade went to her closet and took out a sweater. As she pulled it over her head she looked down. There was blood on the floor. Not much, but enough to remind her of what had happened. She wanted to be afraid or angry, but she couldn't find the feelings. There had been so much killing and always the promise of even more violence just around any of the multitude of corners that were left to sneak past. She felt very alone as she went out of the cabin and into the deserted corridor.

I thought I heard a gunshot as I started down the first of the corridors that, according to Jade's diagram, led to the outer decks. I couldn't be sure.

The ship had a lot of strange noises at this time of night and this was the first time I'd been out of that room for a long time. But it sounded like a gunshot. I tried to put it out of my mind. There was a long way to go before I could get back to my bed.

There seemed to be a lot of commotion around for midnight. Twice I had to let myself into doorways as I heard someone approaching. The first time it was a closet. The second time it was an empty room and it was only after I had shut the door that I heard the sound of steady snoring and realised I wasn't alone. Whoever was in the corridor passed by quickly and I let myself out as quietly as possible.

Exercising in my cabin was not like the real thing. I could feel the sweat seeping through my shirt as I reached a doorway leading out onto the deck. It was just like Jade's diagram had shown. She was good. Some daughter you got, I said silently to Chester, wondering for an instant where he thought Jade and I had gone off to. I almost smiled in the dark. He knew me just well enough to think the worst about my intentions. Then I sobered up in the cold night air. By now he would have sounded the alarm. A weekend we might get away with, but not this long. But alarms were not going to do anyone any good. No one would have any idea where to look.

By the time I'd worked this depressing thought through, I had reached the front of the main cabin superstructure and was looking down at the forward holds. I was wedged in beside a life raft and I could clearly see where I needed to go. Off to the right, down a ladder to the main deck, and then a choice of man-sized hatches set into the huge slabs that covered each of the four cargo holds. I chose the hatch closest to the bridge. If

Jade was up there keeping the watch talking, I could make it. They'd have to be standing very close to the windows to see down the angle I could stay within.

I started to move, took a pace forward and froze. I could see the dull glow of a lighted cigarette a few paces ahead. Someone was standing at the rail smoking. He'd taken a drag, drawn in and caused the tip to glow bright against the dark night. I eased back into the safety of the life raft, fully aware of how close I'd come to fouling up. The man was taking his time, just leaning there and puffing his cigarette. A few minutes later he straightened and flicked the stub of the cigarette out into the air. I could see it make a long arc away from the ship. The man disappeared down the far side of the cabins.

I moved quickly now, across the open spaces and then over the edge and down the ladder. It didn't take long to reach the hatch. It was only dogged on two sides of the possible four. I twisted the mental screws and lifted the hatch. It was pitch black inside but I could see the first three rungs of a ladder leading down into the inky darkness. I went down the first few rungs then carefully lowered the hatch. For a second I worried about someone coming along and dogging the hatch after I was inside. But there was no way I could guard against every possibility.

I hung on the ladder and reached into my back pocket for the small flashlight Jade had provided. Its narrow beam cut through the darkness for a short distance, but it wasn't powerful enough to penetrate to the far side of the hold. I climbed down.

Once on the bottom, I shone the light across some of the crates. The foundation's name and the red medical crosses were stencilled everywhere

I looked. Which boxes were real and which held weapons?

I crossed the hold and searched with the small light until I found the door leading into the next hold. I examined it carefully. There was a green light in a tamper-proof metal screen above it. The door was one of those that could be opened from either side by a lever and a locking mechanism that required a couple of turns of a small wheel set in the middle of the door. What did the green light mean? I guessed it meant closed, because that was the way the door was set.

Holding the wheel tightly and watching the green light I turned it through half a circle. Nothing. I turned it again. The light remained green. But just as I turned it another degree, the green light turned red. I reversed the turn quickly. The light returned to green.

I couldn't take the risk. If that light was, as Jade had suggested, mirrored on the board on the bridge, I was either already in trouble because of that brief flicker to red or I certainly would be if I took the time to open the door, climb through and then sealed the door from the other side. Even worse, I'd have to repeat the drill to get back because I was sure the overhead hatch on each of the holds would be secured from the outside.

Sitting on a crate, I played the light around the hold. A fire axe was mounted on one wall. I went over and lifted it down. Propping the light up on another crate I pried off the lid of one of the boxes. Inside were packages marked 'medical instruments'. They were small packages, carefully wrapped and sealed in oiled paper. I looked at the outside of the crate. Bloody big box of instruments. I pulled out a handful of the packages, opening one to make sure I was seeing the right thing.

They were indeed medical supplies.

I burrowed my way deeper and finally felt the false bottom. Quickly I cleaned away the packages. There were finger grips in the false bottom and I lifted the sheet of plywood away. My flashlight lit up the interior. Hollow tubes. I pulled one out and read the inscription on the side. Mortars.

The fire axe quickly pried open another box, then another. In a few minutes I'd found the shells and the metal pads the tubes sat on. I took the time to put it all back together as it had been when I found it. I couldn't take the risk that someone might make a routine check of the crates. Then I attacked the next three crates. Pistols and M-16s, AK-47s. There was one box of Ingram M-11 machine pistols, a small weapon like an Uzi sub-machinegun. I toyed with the idea of taking one back to my cabin and decided against it. It was just something that could be found and never explained away. As well, there wasn't much chance I'd get very far in a firefight with one gun.

I was about to seal the box when I changed my mind. It wouldn't go back to my cabin, but it would go into the next hold with me. I still hadn't found what I needed and the Ingram might be useful later. I could stash it in the next hold. There was always a chance that Carson's people had put small arms in one hold and the larger pieces—those I was looking for—in another hold.

It was time to do the one thing I didn't really want to do. I had to go across the deck to the next hold. I went up the ladder slowly, not because I wanted to take extra care, but because I was getting tired. But this was the night it all had to be done.

I eased the hatch back. The deck was deserted. I came out quickly and rolled off the hatch coaming and onto the deck, lying stretched out beside the large cover. The cover was elevated from the deck and gave me some protection.

It didn't take me long to make my way forward. By staying low I seemed to merge into the darkness. The second man-hatch was secured by the same two latches. I released them and went quickly down the ladder inside.

It was a perfect duplicate of the first hold, even down to the convenient fire axe on the wall. The first five crates offered nothing but bandages that provided cover for assortments of grenades. They'd do in a pinch but wouldn't give me the edge I needed. I was very tired now. It was an effort to think, much less act.

I decided on doing two more crates and then packing it in and trying to come up with a plan with what I had already found. The first crate was ammunition and magazines. I took the time to wade through it until I found three magazines and the bullets the Ingram needed. I loaded the weapon and put it aside.

There was one more crate. I pried the lid off. Aluminium piss bowls greeted me, their surfaces shiny and new. I grinned at them. There was comic relief to be found, even down here. Then my grin faded as I looked at what lay hidden below. I could start my own war.

They were packed tightly together. Four tubes, complete with firing mechanism and retractable section. Hand-held, shoulder-fired rocket launchers. If I wanted to, if I needed to, I could blow a bloody big hole in the side of the ship with one of the rockets that could be fired out of these sophisticated little cannons. And I knew exactly how they worked, thanks to a certain major in the Philippine Army who decided my tour of his command would be less than complete without an

189

afternoon blasting away at tree stumps and old car hulks.

It took me another half an hour of opening and shutting crates until I found the rockets that went into the launchers. I was getting worried that I would have to go into another hold to find them. But there they were. More than I could use. Now all I needed was a little time to put together my plan.

I sealed the Ingram inside the crate with the aluminium bowls and the launchers. I scratched a mark on the side of the crate with the fireaxe, leaving the top only lightly nailed down. I could free it with my hand. I manhandled the crate with the rockets in close to the launchers.

That was it. I was almost asleep on my feet. My muscles ached and I was not even remotely looking forward to the long hike up the ladder. The only advantage was that I'd spent a lot of time down there in the hold and there were going to be even fewer numbers of late-night smokers perched on the deck. At least I hoped that was the way I would find it.

It was as I had hoped. I had no trouble getting back to my cabin and was soon in a restless sleep. I had more nightmares but I was getting used to them by now. Jade had said they were just a result of the drugs and I was prepared to believe her. She was the doctor. But this morning the dreams were different. I was armed and I was the threat this time. Man after man toppled as I fired all manner of weapons at them. It was like a shooting gallery at a country fair.

I woke when I heard her enter. She looked miserable, as if she hadn't slept. As soon as the door was closed I asked her what was wrong.

She told me about Alberts and his death. I was right. I had heard a gunshot. But it didn't bother me, at least not his death. It was just one less bad guy to worry about.

"We're getting some important company today when we dock," she said.

"Company?"

"Consuelo just told me. All that weaponry is not just for the Sandinistas. It's also for mercenaries Carson's recruited for the Sandinistas, complete with their own commander, a colonel somebody. Can't remember his name. British sounding."

"How many?"

She shrugged. "I don't know. We pick them up this afternoon in Buenaventura and drop them off in Costa Rica just before we hit the US Navy's quarantine line. Apparently they make their way into Nicaragua over the border."

"Why'd they tell you all this?" I asked.

"Because now they need me. Apparently the cover is that they are medical aides, accompanying me and the supplies. At least that's the story in Colombia and Costa Rica. I also have to do the talking if we're stopped by the US Navy. If I'm convincing they'll just note my credentials and sail away. Maybe a question or two from the medico on board their ship just to see that I'm the real thing."

I shook my head. "They've got it all figured out."

"They have that." She looked at me hopefully. "Have you got a plan?"

"I did have until you told me the place is going to be crawling with mercenaries."

"So what do we do now?"

"We wait it out. We move after Costa Rica."

She remained silent.

"I'm going to blow the ship up and we're going to swim ashore."

She looked doubtful. "Just like that?"

"Just like that. I need you to get me some strong string or cord, or wire."

"How much?"

"A hundred feet."

"I'll get it."

There was a knock on the door. I closed my eyes and lay still.

The door opened and someone entered. "They need you in the officers' mess, doctor."

"I'm coming," Jade said.

I felt her get off the bed where she had been sitting and leave the room. The door closed behind her and I waited for a few minutes before opening my eyes. It was a farfetched plan, but I'd seen something like it used in a movie with Richard Burton and Clint Eastwood during the longest escape chase I'd ever seen on film. I'd rubbished the film at the time. Here's these two soldiers escaping, shooting, killing what seemed like hundreds of Germans. And the only injury they'd suffered was Burton's finger being nicked by a bullet as he reached around a door to tug on a string attached to a grenade. Now I hoped I could do that same thing without even getting my finger hurt.

CHAPTER FIFTEEN

Colonel Peter Radcliffe-Jones hated civilian clothes with the kind of passion that bordered on pseudo-scientific mania. But he was in civvies this afternoon—white slacks and navy blazer with a light blue sports shirt—as he stood on the dock watching the freighter being pushed into the wharf by a big dirty-looking tug. He was well rested. It didn't take much to bring him back to full strength. The African campaign had gone well and while the new president wasn't very happy at being cheated out of the chance to execute his predecessor he had taken it all with good grace and contented himself with executing the former president's entire cabinet and all of the supreme court judges, as well as a great number of lesser bureaucrats.

The colonel had beat a hasty retreat in the face of such blatant slaughter. The world's press didn't give a damn about a little African coup but they were drawn like blowflies to the horrors of mass execution.

The colonel disliked playing political games and had spent the past twenty-four hours laying down a trail of money and good wishes through the local political offices. It was all necessary for the next part of the carefully woven plan. He had recruited a number of men to fight for the Sandinistas against the American-backed Contra rebels. Ostensibly his men were leaving the South American country as medical volunteers to assist the December Foundation's medical mission to Nicaragua.

Carson had already briefed him on the problems that had developed around the probing of an Australian reporter and they had, Carson admitted, almost lost the services of the medical cover. But that had been retrieved when Carson presented the doctor with the ultimatum: play out the role or be responsible for the deaths of the reporter and some baby or other. Radcliffe-Jones didn't quite understand the connection of the baby to the story but that was secondary. He already had enough hatred for reporters to want to get his hands on this man, Castle. Reporters had stripped him of victories in the Falklands and in Northern Ireland and he longed for the opportunity to strike back.

The gangway swung over the side of the ship and was quickly secured. The colonel went up the steep steps to the deck where he was met by the ship's captain. They talked for a moment, then Radcliffe-Jones looked over the captain's shoulder to see the black woman standing tall and regal by the rail smiling at him. He was startled, and then instantly pleased. He hadn't known she would be aboard.

He ignored the rest of the captain's sentence and brushed past the sailor, walking up to her.

She folded her arms in front of her, her white teeth flashing. She was wearing white jeans and a white T-shirt that made her blackness very pronounced in the bright sunlight. The folded arms just under the breasts lifted them up toward him. The nipples pushed against the thin fabric, firm and pointed and dark.

He admired her hair, pulled back harshly against the sides of her head and tied tightly in a small bun. Every time he saw her he felt the same stirrings. There was sudden tension. It was as if his life was in great danger, as if he was about to be killed. But he always pressed on. And yet it was all a great secret. No one knew, not even Carson who, he remembered with a certain jealous anger, was known to have slept with her.

She held the smile for a long time. "My colonel looks very fit," she finally said.

"And you look well, Consuelo," he told her.

"There are some things we must do," she said, and without any further words she turned and walked quickly inside the ship.

He followed her. It had always been this way—a perfunctory few words and then a search for somewhere private. As they marched silently down the corridor he thought of the other places they had rushed off to, in so many different parts of the world, on so many missions. It had started even before he had joined Carson's foundation, when he had been the young captain of a famous British regiment and had been assigned to escort Carson the VIP through a former colonial territory then in the grip of a civil war. That had been the first time he had met the African woman.

She opened the door to a stateroom and went inside. He followed her, stopping just inside the door and swinging it shut, backing against it, reaching behind him to turn the key in the lock.

The woman went to the middle of the room and halted, facing away from him, the dimly lit room only heightening the effect of her dark skin and the white clothes she wore.

Neither of them moved for a moment. Radcliffe-Jones remained still, back hard against the closed door, watching her go through the ritual. His chest was tight, as it was before a battle. His nerves were on edge, as if the enemy was close and he was about to make a move that could easily mean his death.

Slowly, without turning toward him, she raised her hands up her sleek sides and behind her head. She removed the little wooden pegs that held the bun in place. Her hair cascaded down her back, creating patterns across the back of her shirt. She shook her head gently, working out the last creases in the coal-coloured hair. Her hands came down and grasped the bottom of the T-shirt. With a fluid motion he remembered from the last time they had performed this slow dance, she lifted the shirt and slipped it over her head. Her back glistened in front of him. She was wearing no bra and he ached for her to turn around.

Her hands disappeared around her waist. There was a moment's pause with no discernible movement and then she stooped very slightly and pulled her jeans down. She was not wearing panties. The realisation excited him. Her nakedness drew him forward. It was his time to move now.

He moved tight against her, she still facing away. His hand touched both her shoulders and waited. It was always her right to make the first moves. His time would come later. She reached up and laid her hands on top of his, then lifted them away and drew them down over her hard breasts. She lay her head back against him.

They stayed like that for long seconds and then she whispered to him, the words clear in the silent room. "Do with me as you will, my colonel."

It was all part of their pageantry, with all the solemnity of a regimental passing-out parade. There would be time later for passion. Now was the homecoming, the reaffirmation of their tenuous links, the merging of opposites, of black and white until there was only a warm grey mist left between them.

He picked her up and carried her to the bed, placing her gently in the middle of it, feasting his eyes on her, letting his gaze move down her face and over her breasts and flat stomach and into her thighs and the slight mound graced with black curls, then past that down each long, perfectly formed leg to feet and toes.

The colonel stood back from the bed and unbuttoned his shirt. He shrugged out of it, fighting his need and working slowly as she had done. He unbuckled his belt and was soon standing naked before her.

Her arms lifted up to him. "Come here, my colonel," she whispered.

He went forward to her and as they touched, the passion was released and the pageantry of the moment dissolved into kisses and caresses. They clung to each other tightly.

Later he could smell the odours they had created together. They lay side by side staring at the ceiling, tired and sweaty. There had never been another woman her equal, he concluded. He listened to her breathing, softer and more controlled now that it was over.

"We could be like this forever," she finally said, not looking at him. "We could go away and lose ourselves in a thousand different places."

"That would be very nice," he said, without conviction. She had never spoken this way before. It had always concluded and he had gone off to find another war and she had—and he felt the anger rise again—always gone back to Carson.

"I mean it," she added. "I know how we could do it and I know where we could get the money to do it right."

He fought the temptation to rise up on an elbow and look at her, to try and gauge what she was talking about. He remained silent.

"I can give us millions of dollars," she said.

He could resist the temptation no longer. He turned on his side and propped his head on a folded-over pillow which gave him just enough height to peer down into her face.

She was looking at him now with eyes set deep in her face, bright and ebony and shining.

"How would you do that?"

She told him about Gerry Roa, about the bank account in Geneva and about the numbers on the small piece of yellow plastic from the baby's duck. "I have those numbers and they unlock a fortune," she concluded.

"And you want to share that fortune with me." It was more an observation than a question. There had never before been any question of a lasting relationship, of something more secure than a momentary passing parade.

"If you would have me, my colonel."

He smiled slightly, toying with the idea of giving all the rest of it away in order to spend his life with her. "I would have you," he said.

Her face clouded a bit, the brightness in her eyes dimming. "Peter, we *could* do it."

"I know that," he answered. "There's very little we couldn't do together."

"But?" She was trying to prompt him.

He avoided her eyes. How could he explain to her? It wouldn't make any sense to talk about the way he felt about his life. He needed to do what he did. It went beyond a woman, beyond even this woman beside him. "What about Carson?" he asked.

She dragged her eyes away and looked back at the ceiling. "He's been good to me for a long time but this is something I'd be doing for myself, for us, Peter."

He was unhappy. "You realise he'd come after us."

She shook her head. "We'd be hidden. You could hide us."

He thought about it. Hiding from Carson would be difficult, even more difficult if they had millions of dollars at their disposal. They'd want to spend the money, want to do things. And those things would have to be done out in public, where they could be seen. Passion would only carry them so far and for so long and then so much more would need to be done. And Carson's long arm could reach anywhere. Carson was part of that worldwide intelligence apparatus. He knew there was nowhere they could feel truly safe. And he knew she knew it too.

Her voice was very quiet, almost sad. "It wouldn't work, would it?"

He ran his fingers along the side of her face, lightly touching her ear. "No it wouldn't." He paused and wished there was some way they could accomplish what she was offering. "Unfortunately, it wouldn't," he added.

She nodded thoughtfully and closed her eyes. "Love me again, Peter, another time, please."

He slid across her, feeling the stirring and the dangers. It was as if they had never been parted, no matter how long and far apart the gap had become. It was like that now. They had always been together. He must never lose her, he said as he entered her once again. As he moved slowly in and out of her, he felt reassured knowing that when it was over this time she would return to Carson who would, as he always did, look after her so well.

Later, the mercenaries trooped abroad the ship. They were tough men, certainly out of place in their assigned roles as medical aides for Doctor Jade Price.

She was on the dock, with Consuelo on one side and the colonel on the other. She had to play out her role too, now. A government official needed signatures and some reassurance—strictly for the record, the colonel had explained to her before they had gone down to the wharf, because money had already changed hands—that these men were indeed what the doctor had been expecting.

The colonel watched the charade. The doctor was pretty, he concluded, but nowhere near the equal of his Consuelo. He glanced at the black woman. She was all business as she stood aloof and grand before the bureaucrat. Their secret was still just that—something only they shared. For an idle moment, as he listened to the doctor answer the questions, he wondered how his life would have been if he had agreed to her plan of recovering the money and then trying to disappear.

He was brought back by the official's last act, the signing of the papers. He watched Dr Price sign her name as the head of the medical mission, assuming responsibility for those who had joined the foundation's staff in Buenaventura.

The official tipped his stained, white hat and left and Consuelo hurried the doctor back up the gangway and inside the ship.

The colonel walked along behind them and then went down another corridor. He wanted to see the reporter. Consuelo had pointed out the cabin but he hadn't had a chance to look inside until now. He opened the medical cabinet outside the door, took out one of the drug bottles and read the label. It would do what was needed, he agreed.

He pushed the door open and stepped inside.

The reporter, this Julian Castle, was lying on the bed. He walked over and stared down at his face. It seemed remarkably composed for someone who had been in a drug-induced coma for so many days. He looked at the label on the bottle with the drip going into Castle's arm. It wasn't exactly the same as food, not by a long shot, but it would keep him alive. Alive! At least until it was time to kill him.

Carson's orders had been explicit. Consuelo and Kasilov were to take the baby, the doctor and the reporter ashore in Nicaragua and then they were to be killed. Officially, others would take the blame. Alberts was already out of the way. Consuelo had done that. He was suddenly proud of her. He would have liked to see her in action. He would personally take care of Kasilov. He had hated the man for a long time. It was, he knew, the professional military man's natural hatred of the spy, of those who cowered in the shadows, who plunged knives into people's backs rather than rushing forward and knifing them face to face like the soldier had to do.

He shook his head. *Anyway, Mr Castle*, he said to himself, *you and I will have a short talk before I kill you. You and your kind have caused me and mine such grief in past years. This will help repay what your profession owes me.*

A few hours later the ship pulled away from the dock and headed across the harbour out to sea. The mercenaries spent a lot of time on the decks. Most of them were young. They were all physically well built. They were outdoor men.

Consuelo asked Jade if she would examine them, give them a quick clean bill of health for the colonel. The doctor had started to complain, recognised the futility of arguing and agreed.

She didn't enjoy examining the men, who spent a lot of the time making verbal passes at her. But it was a relief to be actually doing something again and once she got used to them, recognised them for what they were, soldiers of fortune, livers of life who sold their skills as killers, she was able to set aside their ribald antics and even to throw a few verbal jabs of her own.

There was nothing wrong with any of them. They were all strong as bulls, she told the colonel.

Consuelo was standing near the table that had been erected over one of the forward cargo hatches. "Now, examine the colonel and see if he's eligible for the same clean bill of health."

The colonel gave her a dirty look.

"Come along, colonel. If it's good enough for your troops . . ." Jade said to him.

Radcliffe-Jones stripped off his shirt and let her listen to his heart. She went around behind him and tapped his back with her fingers and listened. There was something there that didn't sound too good. She listened again, wishing the noise of the engines deep below could be muted for a moment.

She said nothing as she wound the blood pressure rubber around his strong arm. She let the little gauge do its job and listened for the pulse through her stethoscope. That was wrong too, she knew instantly.

"How have you been feeling?" she asked him.

He fixed her with a solid stare and there was something about his eyes that frightened her even more than Alberts and Kasilov and Carson rolled into one.

"I'm feeling just fine, doctor," he said, "and that's exactly what you will report. Right?"

She hesitated for a moment.

"I'm fit as a bull, just like my men. Right?" He was pushing her.

She watched his eyes betray him and yet she couldn't escape the fear those eyes evoked in her. "That's right, colonel. You'll pass."

The colonel looked at the African woman. "See. What did I tell you?"

Consuelo nodded and grinned, but while he was shrugging back into his shirt she turned and walked past Jade.

Their eyes met and Jade knew that the woman knew. The colonel was not well. There was something wrong with his heart and his blood pressure was far too high. She couldn't tell exactly what was wrong; that would need tests beyond her capabilities and equipment. But there was no escaping the fact he was very ill, even if he didn't show it.

Two hours later, as she was bathing the baby, Consuelo came into her cabin.

It was an unnatural meeting. Consuelo stood by the baby bath and smiled at Joseph as he splashed in the water and made lots of noise. Jade was holding onto the soapy baby, the front of her shirt soaked from the splashing.

"How sick is he?" she suddenly asked Jade.

She looked up at the African. What could she say?

"Doctor, I want to know."

Jade sighed. "He's got something wrong with his heart and his blood pressure is well over the danger level. I can't tell without getting him into a hospital."

Consuelo looked away. "And you won't get him there unless someone shoots him."

Jade lifted Joseph out of the water and wrapped him in a big towel. One of the ship's officers had told her a little about the colonel's background. "If he was still in the army, they would have given him a medical discharge by now or, at the least, a desk job in some office where there was no pressure."

Consuelo faced her. There was concern in her manner. "That's the problem. He's still in the army. Carson's army. And he wouldn't stand for a desk job, not for a moment. He wants to be right out there with his men, leading them in some furious charge."

Jade understood. "If he keeps that up, it'll kill him. And it won't take an enemy bullet to do it."

Consuelo headed for the door. As she gripped the handle, she paused. "Forget this conversation ever took place."

"What are you going to do?"

"Absolutely nothing. We've all got to fight our battles our own way. I wouldn't ask him to give up what he needs to do to survive—even if I knew how, which I don't." She left the room.

At Quepos, the Costa Rican port authority questioned Jade for half an hour and wanted to see some of the medical supplies that were bound for Nicaragua. The ship was only docked for a few hours but the customs officials were wary.

They had heard of the December Foundation and were impressed with her credentials but, they explained, there had been many attempts to smuggle arms into their northern neighbour and they had agreed with a number of international protocols calling for their country to try and put a stop to the gun running.

Jade protested angrily that it was a slur on the name of her employer that the Costa Rican government would even suggest he could be involved in such unseemly activities.

Consuelo stepped in at this point and suggested it might be more appropriate to let the authorities see some of the equipment.

A few minutes later the authorities left the ship convinced it was carrying the medical supplies listed in the manifest. They had been allowed to pick the hold they wanted to search, even to pick the crates they wished to look inside. All they found was medicine and bandages and they had gone away happy.

A few hours later they were back at sea. Radcliffe-Jones and his men were missing.

"Where are the colonel and his troops?" Jade asked as she and Consuelo sat together in the mess.

"They're going overland. In a few hours we'll hit the American quarantine line. If we're picked up by the US Navy radar, as I am sure we will be, they'll come alongside and want to know all about us."

"And I get to do my act again?"

"Exactly. And this time it will be even tougher. My guess is that they'll have their ship's doctor ask you a couple of medical questions."

Jade nodded.

"Which you'll answer perfectly, doctor, because you know what's at stake."

"I'll do my part," she said stiffly.

"Good. There's a chance they might send a boarding party to search our cargo. The colonel is too well known to remain aboard in case that happens."

"My medical aides wouldn't have passed very close scrutiny," Jade said.

Consuelo laughed. "Not likely. But we did what was necessary. We got them from South America to Costa Rica and that was all we needed to do. They'll be on the dock when we get in. They can travel up the coast pretty fast."

They were all wrong. It was the first time she had seen them make an error. The United States

Navy had not appeared. There had been no challenge to their passage.

She wasn't disappointed. There had been a growing fear in her mind that she would accidentally make a mistake that would cause the Americans to board the ship and search the holds. She doubted they would be as easy to hoodwink as the Costa Ricans had been. But if they had been there at all, it was beyond the distant horizon and the *December Star* had ploughed on through the calm sea and finally slid unnoticed into Nicaraguan territorial waters.

* * *

I was getting impatient. We were getting close to our destination and there were so many things that could delay what I knew had to be done. I kept counting off to myself, trying to see how many minutes I could count until Jade entered the room. I stopped counting on a number of occasions as feet approached. But they kept going past my door and I would start counting again. Finally I heard her footsteps. I recognised them right off. They sounded so different, so much lighter than all the others. It's strange, I thought, how the mind can play tricks and give little bursts of insight. I closed my eyes as she entered.

As soon as she came into my cabin and had given me the injection, the guard went back out into the corridor. He was bored by the whole thing now and that was working to our advantage.

Jade took a man's watch out of her pocket and gave it to me. Once again, she'd done well. I strapped it to my wrist and checked it against hers. She had already synchronised them.

"I've got some money, too. Various currencies. Not much, but it'll help," she said.

"Good work. We go tonight," I told her.

She looked at me uncertainly. "We're going to make it, aren't we?" she asked.

"Sure we are. It won't be easy, but we'll get through." I didn't tell her my secret doubts about the dangers we faced once we got into the water, let alone finally reached the shore. If they caught us, the Sandinistas would hardly be receptive to the truth, and any other story made us sound like American spies—even with Joseph along.

"What do you want me to do?"

"According to what you've found out, we stand off the harbour until dawn and then the pilot boat comes out and takes the ship in."

She nodded.

"I'll go down to the hold at midnight, rig the explosives and then join you and Joseph at the life raft at one a.m. We'll go over the side right where the bridge wing overhangs the side of the ship. That gives us maximum protection from the bridge watch."

"It's a long way down."

I grinned. "You go first, with the life raft. I go right after you with Joseph. With the lifejackets on, we'll bob around, find each other and get on the raft and then row ashore."

"You make it sound so simple."

I shook my head. "It isn't. But it beats staying aboard and facing whatever they've got planned for us."

She agreed, and we went over the details a few more times. It was a crude plan but it was the best I could come up with. To stay aboard meant certain death. No one was going to want us free to tell what we knew.

She clung to me for a few minutes. I kissed her softly and let the warmth of her body seep through my clothes and then she went back to her cabin.

I watched the minute hand as it swept up toward the top of the dial. As it reached 12, I left the cabin. No one was there in the corridor. I padded along the length of it and out into the night. It was warm and not too far off was the coastline, marked only by a few twinkling lights. I knew the distance would be greater than it seemed. I only hoped the currents were going in the right direction.

There was no one on the forward part of the ship. I climbed swiftly down the ladder to the cargo deck, then crouched and moved swiftly along the edge of the large hatches until I was beside the man-hatch to the hold. The hatch was still only secured by two dog-latches. I swung them away and climbed in. It was difficult this time. I had the cord and the flashlilght in one hand and used the other to grasp the rungs.

On the floor of the hold I quickly retrieved the fire axe from the wall, located the undisturbed crates I had placed in position, retrieved the rocket launcher and loaded it. All it needed was to have the safety catch removed and be aimed at the crates of rockets. The Ingram was still loaded. I kept it nearby.

Now for the safety precautions. I took out five grenades from their crates and placed them around the floor of the hold, wedging them between crates so they wouldn't fall over. The ball of cord was unrolled. I fastened the end to the ladder behind a rung about halfway up, weaving it back and forth in such a way that anyone stepping on the rung couldn't avoid tangling his foot in the cord. I ran the string around the back of some crates and then to each of the grenades, making a loop through the safety pins. I had no idea if it would work but the principle made sense, and it had worked for Burton and Eastwood. One good tug on the string would pull at least some of the pins loose and that would do a lot of damage, I hoped.

I worked steadily, watching the clock and knowing I still had enough time. By 12.50 I had only to tie the second piece of string to the trigger of the rocket launcher and secure it. I was on schedule.

I picked the heavy weapon up and suddenly stopped. The ship's engines were loud, thumping steadily along. I was used to their noise and it receded into the background. But there was a new noise now. Feet were running along the deck. Someone was lifting the overhead hatch where I'd come in. It swung back with a clang. Light streamed through. There was a spotlight or something focused on it. I heard voices now.

"He might be in there. Take it easy," someone said.

"Check the woman. Make sure she's in her cabin. Guard her."

I recognised Kasilov's voice.

I picked up the Ingram and looked at my watch. Five minutes to go. If they'd just held off for five minutes more. I wondered what had gone wrong. But there were too many possibilities to canvass.

"Get someone in the next hold to cover the hatch down there," Kasilov ordered. Feet ran swiftly across the metal above me.

A set of legs swung over and touched the first rung. I didn't stand a chance. If they reached the string the grenades would go off. I'd be blown to pieces.

I levelled the small machine pistol at the top of the hatch and pulled the trigger. The gun fired, the sound deafening in the metal room and the bullets ricocheting around above me. The legs were yanked out.

There was yelling on the deck above but I

couldn't make out the words. My ears were ringing from the sound of the gun. There wasn't any way out. I aimed carefully and fired another short burst. Most of the bullets went through the hatch, a few hit around the metal edge and ricocheted back. If I kept this up I was going to get hit by my own bullets. No one fired back. I knew why. There was just too much ammunition in the hold.

I crouched down behind the crate and thought quickly. It was a crazy idea, mad, but I didn't have a lot of choices. I fired another short burst then dropped the Ingram and picked up the rocket launcher. It was still armed. I ran across the hold, as far away from the outer side of the ship as I could get. Some of the crates here were larger than others. I got behind them, then stood up and aimed the rocket launcher at the wall across from me. I needed to punch a large hole through the side, at least big enough to squeeze through. I tried to guess where the waterline was. The hole had to be above the waterline.

I pulled the trigger. There was a massive explosion on the other side of the hold. It threw a crate back against me. I had guessed wrong. It was under the waterline. Water gushed in like a decapitated hydrant. It was a big hole and there was no way I was going to be able to fight the pressure of the water. I raced back to the box and pulled out two more rockets.

The water was filling the hold fast. It was moving up my legs. Somewhere I heard shouting. I aimed higher up the wall and fired again. It worked this time. I was ready for the explosion, tensed against the blast. It ripped a jagged hole in the side of the ship. I needed more time. I loaded the second rocket, twisted around and fired at the watertight door leading to the second hold. The rocket exploded on the door, blowing it apart and off its hinges. Water surged through it. The water was climbing up to my waist and rising quickly.

I threw the rocket launcher down, grabbed the Ingram and started fighting against the rushing water towards the hole in the side of the ship.

Glancing back I saw a body coming down the ladder. It was Kasilov. He was still two rungs above the cord and the water was rapidly rising. I had no idea if the grenades would explode under water but I guessed they would. I sprayed the Ingram's bullets across the room, watching almost fascinated as they hit the wall, throwing up sparks. They cut across Kasilov's body as he tried to turn, pistol in one hand, holding onto the ladder with the other. He let out a frightened and painful yell and fell clumsily from the ladder, hitting a crate and then splashing into the water. He lay face down, not moving.

The Ingram coughed and went silent. It was empty. I dropped it and made for the hole. A gun fired from the upper hatch, the bullet plopping into the water nearby. They were getting more desperate.

The water was higher, climbing toward the second hole in the wall. I was almost there when there was a terrible grinding sound. The pressure was building up, buckling metal plates. I was swimming. My feet were off the floor. I reached the hole as the water covered it. There was a swirl of new water entering, but the rush was no longer strong.

I gripped the ragged edges of the hole and pulled myself through, holding my breath and completely covered by water. My feet touched the edge of the ship and I pushed as hard as possible. I needed all the distance I could get to clear the ship's propellers. I pulled with my arms through the water, kicking wildly. My lungs hurt. I needed air.

I struggled for the surface, breaking out into the night but still too close to the ship. I took a quick breath and went under, pulling myself through the water. The sound of the propellers was loud, the thumping of the engines pounding in my ears. I went back to the surface again.

The stern swept past me as I dived back down, swinging my body so I was swimming away from the stern. A blast of water from the propellers caught me, twisting me over and over and thrusting me even faster away from the ship.

When I came back to the surface the ship had moved away. I could see figures running all over the deck. It looked like it had heeled far over.

Then, for the first time I thought of Jade and Joseph. What had I done to them? Had I killed them both?

Without warning, there was a blinding flash in the water. A huge explosion ripped open the night. The ship was exploding. Flames shot into the air. I ducked under the sea but quickly surfaced. The horrific noises under the sea were unbearable. The night was turning into day as the ship continued to be racked by explosions. The fires were fierce.

The flames spread quickly. The surface of the sea started to burn. The oil tanks had ruptured. I struck out with my arms and legs, trying to put more distance between me and the furious inferno. As a wave lifted me I spotted something floating ahead of me, well beyond where I was swimming. The wave dropped me down and I lost sight of it.

The next wave carried me even higher and I could make out a life raft. I couldn't see much. It looked empty and my spirits collapsed. She'd managed to get the life raft over the side.

I struck out for it. The next wave that lifted me brought an incredible feeling of elation. Jade's head was looking over the side.

I screamed her name but she couldn't hear me. I kept swimming. There was a current but it wasn't strong. I thrashed through the water until I was closer.

Yellling her name, I watched her look in my direction. Then she saw me and her hand came up and waved frantically. She took out a paddle and started beating at the water.

I stroked the water more calmly now, trying to save my energy and get to the raft with a steady movement of arms and legs.

Soon I was alongside. She reached down and grabbed my arms, helping me roll over the side. Joseph was there, life jacket secured tightly around his little body. I was never more pleased to see anyone in my life.

We just lay there for a minute, me gasping, Jade sobbing and Joseph screaming his head off.

Finally she spoke. "As soon as I heard the gunfire I went over the side," she said. "First the raft, then Joseph and me. I lost him when I hit the water, but he bobbed up right beside me in that jacket."

She was still sobbing as she talked and I pulled her against me with one hand and swept Joseph in against both of us.

"I thought I'd lost you," she cried.

I had thought the same thing, but I said nothing.

We looked back at the ship. It was some distance away now, dead in the water, burning brightly and heeled far over. I guessed it would soon be under.

I told her about the rocket launcher. My guess was that the explosion that tore the door apart between the two holds had let in enough water to destroy the watertight integrity and the grenades must have exploded about that time, to set everything off.

213

Neither of us had any explanation for why the crew had come onto the deck and found the hatch unlocked. Maybe someone had looked into my cabin and found me gone.

I roused myself. I was stiff and sore but we had to get to land, and quickly. There would be search craft coming out from the harbour soon. It would take them some time but I didn't want to be found drifting in the sea.

The shore was some distance away but there were two paddles and the current was sweeping us south along the coast but steadily in towards a point of land that stuck far out into the sea. I pointed to it and we were both quiet as we paddled strongly.

We beat the current and the searchers. It was still dark when we were able to abandon the raft and swim the short distance to a sandy beach. Then the surf picked us up and swept us into the sand. I had Joseph tied by my belt to my arm and although he didn't like the ride and screamed louder than the roar of the surf, he bobbed along in his life jacket and made it to the shore in one piece.

We climbed shakily up the sand into the protection of the trees and then collapsed in a heap. We had come a long way but we were far from being safe. The ship had disappeared, either over the horizon or sunk. I couldn't have given a damn either way, I realised.

There was some activity in the distance, lights flashing on the sea as searchers went to work but we weren't in any danger from them—at least not yet.

Jade comforted the baby, rocking him gently and speaking soothingly. The warm air took some of the discomfort out of being wet.

By first light I had taken a quick walk north and south. We were in a small cove which was part of a large bay. I saw no one and no huts or roads, absolutely no sign of life. Where we were holed up looked safe enough for the time being but we would have to make a move at some point— farther inland and, hopefully, to some food and shelter. We had the money Jade had taken from the ship.

I knew only one name in the whole country. My only point of contact was in Managua—at least seventy kilometres away. And the contact, a reporter with Canadian Press, might not even be in the country. It had been more than a year since I had heard the man was in Managua. A year can be a long time in Nicaragua. Most reporters would have worn out their welcome in that time in a country where the politics were so volatile and truthful reporting was usually an invitation to expulsion. Things looked decidedly bleak.

CHAPTER SIXTEEN

Carson was ashen-faced and livid with anger as he forced himself to concentrate on the voice of the equally irate colonel on the telephone. Radcliffe-Jones was calling from Managua, from the office of the defence minister and a three-way discourse was going on. The minister was ignoring the facts. The ship was gone and the weapons were gone. As Carson stared unseeing out his window across Sydney harbour, he couldn't believe how badly the whole operation had disintegrated. He had suffered reverses in the past but nothing on this scale. In the past there had always been enough warning for him to abort a failing mission.

For an instant he tried to set aside his anger long enough to assess whether he had missed some danger signal. No! The only problems had been solved. Jade Price had been threatened into submission. But had she?

"How did Castle get free? He was supposed to be drugged!"

"That's what I thought, too," the colonel said.

Carson could hear someone talking urgently in the background. "What's that?"

"The minister wants to know what will happen to his down payment."

Carson stamped his foot in frustration. "Tell

the sonofabitch he'll get his money back when I'm good and ready to give it to him. Can't he understand? We've lost much more than he has. Consuelo . . ." He closed his eyes and visualised the African. He spun around and stared at her desk on the far side of the office. He should never have sent her. "And we've still got the problem of possibly having Castle and Price at large."

"I want him. I'll get him," the colonel said with a cold, controlled fury.

"More than that," Carson added. "You have to get him, or we could all be in deep shit. Between the two of them they have enough to hang both of us."

"I think the defence minister can help, for a price," the colonel said.

Carson didn't even hesitate. "Tell him that if he helps, I'll replace the entire lost shipment for free. Tell him that, but tell him it has to be based on results and we'll expect the full cooperation of his government."

"I'm sure I can convince him that it's in his best interests."

"That, too. There'll be a handsome bonus for him if he's able to deliver Price and Castle."

"I'll do that but I want to deal with the two of them in my own way," the colonel demanded.

"You do whatever you want. Just make damn sure they don't talk."

The colonel was silent. Carson could imagine what would happen if he managed to catch them.

"Peter, I grieve with you for the loss of Consuelo." It was one of the few times that he had ever used the colonel's first name. "I know about the two of you and I just want you to understand that, in my way, I feel the same loss as you."

"Thank you, sir," was the colonel's only reply.

Carson had not expected much more in the way

of a response. The colonel had no way of knowing how Carson had found out about their relationship. Radcliffe-Jones wouldn't understand why Consuelo had told him of her liaison with the soldier. Carson also knew there was no real reason to tell him what she and Carson had shared. He wondered if the colonel was really bothered by her death. He guessed he would be touched by it. But the subject had already passed.

"I'll go now and get all this under way. I'll keep in touch," the colonel said.

"Don't fail, Peter, or we'll all go down."

The line went dead. Carson hung up the telephone and walked back to the window. Many things had to be done. The press was already clamouring for answers to too many questions but the cover story about the ship carrying medical relief for the peasants of Nicaragua was holding. There was no reason for the story to spring a leak, unless Castle and Price surfaced.

He left his office and went down the corridor to his war room, seeking solace in more concrete matters. Nicaragua was only one thing that was happening today; there were so many other deals under way.

He entered the huge room and ran his eyes over the large displays of maps and figures. A duty officer followed him around, giving him an update on a number of potential trouble spots, listing options for aid projects and possible weapons and expertise sales for each new development. It was a routine that could calm him.

It was a macabre sort of sales report and territory discussion. Marketing his products was easy. He had sales offices and managers in so many places, just waiting to be dispatched with their offers. South East Asia and Africa were the best sales targets on this day. New products and new overtures were waiting for his final approval before they could be made. There was an urgent query from the office responsible for South America. A low-profile dictator wanted to know if certain high-tech jet fighters could be provided. He nodded an affirmative and gave a price. He knew where they could be bought and he was offering a price he knew the dictator could afford. The low profile would help. Only fools wore their intent loudly on their sleeves. It was a theory that had served Carson well.

Carson enjoyed this part of the daily routine. But today he was clearly worried. It could all come apart if he was unlucky this time, and luck was one of the few commodities he hated counting on because he couldn't buy it and was unable to guarantee the result.

He went back to his office and opened a small safe in the wall behind an original Picasso that showed a clown juggling bottles. There was a red file inside, sealed with a piece of wax. He checked the seal, not expecting it to be broken, carried the file to his desk and laid it carefully on the highly polished surface. It was his fallback position, prepared and updated from time to time but never used. He wondered how many files like this one existed in various government offices and the like around the world.

He broke the seal and opened the file. The title was cryptic: DECEMBER CLEANUP was all it said.

Turning the page he started reading once again the details he already knew off by heart. Consolation and escape were contained in these pages because it was a plan that would divide the December Foundation into two parts—one open and showing nothing but the already established public face, the other disbursed to the far corners of the world all those operations that might risk discovery of illegality and impropriety and bring scandal down on him.

December Cleanup provided him with—what was that wonderful word the intelligence agency people liked so much? *Deniability*!

If he was given the time he would be able to cloud it all over, move all the bits and pieces out of Australia under phony names and hidden corporations, the ultimate cutouts, so no one could juggle it back together. But it would take time and it would mean dislocating so much. He didn't want to act until absolutely necessary.

He turned and read through more of the plan's detail. He would leave Sydney. Everything could be coordinated from his island estate in northern Queensland. He would, in military terms, shift his flag to where he could better control access to himself, his key people and the core of his operations.

The backup networks were in place, but time remained the critical factor. If the colonel did his job, none of this would be necessary. If the colonel failed, Carson would need time to act.

Radcliffe-Jones spent an hour with the defence minister in his Managua office working out the financial details of the new arrangement. The arms shipment to replace the lost equipment at no cost was easy to conclude. It was, the minister agreed, a fine gesture. He was less happy when he realised it was tied to results—finding and delivering Price and Castle.

"I assume 'dead or alive' will be sufficient?" the minister asked.

"Your assumption is half right," he answered. "I don't care what you do with the woman. Give her to your troops, for all I care. But the man, Castle, is to be delivered to me alive."

The minister nodded and waited for an explanation.

The colonel ignored him and moved on to the matter of the minister's personal renumeration for services expected to be rendered. They haggled for a while, the minister convinced it was worth a great deal of money to his personal account in an overseas bank. The colonel finally agreed. They were wasting time, he realised, and he wanted Castle wrapped up as quickly as possible, preferably while the colonel's anger was still at fever pitch.

He left the minister's office and went downstairs to the jeep the military had assigned him and the driver, one of his own men, headed for the military camp on the outskirts of the city.

He idly watched the passing street scenes. It was a decaying city. It had always been that way, although there had been a lot more colour in the streets under the dictator Somoza. He remembered the gaudy parties that had taken place in those days. The blight of poverty had changed little under the new regime, despite the promises that had accompanied the revolution.

It was different inside the military camp. Few expenses had been overlooked there. This was Nicaragua's dilemma. As long as the Sandinistas felt threatened by the United States and the US-backed Contra rebels operating across the border from bases in nearby Honduras, the lion's share of the national budget went to defence.

It was those rebel bases that he and his men had been hired to attack. He loved the lack of subtlety in this mission. The Sandinistas decried the use of mercenaries by the US to train and arm the rebels, and yet that same regime was prepared to hire mercenaries to do the one thing their forces were incapable of doing—crossing the border into

Honduras to attack the Contras right inside their own bases.

He had no problem with the assignment. It was just another job to him and he knew damn well that he would succeed in causing considerable damage to the Contras. He also knew the bases would be back in operation soon after he departed. While he had little respect for the Contras' fighting ability, he had the utmost respect for the Americans' logistical support. They could replace anything he destroyed far more quickly than he could return to take it out a second time. And the second time, the bases would be much more difficult to penetrate.

By the time he returned to the army camp, the local commandant had received his instructions from the minister.

The defence forces of Nicaragua were at Colonel Radcliffe-Jones' disposal, he was told courteously. He took a few minutes to change into army fatigues, complete with the two pips and crown of his former British rank, and went to the operations centre.

A large map of the country was displayed on the wall. While senior commanders made notes, he swiftly assigned search sectors. The coast was to be patrolled rigorously, particularly to the south of the site where the *December Star* had sunk. The main roads leading to Managua were to be blocked in a number of places and roadblocks were to be set up throughout the capital. The borders were to be sealed both north and south.

Carson had sent pictures of Castle and Price over the facsimile machine and while they weren't good quality, they were to be reproduced and handed out everywhere. The newspapers were to run the pictures, with names and allegations of crimes against the people and a reward was posted for information leading to their capture.

Within a few hours the operation was moving into high gear. Radcliffe-Jones was alone in the room. He sat and stared at the map, trying to decide what he would do if he was a reporter trying to escape from a strange country. He knew of only two things that made sense. Let someone outside Nicaragua know of his plight—and there was nothing the colonel could do about that line of thought right now—and make contact with someone he could trust inside the country. Who would Julian Castle know in Nicaragua? He shook his head. Another reporter, maybe?

He left the room and went into an outer office. There was a young officer who had been assigned to act as his Nicaraguan aide. The colonel had a command structure for his own men but this was his link to the defence forces.

"How do you keep tabs on foreign reporters?" he asked the officer.

The man was filled with the self-importance of his new assignment and he obviously wanted to prove his worth. "There aren't many of them and they are all in Managua. They have to be escorted if they leave the capital," he said eagerly.

"Is there a central registry?"

"Ministry of propaganda has a complete list and is supposed to know exactly where they are at any time. So many of them are troublemakers."

The colonel grinned. He agreed completely with his new aide's assessment. "Get me a copy of the list."

"Yes, sir." The officer picked up the phone and the colonel left the office and walked outside. His own men were waiting for him. He had served with most of them before. He knew their individual worth and, more importantly, he also knew how well they could operate as a cohesive unit.

His plan was simple. While the military scoured the country, he would assign his own men, armed with pictures, to the most obvious candidates among the foreign press, to secure the post office, telegraph office and everywhere else he could think of where Julian Castle might surface.

"I'll get you, you sonofabitch," he said out loud as he crossed the paved parade square to where his men were waiting. "And when I do . . ."

CHAPTER SEVENTEEN

I had to get the three of us into the capital as quickly as possible. We stood out too much if we stayed in the rural provinces and there was no way we could stand up to any scrutiny by local guardsmen and policemen. At least in the city, we might be able to stay lost in the crowd. By mid-morning we were on our way, tucked into the back of an old truck, piles of bamboo on one side and bags of rice on the other. Jade's money had bought us some help and the aid was further guaranteed when we let the driver make his own choice of what currency he was paid in. He chose American greenbacks. I didn't have any idea how far we could trust him, but I also didn't have a lot of choices. He got into the spirit of things right off, making a place in the centre of the bags where we would pass at least cursory scrutiny without being seen. We clambered aboard and set off for the capital. It was a bumpy ride, uncomfortable and seemingly endless.

There was a lot of troop movement that increased as we travelled closer to the capital. Were they looking for us? I couldn't see that as a possibility, not unless the colonel that Jade had told me about was much more powerful than I could visualise. If he was, we were heading into more danger than I knew how to handle.

Jade and Joseph were hungry. It had been a long time since we had eaten. I told her I felt sure we would be able to find a way to put it all together in Managua. Mentally, I crossed my fingers.

We entered the capital. It grew noisier as we rattled through the narrow streets and our entrance was most marked as the odour changed from the clean smells of the green countryside to the dirtier, polluted city air. The driver stopped the truck and moved aside the bags that protected us. It was the end of the line. We dropped off the tailgate to find ourselves in a large central square. It was busy with street merchants and throngs of people. I looked around, bewildered at the strangeness. I asked the way to the nearest public telephones and the old driver pointed across the square to a post office.

We started across the crowded square. There were wooden stalls along the way, and vendors of fresh fruit and bread rolls. The sight added to our hunger. We stopped and bought some buns. We started walking and eating.

Halfway across, Jade grabbed my arm. "Turn away! Quickly!" she said, spinning us around. "Let's get out of here!"

I moved with her. "Why?"

"When you get a chance, look back carefully. The two men in the striped army suits, the Anglos with the rifles. They're part of Radcliffe-Jones' mercenaries. They were on the ship. They got off in Costa Rica."

My heart sank. I picked up speed and steered us down an alley. Things were getting more complicated. I was getting desperate.

Roy Woodley was the Canadian reporter's name. The last time I'd heard of him he was with Canadian Press, a wire service, in Managua. The knowledge was twelve months old. It was a long shot. We passed a small green park across from a Catholic church. The park was well tended; the church looked as though it was in need of urgent repairs.

I turned to Jade. "I'm going to need your help on the next stage."

"What do you want me to do?"

I turned back to the park. A few mothers and children played on the logs that had been arranged in the form of squares. We sat down on a bench. "You're going to stand a much better chance of contacting Roy Woodley than I am."

She nodded. "Where do I find him?"

"Good question." I'd been thinking about it for hours. There was a known fact about foreign correspondents in a strange city. They all seemed to congregate in the same hotels and watering holes. I didn't know which hotel it was in Managua but other journalists would. "You're going to have to find your way to a newspaper office in the city, any one will do—and ask where the foreign reporters are staying."

She frowned. "And they'll know?"

I grinned despite the tension. "They'll know where the local hangout is and from there you should be able to track down Woodley of Canadian Press. Someone will know."

"What will you do?"

"Joseph and I will stay here. We'll alternate between the church, the playground and an occasional walk around the block." I looked out at the fat mothers with their noisy kids. "Who knows, maybe someone will adopt us."

Jade almost laughed. "I'll go now. It could take some time."

I took her hand. "Time is the one thing we don't have one hell of a lot of."

227

"I know that," she said, seemingly reluctant to withdraw her hand from mine. Finally she did, giving me the baby and walking off down the narrow lane without looking back at the two of us. I looked down at Joseph. "Okay, kid, just you and me! Right?"

He mouthed something that I took as acknowledgment.

Two hours later Jade had part of what she needed. A small daily newspaper had provided the name of a hotel where some of the foreign journalists could usually be found. She had spoken to a curious deputy editor. The whole tone of the newspaper office was so unlike those she had been to with her father that she swept naturally into a guarded stance. Government control here was all-pervasive; it even reached into the press, the one institution she knew should be free. As she talked with the man about her quest to find a friend of a friend, she wondered if there had been some fundamental errors in her stance back on the streets of Washington.

By the time she left the editor's office she'd agreed with herself that what she had been doing back home had been correct. She wasn't condoning the Nicaraguan political system; she was merely protesting against her own government's interference in the sovereign affairs of another nation. There was a principle involved. As she walked through the streets, cringing slightly at the sight of police and military uniforms, she could feel the principle slowly eroding.

The hotel was fancy compared to most of the buildings she had seen in the capital. It made sense, she thought, as she walked up the wide front steps. If this was where the foreigners stayed, then it was logical to have them in comfortable surroundings so they would say nice things when they arrived back home.

The lobby looked as impressive as the facade. For a moment she caught her breath. It was as if she had walked out of Managua into a hotel in any one of several Western capital cities. She crossed the lobby towards a door that led to a bar. Pausing just inside the doorway, she took in the room. There were very few people. She discounted most of them, her attention going to a corner table where three men sat. One had a camera propped up on the table in front of him. He was changing a lens. The other two were lounging back with glasses of beer in their hands.

She walked toward them and they looked up as she approached. Two of them were young, one was middle-aged. She met his eyes and smiled. "Hello," she said.

They all grinned, the two younger men already eyeing her figure.

"I'm looking for a reporter named Roy Woodley."

"Canadian Press?" the older man said with a firm British accent.

"That's right."

"Well, to find him you'll have to go on to Toronto. He left here about three months ago. Webster here," he pointed at one of the young men, "replaced him."

She felt the disappointment explode in her heart. Her body sagged a little.

There was immediate concern around the table. "You okay?" one of the men asked.

The photographer stood up and offered her his chair.

She sat down and nodded her thanks.

"You look like you need a drink."

"That's an understatement," she managed.

He signalled a waiter and ordered her a beer.

"So why don't you just tell us what the problem is and we'll see what we can do to help?"

She looked at them. Julian had given her no other names and there had never been any discussion of what she should do if she didn't find Woodley. It wasn't an oversight, she knew. He just didn't have any other options.

"You an American?" the photographer asked.

She nodded.

"You're not particularly welcome in this country right now."

"That's part of the problem," she admitted. The beer arrived and she took a long sip. She wasn't going to get anywhere if she didn't tell them something. "My father is Chester Price from New York . . ."

The older man interrupted. "I met him once, out in Hong Kong."

She grinned. "You know my father?"

He shook his head. "I met him. Don't know him. I remember a big guy, looked like a former boxer."

She laughed lightly. "That's him."

"Is he here?" the man asked curiously.

"No. He's in Manila. But I'm here with another reporter, an Australian named Julian Castle."

There were blank looks around the table.

"So what's the problem? Australians can show their heads here without any worries."

"Not here, not now. At least not us. There's a lot of people looking for us."

"As in *official* people?" the photographer asked.

She nodded, knowing she was getting in deeper all the time. Her fingers held the damp, cool glass tightly.

"What do you want from us?" the older man asked, leaning forward toward her.

"We need to get out of the country."

"Where to?"

"Anywhere."

The young man, Webster, who had said very little, moved closer to her. "We get caught helping you, we're all in trouble." She recognised a Maritime provinces accent. "You could be a CIA agent for all we know."

The other two men said nothing.

"I'm not CIA or FBI or anything else. I'm Chester Price's daughter and I'm scared and I need your help." It was an effective plea made even more poignant, she knew, because it was exactly how she felt.

The older man nodded slightly. "I understand." He spoke to the other two. "No need for us all to take any risks. Why don't you two take off and I'll see what I can do?"

They agreed and left the room, one moving toward the elevators and the other going out the front door.

"Watch this," the man said, pulling back the blind on the window beside the table.

Jade looked outside as the young photographer walked down the stairs and started along the sidewalk.

"The man in the black jacket across the street."

She saw him. He was watching the photographer and started to walk along the street on the far side, keeping up with him.

"Every one of us has our own little government watchdog. We leave this hotel, they follow. We go inside a building, they wait outside. If we lose them, we're expected to wait until they find us again. We know they're there and they know it. It's for our own protection they say. But that's bullshit."

She pulled back from the window. "Then I'm putting you in great danger, asking for your help."

The British accent suddenly dropped away, to

be replaced with distinct Americanisms. "Not really. There are lots of ways to beat the system here."

She was less shocked than she should have been. Too many things had happened to her. Shock was a word that was rapidly sliding out of her emotional dictionary. "Who are you?"

He grinned, the British clipped tones back in place. "Let's just say I work for an organisation, as a sort of sideline to my reporter job, that would like very much to help you."

She wanted to ask but she knew it would be foolish. He would never admit it even if it was true. "How can you help?"

"I'll put you in touch with a man I trust. He runs a network of people who should be able to get you out of the country. Now, where's your friend Mr Castle?"

She looked at him for a long moment, not quite able to decide.

He grinned. "At some point we're going to have to start trusting each other. Remember, I have only your word for who you are. Now it's your turn to accept what I've said."

She nodded and told him about the church and the park. For the first time she also mentioned Joseph. He laughed gently, as if babies were some kind of soft spot in his makeup. He took out a small piece of paper and a pen and drew a crude map and wrote in some street directions. The three of them would have to get themselves to the house marked on the map. An old lady would let them in and take them downstairs to a basement. They were to wait there.

They finished their drinks and he took her into the lobby. Instead of going out the front door he led her along a corridor and down a flight of narrow steps to a door at the rear of the hotel.

"You'll be okay going out here. Our watchdogs don't monitor this door. It's for special occasions."

"They know about it?"

He grinned at her. "Sure they do, but the explanation's simple. A sort of unwritten code. We use it for liaisons with girlfriends, to go to pick up some smokes. That kind of stuff. We never use it when we're working as reporters. We always go out the front so they can do what they're paid to do and tag along with us."

She shook her head.

"They're just doing a job, like the rest of us. They want to keep it simple, just like us. So, in this case we'll just pretend you're my girlfriend and I'm showing you out the servants' exit."

She suddenly felt an overwhelming sense of gratitude to whomever this man really was. As he held open the door for her, she leaned close to him and kissed him on the cheek. "Thank you," she said.

He looked surprised. "And thank you! Now, take care and keep your wits about you."

She nodded and started off down the alley.

* * *

The man who arrived in the basement to which the old woman had shown us was most unsavoury, but I was well past the point of caring. The long wait in the park had worn my nerves raw and the move to this house had proven difficult. Police and soldiers seemed to be everywhere.

The man smelled of garlic and looked as if he hadn't had a bath in months. His clothes suggested street bum. We made no attempt to shake hands. He gave Joseph a dirty look and eyed Jade lewdly.

I was about to make a comment.

"We have to go now. Come," he mumbled, turning and leaving the room.

We followed him out. I knew we were taking a risk but the options were down to one—either go with this guy or get picked up by the increasing military patrols.

Outside there was an old sedan that looked about as reliable as the man who had been sent to take us out of the city. He was already behind the wheel, drumming his stubby fingers on the steering wheel. We climbed in.

As we started down the street, the man explained what we had to do. "I got a dozen of my people on pushbikes and motorcycles. They're going to find the way through the roadblocks for us. They been working on it for hours now." He lifted a street map up and handed it to me.

The map had large red Xs on various streets and roads. There were black lines along other routes.

"We go on the back streets, the bike people out front. If they find a roadblock they warn us before we run into it and we turn back and find another way through."

"That's good planning," I told him, impressed. Clothes, they said, don't make the man. Maybe I'd underestimated him.

He laughed. "Courtesy of the American government. They trained me for this kind of thing."

I glanced at Jade. She was showing no emotion. She was coming full circle. From wanting to help the Sandinistas, she was now being saved from them by the same men she had professed such disgust about her government's involvement with. This was not the time, but she and I were going to have a heart-to-heart talk about all this pretty soon.

We were driving slowly down back streets. A boy on a motorcycle came roaring down the street toward us. We pulled over. The boy shouted something and we turned around.

"New roadblock up ahead. They do this kind of thing sometimes. But they only have so many men they can deploy. The boy knows where they moved from and it is clear so we go that way now."

We went off down a new series of streets, winding back and forth. Twice more we were warned off a certain course in time. Gradually we worked our way into the outskirts and then farther out.

We were now well out of the city. The slums had given way to stretches of jungle and occasional shacks.

"I don't suppose you two had anything to do with that ship that went down off the coast?" the man with the garlic breath asked.

I stared straight ahead at the road, wondering how to respond. The guy was risking his life for us. It seemed entirely selfish to lie about it.

"Rumour has it that the ship was carrying medical supplies for the peasants. Be a damn shame if that was true. The one thing these people need are medical supplies," the man continued.

Before I could say anything, Jade spoke. "The rumour was wrong. The ship was filled with weapons for use against the Contras."

The man nodded, satisfied.

Off to the right, as we hit the high ground, I could see the blue waters of Lago de Managua. The long lake gave the whole scene the look of a summer holiday expedition. As I watched the scenery, the driver handed me an old map.

"We're going to near a place called Mina El Limon."

I found it on the map, about halfway between Managua and the border with Honduras. "Then where?" I asked.

He shrugged. "Then somebody else gets you and I go home and forget you."

A few hours later we took a dirt road to the right and drove for a few minutes before we stopped in a clearing in the jungly forest. The driver got out, motioning us to do the same thing.

We stood there in the growing heat. Flies swarmed and buzzed around us.

There was some sound from up the road, a big vehicle, maybe two. Jade stiffened and I looked for somewhere for us to hide in the nearby bushes.

The driver looked at us and laughed. "You should get an ear for this kind of thing, my friend. The Sandis never tune their engines. That one coming is tuned. He's on our side."

A jeep and a large truck rumbled around the corner. There were soldiers in the two vehicles. They came to a halt. A soldier, an Anglo in an American Army uniform, got out of the jeep. He had a green beret on his head and the gold oak leaves of a major on his collar.

"You okay?" he asked as he came up to us.

We shook hands and told him we were still in one piece. "And damn glad to see you," I told him.

He turned to Jade. "Dr Price?"

She nodded.

"Perhaps now you won't be so fast to condemn us, Doctor." The major said it without rancour and didn't wait for a reply. "You two ready to leave Nicaragua?"

"What are we going to do?" I asked, wanting to know how the major knew so much about Jade but needing, even more, to get out of there.

"We're going to drive you a few miles and rendezvous with a chopper, just outside Villanueva, which will lift all of us neatly over the border into Honduras."

"Then what?"

236

"You'll be taken to a Contra base with me, then turned over to a representative of the United States government and then, after a short chat, you'll be able to go home."

The major indicated the jeep and we climbed in. The drive was only short, over a couple of hills and through a valley. The major spoke into a radio and in a couple of minutes we could hear helicopters. There was a big Huey transport and two Cobra gunships. The Cobras swung around us, covering the Huey as it set down in the middle of a clearing. The major turned over the jeep to a rebel soldier and joined us in the helicopter. We lifted away.

* * *

Radcliffe-Jones had it all figured out. The Sandinistas had a good intelligence network out there in the field and, while they couldn't nail Castle and Price in the city, the network had pulled together enough information to give the colonel and his men a decided edge. He even had radio confirmation about the arrival of the helicopter to pick up some people near Villanueva. But by then he'd been on the move long enough to have four big Russian-built Mi-24 Hind helicopters in position just inside the border. Cuban pilots, well trained in the Soviet Union, were at the controls and each chopper carried some of his best men.

He looked out the window of the chopper. She was one of those big helicopters with the weapons' wings drooping off each side. They had cannon, Sagger anti-tank missiles and rockets. They'd do the job.

The colonel listened to a burst of static over his headphones. The Cuban up front made a comment and the chopper veered hard right. They had a fix on the three helicopters that were now

237

scurrying toward the border. They had just crossed near Somotillo on the Negro River. He looked at his map. All four of the Hinds were within range. It wouldn't take long for them to intercept.

"Attention all flights," he said into the microphone. "One and Two take out the gunships, Three and Four go after the transport. Bring it down in as much of one piece as possible." He knew he was asking a lot, but if they could take out the rear rotor assembly that would be enough. He still wanted Castle alive.

The minutes ticked by quickly as the Hinds hurtled along at treetop level. They had speed and the advantage of surprise. They were also coming in from an angle to the rear of the fleeing helicopters. It was a textbook position. He couldn't fail now. *For Carson and Consuelo*, he thought suddenly. *And for me*, he added with satisfaction. *Castle is for me.*

One of the other Hinds got there first. There was a quick radio message and a slight alteration of course. Then he saw the three dark shapes ahead. "Let's get them," he ordered.

One of the gunships went up in a ball of flame and dark smoke almost immediately. The other peeled away, returned and fired a burst of rockets that cut down one of the Hinds but found itself caught in a pincer movement and rapidly fell from the sky, exploding as it crashed out of sight into the jungle below.

They concentrated on the lone Huey transport. The small chopper was hopelessly outnumbered, three heavily armed Hinds to one heavy machinegun mounted on the side of the Huey. But the pilot of the Huey was good, the colonel realised. The helicopter swooped low into a ravine and twisted and turned its way through the gully. The Hinds had to stay above. They fired, but the small target below yawed back and forth and the rockets and cannon fire exploded and bit into the jungle below.

They were getting too close to the border. "Come on! Get him!" he yelled.

A burst of cannon fire raked the Huey's side. It reeled from the impact, then lifted and slid quickly to the right. It was going down now, dropping toward the ground. The Hinds could get it, could blast it out of the sky. "Hold off. Follow him in," the colonel ordered. He didn't want to see the Huey disappear in a fiery explosion, which he knew could so easily happen now the helicopter was wounded.

The Huey kept moving forward, almost limping through the air. It was making for a small clearing half a kilometre ahead. He'd let it get there and then they'd go down and claim Castle. Already he could feel the added adrenalin pumping as he reviewed swiftly what he was going to do to the reporter.

The Hinds slowed and followed the Huey down, the colonel's chopper the last one in the line. He watched the small helicopter touch down. There was no movement. No one left the ship. The colonel's hairs suddenly bristled on the back of his neck. There was something very wrong about the scene. The other two Hinds were now almost down.

The whole jungle around the clearing erupted with specks of gun flashes. It was a trap! "Pull away!" he yelled, feeling the Cuban pilot's instinctive lifting of the heavy craft. Bullets ripped into his Hind.

Ahead, rockets scored on the two leading Hinds. They swayed drunkenly in the air, too slowed down to make escape possible. One twisted on its side and crashed into the field. The second was on fire and disappeared into a nearby ravine.

The Cuban pilot was fleeing. They had spun around and were pulling back from the field. He looked behind the ship. Small figures were running from the Huey toward the nearby jungle. They were going to get away! He knew there was no way he and his men could get in there. He stared out the window, knowing the seriousness of the defeat. His eyes fixed on a position on the ground, sweeping along, not focused, not seeing what was flashing past. He was a long way away, his mind working on nothing but the hatred of it all, the hatred that had driven him to let the Huey escape. They'd had him. All he had to do was order the Hinds to fire and they would have blown him out of the sky. But he'd held back until it was too late. Castle was still alive. *So am I,* he thought, *and as long as I'm alive I'll hunt for the sonofabitch.*

The Contra camp was a forward outpost, nothing too grand, but certainly effective. I stood with Jade and the major and looked back at the clearing. There were two helicopters there, one burning and one ripped to pieces by cannon fire. Jade shivered beside me and tried to calm the crying baby.

The major introduced me to the camp commander, a Nicaraguan, and we spent a few moments going over the possibilities. He'd picked up the major's distress call and had talked the Huey's pilot into the clearing. It had all happened so fast. The Nicaraguan was extremely apologetic for letting one of the Hinds escape. The major reassured him there'd be another time and place when the Hind could be brought down.

Two hours later we were in another helicopter on our way to a larger base, well inside Honduras. This one was on a much bigger scale. There were temporary buildings and a paved landing strip. A

C-130 Hercules was on the runway. The United States Air Force markings were clear in the hot sun. There was also a small executive jet parked off to one side.

It was the man in the jet who was waiting for us. He looked like a bank clerk but when he opened his mouth, the sound was strong and his first words belied the physical image. "I'm Michael McQueen and I'm with the Central Intelligence Agency. I've got a few questions for you and then we'll be on our way."

"Where to?" I asked.

"Depending on the answers you give me, probably to Panama and Australia."

"That sounds good," I said. "Let's talk."

Jade interrupted. "I'd like to call my father."

McQueen nodded. "We're taking my plane into Tegucigalpa. As soon as we get there I'll make arrangements for that—and for the baby."

Jade looked concerned, holding Joseph closely.

"What arrangements?" I asked.

"Our people in Manila can get him back to his relatives there." He paused. "If that's what you want."

I looked at Jade. I knew the bond that had formed between them, between all of us. Giving up the baby was going to be difficult for her.

She was looking down at his little face. His finger was pointing up at her, wiggling back and forth. She finally nodded. "It's what would be best."

McQueen spoke softly, recognising the moment for what it was. "That's fine, then. The little guy obviously has lots to thank you for—and he probably will as he grows up. Let's get to my plane."

It didn't take long. The sleek executive jet lifted away from the sweltering runway and curved off toward the Honduran capital.

As soon as we were airborne, McQueen started his debriefing. I was amazed at how much he already knew about Carson and the foundation.

"We've identified the guy who has been chasing you through Nicaragua. He's an ex-British colonel, now a mercenary working for Carson. Name's Peter Radcliffe-Jones. He's good and he's got a lot of pull with the Sandinistas. He's been virtually in command of their military for the past couple of days."

"He almost caught us," I added.

McQueen nodded.

"If you know so much about Carson, why don't you shut him down?" Jade asked.

McQueen looked unhappy. "Dr Price, that's a very good question and you're not the first to have asked it. The answer, given your own background, is not something you're going to want to hear."

"Try me," she said shortly.

He turned to me, "You can't write anything about any of this."

I shrugged. I'd been here before with the CIA. They were rescuing me and this was certainly not the time to start talking about freedom of the press.

He accepted the shrug as acknowledgment of the prohibition. "Carson operates because my political masters choose to let him operate. He has proven to be very helpful at certain times in the past. And we're also not always sure just what he is up to."

"Like the Nicaraguan gun shipment?" I threw in.

"Exactly. His network is extremely sophisticated and we have to weigh up those of his activities we don't like with the things he does that we approve of—in fact, in some cases, have actually asked him to do for us."

Jade looked angry and McQueen noticed.

"It's not always a cut-and-dried world, doctor," he told her. "Certainly not the way you might have seen it in the past. We can't solve problems marching in the streets."

"But he tried to kill us. And he's killed others."

He inclined his head in agreement. "And if it will be any consolation to you, I think he's gone too far this time trying to deliver weapons to the Sandinistas. That's going to cost him plenty in Washington. Those who have supported him in the past will find it very difficult to stay on his side now. He's stepped well over the line this time."

The rest of the questions were technical. They started with Jade being recruited and they worked their way through my involvement with the Roa money. The plane landed and we were whisked to the American Embassy. The questions continued, broken only by our opportunity to talk with Chester.

The big man sounded uncharacteristically bright at the sound of our voices. He was full of questions and gentle admonitions about making excuses for my absence to my editors and what I'd involved his daughter in. He seemed to be pacified by my comment that I didn't think he was going to have any more worries about her marching in the streets.

It was all happening very quickly. There was food, showers and a change of clothes but there was no time for sleep. A Starlifter transport was waiting at the nearby air base. We could rest on the way home, McQueen told us.

At one point during another battery of questions, the telephone rang. McQueen picked it up, listened and then hung up.

"I was right," he said, grinning. "Washington's upset."

"They tell you to get him?"

243

"Not yet, but I think they might. I'm going to Australia with you, just in case."

There was only one last thing to do. Joseph had to be handed over. A woman who worked for the Embassy would look after him until arrangements could be made to fly him back to Manila and then pass him on to Gerry Roa's relatives.

It was a tearful farewell. Jade didn't hold back her emotions and I could feel a lump in my throat as well. Joseph had been part of the team and he had performed admirably. I hoped that some day in the future I'd get a chance to tell him that.

The drive to the waiting transport was short and as we climbed aboard I asked about Colonel Radcliffe-Jones.

"He's running, he's dangerous and I have no idea where he is," McQueen admitted.

"If I was him, I'd run straight back to Carson in Sydney. They both need each other."

McQueen nodded. "It's a possibility. By the way, Carson's got a place up in north Queensland. An island. We gotta check that out as well."

As the Starlifter taxied out onto the runway I was left with my own thoughts. Would Carson know he was in trouble? He'd be even more dangerous if he knew the walls were closing around him. If the colonel was with him, it would be one hell of a fight to take him. Whether I could write about it or not was secondary now. I just wanted to be there at the end, whatever it was going to be.

CHAPTER EIGHTEEN

Carson looked out across the Great Barrier Reef toward the empty horizon as the Bell JetRanger churned its way through the early morning light. DECEMBER CLEANUP was well under way and the next few days would tell whether or not he would get away with it.

He was prepared for failure, for the total collapse of his international network. He could, with regret, give it all away if that was what was needed to escape what he knew he would never be able to stand—capture, a courtroom and the public humiliation. And the bottom line of the cleanup operation was designed to get him out of sight, to cut him off from the foundation and whisk him away to any number of retreats that had been hastily prepared for this possibility. Most of them were in countries in which he really didn't want to live. But beggars couldn't be choosers, he lectured himself, and he'd still have enough millions to isolate him from whatever lurked outside his door. No, he concluded as the helicopter turned north toward a speck appearing in the distance, where he was going now was just a stopgap place. If he could hold here, he would be happy. If not, well, his personal freedom was the most important consideration and he was prepared to run a long way and hide for a long time if that was what proved necessary to guarantee that freedom.

He wondered how the colonel felt about his personal freedom. Radcliffe-Jones would already be on the island. Carson had sent one of the foundation's jets to pick him up, with some of his key men, and carry them to the island. Security could still be found within a circle of trained guns.

What he really wanted to do was to fly 100 kilometres further out to sea, to see the physical existence of one of the last paragraphs in the cleanup plan, the *Anastasia* a thirty-million-dollar motor cruiser. He had only had time to inspect her briefly in Monaco three years earlier. He had admired her grandeur but he had never sailed in her. The ship had been purchased in the name of a corporation that had no traceable links with Carson, and she had remained cut off from him. Now she had sailed halfway around the world and was stationed 100 kilometres away. And how he ultimately would get to this ship, part of the plan, was as creative as the *Anastasia* herself.

Another clean company had bought a Canadian deep sea research company that built and operated sophisticated, hi-tech submarines for commercial and scientific purposes. The company had built six submarines, only five of which appeared on its books. The sixth was in a special mooring at his island, below ground level at the sea's edge. Its hangar was located directly under the island's electrical generators. Like the *Anastasia,* the sub was a secret to everyone except his closest aides. Even Peter Radcliffe-Jones was unaware of its existence.

The helicopter was coming up on the island. It spread out below like a giant tear whose short tail curved around to provide a naturally protected bay. A large piece of reef rested, as if it had been placed there on purpose in order to complete nature's scheme, in such a way as to seal off the lagoon. There was dense jungle vegetation at the narrow end of the tear and back along most of its widening length. A magnificent single-storeyed mansion that spread out from its position above the sand line and along the beach in both directions dominated the large, bulbous end of the island. The main, cathedral-style building was perfectly centred on the long stretch of pristine beach.

As the chopper slid over the buildings and descended in a slow graceful curve toward the manicured lawns, he took in the helipad, the giant swimming pool and various bungalows. He had done considerable entertaining here. Some of the world's richest and many of its most powerful men had walked his beaches. The island was not a secret, but it was part of his escape plan. No one could approach without his sophisticated radar warning him and as a private estate he could control the approach of sightseers and the press.

The colonel was waiting for him. There would be no recriminations. There was precious little time for that. He knew he had set the colonel a difficult task. Finding Julian Castle had proved too difficult but Carson could, with uncharacteristic generosity, he realised, forgive Radcliffe-Jones' failure. Perhaps, he thought, it was only because he now needed the colonel's counsel.

The chopper settled fully onto its skids and the pilot shut down the engines. Carson opened the door and stepped out into the warm, humid air. There was the pervasive smell of orchids. He took a deep breath, then bent over and went out from under the rapidly slowing rotor blades.

Radcliffe-Jones came forward. "Good to see you, sir." The colonel offered his hand.

Carson shook the extended hand. The grip was still firm. "I'm glad to have you back, Colonel." He watched the officer carefully. There were signs of strain around the man's eyes that he hadn't seen before. And the eyes themselves looked tired, as if they needed rest, not just sleep, but long, unbroken rest in some quiet, peaceful setting. "Let's go into the house. We have a lot to talk about."

They walked across the closely cropped lawns toward the main building. They made small talk. Around them men who served the estate worked in the gardens and clipped branches from trees that encroached on the rocklined walkways. A man was cleaning the deep part of the vast swimming pool. There were also signs that this was much more than a mere mansion. Amid the splendour there was a facade of formality. Men in military fatigues carrying rifles and sub-machineguns patrolled the vast yard and beyond. Carson could see at least two men sauntering along behind them as they approached the house. The colonel had ordered bodyguards. Damage control was already in place.

Inside the building there was the same attention to detail as outside in the yard. Everything was neat and orderly. A maid passed by carrying fresh towels.

"Let's go into the study," Carson said, leading the way.

It was a huge room, filled on three walls with floor-to-ceiling bookcases. The fourth wall, where the door was, was for paintings and there were many, the whole gallery tastefully arranged by someone who had great creativity in such things. The room was long, three times the length of the average lounge room and the ceiling was high.

Across the thick white carpet was a modern desk

without drawers. Carson ignored this and indicated the lush black leather sofas set in an almost complete square around marble coffee tables in the centre of the room.

The two men settled into the seats. "So what does it look like from your side?" Carson asked.

The colonel flipped a hand out casually, palm up. "A holding pattern. Castle and Price made it out to Honduras with the help of the US Army. I picked up some information from a contact in Tegucigalpa that civilians then stepped in and took over from there. Probably State Department or CIA."

Carson frowned. "It was CIA. Our Washington office confirmed that."

"Your friends in Washington going to be able to help this time? They've done well by you in the past."

Carson looked thoughtful. "I'm not sure this time. They're very wary. If it happened anywhere else except Nicaragua ... They've got divided loyalties about what should be happening down there."

"So we may be on our own?"

"Yes."

Radcliffe-Jones smiled. "If it comes to the crunch I'd prefer it that way. It's much easier to run the battle if you know exactly where you stand. How do you want it handled?"

Carson looked hard at the colonel. There was no easy way to say what had been in his mind for some days. "I don't want to fight, Peter. If it comes to a final assault I just want to get away in one piece." He sighed. "I have no stomach for public vilification. I'll just disappear and retire. I've made the appropriate arrangements."

The colonel stared at him. "I don't understand. You'd just give up?"

Carson's head bobbed slightly. "And slink away into some small corner of the world. I've done my bit. If I'm to be cheated out of continuing, well, I can live with that."

The colonel was getting angry. "I want Castle. I don't want to be cheated out of that."

Carson grinned. "I thought you might feel that way. It's set up. There's a bank account for you in London. Three million pounds sterling. Just waiting for you. It'll pay your way for however you want to handle it."

The anger faded away quickly. "That's very generous."

Carson waved an idle hand to dismiss the comment. "You've done well for me, Peter. It's the least I can do for you. You've put your life on the line so I could make money. All I'm doing is giving you a bit of what you've earned me. Sort of severance pay."

The colonel chuckled. "That's what they call the golden handshake, isn't it?"

"More like platinum . . . but you're worth it, my friend."

"What are you going to do?"

Carson looked away. The colonel knew nothing of the submarine or the *Anastasia*. "I have a couple of options. I'll choose one in a few days. If things go bad, I'll stay there. If not, I might come back and see what can be salvaged. What about you?"

The colonel rubbed a thumb on the inside of his opposite palm. "I'll give my men a break for a few days, then start looking for Castle. I don't care about the woman but I want that reporter."

"Enjoy yourself while you're here." He got up. "Now I need some rest. I'll see you for lunch."

The colonel nodded and walked out of the study. Carson followed slowly, turned as he passed through the doorway and went down a carpeted hall. He stopped for a moment by a double set of doors and then went inside. This was the room Consuelo had always occupied when they were on the island. He looked around at the huge bed, the vanity unit and the sliding doors that opened out onto a private patio and ground-level spa pool. There was another door. He went to it and pushed it open. It went into a suite of rooms that Consuelo had often occupied. They had both passed through that doorway many times in past years. He missed her.

He crossed through the anteroom and went into the main bedroom. His clothes had been taken out of the suitcases that had been aboard the helicopter. His pyjamas and dressing gown were lying on the bed. He walked over to a small French desk. His briefcase was there. He turned the combination lock and opened the case. There was only one document in the case: DECEMBER CLEANUP.

He took the document out of the case, turned to the last page and ripped it cleanly from the folder. He left it on the desk, then took the rest of the document and ripped it into small pieces as he walked across the floor into the bathroom. He flushed the toilet and watched the small pieces swirl around and around in the water and finally disappear with a miniature roar down the tubes.

"Get Castle, Peter," he said after the papers had disappeared. "Get him for all of us!"

* * *

Peter Radcliffe-Jones was with Markham, Carson's personal security chief. They walked along the beach in front of the main house. The colonel liked Markham. He was a professional cop, inside and outside the force. For the past ten years he had been outside Scotland Yard, guarding Carson and overseeing the vast security network that protected the foundation's activities. It wasn't a spying job or a dirty tricks role, as played by Alberts and Kasilov. His wasn't even a military role like the colonel's. It was straight domestic security.

The colonel and the security chief weren't close but each had respect for the way the other carried out his assigned functions and there had never been any power play between them. They had been talking about Kasilov.

"I never liked that mother-fucker," Markham said with his Cockney accent that had never quite disappeared even though it had been exposed to a wide variety of languages and dialects. "Figured he'd do bad for the old man someday. Alberts wasn't much better but at least he came from a country with a little class."

The colonel grinned. Markham's hobby horse was that Russia remained a bleak intellectual wilderness peopled with barbarians, while England had become a bleak intellectual wilderness peopled with former heroes now in decline. Markham argued that the United States was now at the height of its capacity and Australia was on its ascendancy—if it could shake its way clear of Labor Party socialists who seemed intent on grinding everyone down to the lowest common denominator.

"But you didn't come out here to listen to me rant and rave, now, did you?" Markham asked.

"No. I didn't. I wanted your assessment of what's going to happen."

"Ooh," said Markham with pursed lips that made his round face tighten dramatically. "I think it's all over and we'll be lucky to get out of here with our skins in one piece. I'm a copper and while I might have given that all up a decade ago to join you people, I still think like a copper."

The colonel listened, liking the way Markham developed his point.

"And if I was still a copper and this was my case, I'd be thinking about an arrest right now. Quite aside from the things I know because of my position here, thinking maybe just from that doctor and her reporter friend's point of view I'd have enough evidence and probable cause to get me a warrant and to break down the doors here and haul the old man, me and you, and a dozen others off to the slammer."

The colonel nodded. "And you think they'll do that?"

"Hard to say. Carson's got lots of mates in high places. If it wasn't for the reporter and the doctor he might be able to paper it over."

"But you don't think so?"

Markham sighed. "I'm not worried about the locals but you guys got caught in Nicaragua and that's sure to antagonise some very important people in Washington."

"What are you getting at?"

He stopped walking along the beach and turned toward the colonel. "If I was a betting man, which I am, I'd lay odds at three-to-one that Washington will try to shut us down without publicity, if . . ." He paused.

The colonel picked it up. "If Castle and Price don't talk publicly."

"Right."

"If they keep quiet long enough for me to find out where they are, we won't have to worry about them ever talking."

Markham shook his head sharply. "Peter, shut up about that kind of thing. I don't need to know and I don't ever want to know."

The colonel looked at him blandly.

Markham looked away, flushing darkly. "I just

don't want to know about such things. I keep my head together here because I don't know about operations. I'm strictly involved in security and the old man's safety. What you and the others do is your own business. I just don't want to know." He turned abruptly and walked away.

The colonel stood still, watching him walk away on the white sand. *Sorry, my friend,* he said, only to himself. Markham still saw himself as a cop, doing a cop's job. Defending and protecting the weak and the innocent and the unaware. Only no one among them was weak or innocent any more.

CHAPTER NINETEEN

"I was right," McQueen said, putting the telephone down in the small office they'd assigned him at the Australian Air Force base at Richmond, a short distance from Sydney. "Thanks to the evidence put together by you and Dr Price they're convinced he went too far this time and they want him taken out."

"Taken out?" I asked. "Exactly what does that mean?"

McQueen grinned behind his spectacles. "Out. O-U-T. What the word says. Mr Carson of the great bandaid is to be taken out of action, convinced to retire to a secure little compound probably somewhere in southern Florida."

My curiosity showed.

"This is all off the record, Julian."

I grinned. I hadn't thought like a reporter for a long time. "Undoubtedly. But tell me how it works."

"Just a second." He picked up the telephone and called an extension. "This is McQueen. Find Captain Sharpe and ask him to come to my office." He hung up and turned back to me.

"You were going to tell me about how you're going to isolate Carson."

He laughed. "I could get hanged for telling you this."

I waited.

He shrugged. "As I've said all along, you've earned the right to know a few things. We're going to shut Carson down but my guess is that he's already taken steps to divorce himself from most of his covert operations. So we need him in one piece to dismantle all that for us."

"If he'll do it."

"Oh, he'll do it. I have no doubt about that when we present him with the alternatives."

"What alternatives? It sounds like publicity would be as bad for you as it would be for him. You've obviously been granting him tacit approval for many of his operations during the past years."

"Who said anything about publicity? And before you ask it, we're not really into murder. 'Terminate with extreme prejudice' is a line for the movies, not for us. We're really much more subtle—at least some of us are. Carson has powerful enemies in a number of capitals, and all we'd threaten him with is the unpalatable option of turning him over to one of them."

"That's the same thing as murder," I argued.

"Is it?" There was a smile on the CIA man's face. "We'd prefer not to see it that way."

There was a pause for a moment. I knew it had to come sooner or later.

"I really can't let you come on this mission, Julian—if it goes ahead," McQueen said. His tone suggested he knew I wouldn't take the news quietly.

"I want to go along. This guy almost killed me. I want to be there when you take him out."

McQueen just shook his head.

"I'll make you a deal," I said, keeping my voice low, as if it sounded more threatening that way.

"You let me come along, and I'll let you tell me what I can and can't write about what I observe, about what I've already been through." I was making a sacrifice, but that didn't worry me. What concerned me more was missing out on the final chapter.

"Is that the extent of your blackmail?" McQueen asked.

I nodded. "What I could write so far would keep your government and my government arguing and calling each other nasty names for years."

He sighed, the closest I'd ever seen to McQueen without all the answers. "You'd do that, would you?" he asked.

"Absolutely. I want in on this."

"I can't be responsible . . ."

"I'm not asking you to be."

There was a long moment's silence. "Okay, I'll accept your deal. You're in—if we go, you go. But try and stay out of the way of the professionals, will you?"

I grinned. "I'm supposed to be a non-combatant, remember?"

There was a knock on the door. McQueen opened it and let a young Australian army officer enter. I instantly recognised the little wings and short dagger insignia of the Special Air Services regiment. SAS! McQueen had some serious pull somewhere up high in Canberra.

McQueen introduced us, leaving out the part about my being a reporter. "We've been given the green light by both Washington and Canberra, Captain. You have a plan ready?"

Captain Richard Sharpe was all business. "I certainly have, sir. Given what you've been able to tell me and from what we've gleaned from maps and a high-level recce flight, we'll have to go in by sea. Carson's got low-level radar installed and he'd pick us up in the air as soon as we left the mainland. If he's got a method of escape he'll be on it and out of there before we arrive."

"You think he's got a way out?" I asked.

"All we've been able to locate is a helicopter. Nothing special about it. There are a couple of smaller boats moored in the lagoon. There's a big dock . . ." He took a couple of photographs out of a folder, ". . . right here." He pointed to the end of the lagoon. "But no boats around to use it."

There were four photographs. Two were normal blowups of black and white aerial shots. The other two were high-intensity infrared. I'd seen something like them before. There were differences between the two pictures. I asked about them.

"This one was taken late yesterday, and this one," he picked up the second picture, "was taken on a routine RAAF survey of the island done three years ago as part of a marine parks environmental mission."

"He's done some building between the pictures," McQueen commented.

"We've been able to account for most of it."

McQueen looked at him. "And what haven't you been able to account for?"

Sharpe pointed at a bright red blob on the edge of the high water line on the second picture. His other hand pointed to the same place on the first picture. "This photograph measures ground heat, major equipment, that kind of stuff," he explained. "Between the first and second photographs, something major has been added to this location. It has more than tripled the energy output recorded by the film."

I picked up the black and white picture and looked at it closely. "Looks to me like a generating plant or a boatshed."

"More likely a generating plant. We can't be sure but we can't find another building suitable. But it's curious because he's either built a massive generating capacity or something else has been added between these pictures."

"Why's the water a darker colour in front of the shed? It looks like it's deeper," I asked.

"It is deeper, like it's been dredged," the captain said. "Probably to get the generator installed in one piece. They could have brought it in a barge and run it right into place."

I picked up the first picture. "There's only one problem with that theory."

McQueen looked at me. "What's that?"

"There's no channel on the first picture."

We all searched the photographs and agreed. The channel leading from deep water to the generating plant only appeared in the most recent pictures.

We speculated for a few moments. I suggested a submarine.

Both Sharpe and McQueen grinned. "This is real life, not James Bond," McQueen said. Sharpe was more diplomatic but his expression suggested minor toleration for the suggestion.

"Whatever it is," the captain said. "Let's not worry about it. We can have a look when we get there."

For the next hour we went over the details of the captain's plan. There was to be maximum surprise and minimum violence. The captain was good. He had options and he was flexible enough to see merit in some of McQueen's ideas. I kept an eye on McQueen. The one thing he didn't seem to be was a specialist on this kind of thing. He was the librarian or clerk type but it was obvious he knew a lot about infiltrating enemy positions. The captain nodded thoughtfully and by the time we were finished, the Australian's respect for the

259

American CIA man was shining through. They were both professionals. I was feeling like the odd man out. I'd felt that way ever since they'd both mocked my suggestion of a submarine. I couldn't get it out of my mind, as if there was some clue I'd heard or read that made it a possibility.

Finally a plan was hammered out and accepted. The captain left to work out more of the details with his men. McQueen excused himself to report to his superiors in the Langley, Virginia headquarters of the CIA and I wandered outside. Jade was off the base, with an escort, picking up some appropriate clothing. I was okay, I was dressed in army fatigues, but she insisted on jeans or something a little less military.

They'd assigned us adjoining rooms in the officers' quarters. As I let myself into my room I could hear the shower running in her room next door. I waited until the shower was turned off, gave her a few minutes to get dressed then knocked on the door.

I heard her pad across the floor, unlock the door and open it.

She stood back, resplendent in blue jeans, a white blouse and a jean jacket.

"Who paid for all that?" I asked, letting my admiration show through.

"Courtesy of McQueen," she said happily.

"I should be making notes. Not so long ago you would have called the CIA public enemy number one. Now it's paying for your wardrobe."

She crunched her face into a scowl, then grinned and laughed. "What the hell. It's all taxpayers' money anyway. You should get something too."

"I'm an Australian. Remember?"

She shrugged as she moved away from the door and let me in. "They probably wouldn't have recognised the difference."

There was a moment of awkward silence, then she fixed me with a look of determination.

"So what's the plan now? When do we get Carson?"

I had to give her points for fortitude. "We're going after him on his island."

"I'm ready," she said seriously.

I let my eyebrows arch so she would be warned about what was coming. "Jade, I really don't think this is the kind of mission you should go on."

The anger was instantaneous. "Bullshit! You're going after the man who tried to kill both of us and you're telling me I shouldn't go along. Julian Castle, you're sexist." Her voice was loud in the small room. "If I was my father, you wouldn't be saying I couldn't go."

"It's not sexism, Jade. It's concern for your safety," I argued.

"Well, don't be so concerned. I'm a big girl in case you haven't noticed." Her eyes blazed.

"I've noticed."

She flushed a little but didn't back down. "So if I'm big enough for you to notice *that* then I'm big enough to go with you after that sonofabitch who almost killed us."

I shrugged. The only position I had left was a copout line. "It's not really my decision anyway. It's McQueen's."

"Then I'll see him," she said, turning abruptly and walking out of the door. She slammed it shut behind her and left me standing in her room feeling like a fool. *Some gutsy broad*, I thought, adopting my most sexist stance before surrendering in the face of obvious defeat and walking back into my room. I left the door open but she didn't return.

For an hour I lay on the bed thinking about her, Chester, and all the others who had peopled the past few weeks. All of this from a chance remark

261

from a servant in the shattered remains of Marcos' Malacanang Palace. The ex-dictator was sitting on a beach in Hawaii, enjoying the protection of Washington and, probably, counting whatever shekels he'd been able to escape with. The television news was talking in terms of billions of dollars. For once I didn't think the TV glamour boys were exaggerating.

There was a knock on the door. I swung off the bed and walked to the door. It was a soldier.

"Captain Sharpe's compliments, sir. The troop is ready to move and he'd like you over at Operations right now."

I nodded. The SAS didn't waste time. *Who dares wins*, I thought as I walked with the soldier across the base to the operations centre.

Richmond was an air force base but it was also set up to handle a wide array of missions, and the SAS people had been given a set of offices for their planning.

Sharpe was briefing some air force officers and his team leaders beside a map when I entered. He acknowledged my presence with a nod and continued on.

"We'll use the C-130 to get us here." He pointed at a map and a small airstrip. "A couple of trucks have been commandeered to carry us and our equipment to this bay and we go into the water there. If the weather holds we start off at dusk, cross these straits and take our time going in."

I listened carefully, watching the men gathered around him nodding acceptance of the plan.

"We'll go ashore at the far end of the island, use the darkness as cover to move in close to the compound, then wait for dawn. I want the light to see what's going on. I want the helicopter and the boats in the bay put out of action, everyone rounded up and Carson out of there as quickly as possible. Okay?"

There was a chorus of muted agreement and the briefing had ended.

As Sharpe walked over to me, McQueen entered the room followed by Jade. My heart sank as I watched her grin at me with more satisfaction and defiance than were needed.

McQueen said only one line, mostly to the captain. "Doctor Price is coming along."

Sharpe just shrugged. It didn't seem to bother him at all. I kept my mouth shut. She had the backing of a man I couldn't argue with. I wondered how she'd done it.

"Let's saddle up, people," McQueen said.

The big Hercules C-130 was sitting on the tarmac. The equipment was all aboard and the SAS troops were filing up the big ramp that had been lowered from the rear of the transport. Sharpe, McQueen, Jade and I were the last aboard. Sharpe went forward to talk with the pilots and McQueen took a seat beside a sergeant. I sat down near the ramp and Jade quickly joined me.

The web belt seats were uncomfortable. I squirmed to find a position for the long ride north. Jade seemed cool and relaxed. I knew there wouldn't be much time for conversation once the big engines started. I'd ridden these monsters before.

"How'd you convince McQueen to let you come?" I asked.

She smiled, a picture of innocence. "Simple. I told him I'd burn my placards and refrain from any more street marches. Even admitted he'd make me a convert if he'd let me come."

I laughed. "You drive a hard bargain, lady."

She grinned widely. "Wasn't much of a bargain.

He's already converted me. Maybe, just maybe, we need people like him." She sobered a bit. "I can't shake the feeling we'd both be dead if he hadn't come along, but even more important, creeps like Carson would go on plying their evil trade."

"Your dad would puff up with pride if he heard you talking like this."

She tossed her head frivolously. "Let's not get carried away, Julian. I can't let my father get the idea that I think he was right all the time."

The cough of the engines made the aeroplane shiver and the quick revs that followed made conversation impossible. I settled back. She reached across and took my hand. I felt the slim fingers tighten on mine. She made no attempt to let go and I leaned back and closed my eyes and thought of this impetuous young woman beside me. I wondered if whatever we were sharing could continue once we were out of this mess and back in the boring Real World.

A few hours later I was brought out of a restless doze by a distinct change in the sound of the engines. The lessening of the roar was followed by a tilt to the right and the lowering of the nose. I could see nothing of the outside from where I was sitting. The soldiers had long ago finished their final equipment checks. They were sitting quite still, in various states of psyching themselves up for whatever lay ahead. I looked across at the half of the troop I could see clearly. They were a mixture of ages and builds. The SAS was one of those world elites. If I had to be going into something like what lay ahead—and even Sharpe had admitted he wasn't sure exactly what we'd find—then these were the kinds of men I would want on my side. Carson's thugs like Kasilov and Alberts would be no match for them.

A few minutes later we hit the ground with a solid thump. The weight of the Hercules settled onto its springs and wheels and there was a scream as the engines reversed, then the noise abated as we taxied somewhere on the field. As soon as we stopped rolling the rear ramp started lowering. I squeezed my eyes together as the north Queensland sunshine filled the rear of the plane. The hot air swept inside the plane like a wave thick enough to cut.

Sharpe led the way out and Jade and I followed the first troops. McQueen had changed clothes. He'd given up the three-piece suit for army fatigues like mine. Jade was the only one dressed in anything different. I was still amazed that no one was giving her presence a second thought. I was really out of step these days.

The airfield was deserted. It wasn't used by anyone, it seemed. There were small bushes growing on the dirt runway and no buildings in sight.

There was nothing much for me to do. The troops had their orders and their methods of operating and for us civilians to lend a hand would have just fouled up their tightly knit and methodical way of doing things. We stood off to one side as they quickly unloaded the rubber boats and various other items.

Within a couple of minutes two large trucks rolled onto the airfield. They were moving vans with logos of a well-known company on the side. The drivers were in civilian dress but as they stepped down from the cabs and talked with Sharpe it became obvious they were his men. I wondered how the bill for the use of the trucks would show up on the company's accounts. Some manifest, I thought as I watched the hardware being loaded.

Jade was still beside me. She wiped some sweat from her face and shrugged out of the jean jacket. The white blouse glared in the sunlight.

A sergeant came over to us, accompanied by a young soldier about the same size as Jade.

"Doctor," the sergeant said to her, "you can't come with us with that white shirt on. It'll show up too much in the dark. This man has an extra shirt that should fit you. Would you care to change?"

"Sure," she said quickly, then paused for a moment at the implication.

I toyed with the idea of letting her figure it out on her own, and then relented. She was getting to me. I wondered if I was acting out of protective jealousy, or just trying to be helpful. "The cab of the truck would be the place to change," I suggested.

She nodded with some thankfulness and went off to change.

The sergeant grinned at me, then turned and went back to his men.

It didn't take long and we all climbed into the trucks. The drivers sealed up the doors. It was instantly hot and sticky. There were small hatches in the roof and they had been sprung to let in some air but it didn't help much. The smell of men and the canvas boats quickly filled the van. I was wet with sweat. The rough fatigues were itchy and I tried to ignore the urge to scratch. No one else was doing it.

Thankfully, the drive wasn't long. After a steep incline that had us all clinging to whatever handholds we could find, the floor levelled out and the truck stopped. The doors swung open and we climbed out.

We were in a small cove. There was a terrific beach with high rock bluffs at both ends. We

266

wouldn't be bothered. Sharpe had the only access road blocked off by a couple of military policemen and an explanation that some kind of army manoeuvre was taking place nearby.

For half an hour everyone worked hard, assembling the canvas and rubber boats, attaching specially muffled engines and starting them briefly. There was an assortment of weapons, handguns, rifles, sub-machineguns and shotguns. There were also stun grenades, smoke grenades and a few high explosives. Sharpe was prepared for everything and hoping he could get away with using as little of it as possible. He didn't want to attract any attention beyond the island and that was going to be difficult enough. I kept thinking of how great a story this would be, particularly if I'd had a camera or one of the photographers from the newspaper. But McQueen had been adamant about that. Julian Castle was no longer a reporter, at least for the duration. We'd talk about what, if anything, could be written when it was all over.

When everything was ready there was still more than an hour until it would be dark enough for us to move. Rations were produced from a crate and we all ate the uninviting contents. Jade was given a choice: grin and bear it, or go for a walk, Sharpe explained. His troops were going for a swim and swimsuits were not standard issue.

She accepted his invitation gracefully and opted for a walk up the beach. As much as I wanted to swim, I volunteered to go with her.

The sand was hot and by the time we reached the first of the rocks we could look back and watch the soldiers in the water. They were clowning around like a bunch of schoolboys. She grinned and followed me around the bluff. On the other side there was a break in the rocks and a small piece of sand just wide enough for us to sit together. The water lapped at our feet, blue and inviting.

"We've been through a lot, Julian," she said, as she took off her running shoes and socks and wiggled her pale toes in the sand.

"It's not over yet," I said, wishing it was. "Although it's getting damn close to some kind of conclusion."

"And when it is over, what will you do?"

"Back to Manila, I guess, and try and do what I'm supposed to be doing now. Reporting the news."

"My father likes it out there, too," she said.

"He's good at it."

She nodded. There was a break for a moment and then she said gently, "I wonder if they'd take a reformed activist, turned doctor in Manila."

I looked at her and she smiled a little.

"I'd like to spend more time with you when it was quieter," she said.

I took her hand tentatively. "I'd like that too." I meant it. She'd grown on me. It hadn't really shown up clearly in my mind until we'd thrown a few words at each over her coming on this mission.

For a moment we looked at each other. "Let's swim," she said suddenly.

I grinned helplessly. "Swimsuits aren't standard issue, remember?"

She stood up, quickly unbuttoned the army shirt the soldier had given her, stripped it off and stood there in front of me. Her breasts shone whitely against the rest of her tanned skin. Then she reached down, released the clasp of her belt and pushed the jeans down her legs. She turned away toward the water wearing only panties, then paused and seemed to think. Her fingers tucked into the elastic and she pulled the panties down and tossed them onto her jeans. She laughed at me.

"C'mon, don't just sit there gawking." She ran into the water and dived straight into the shallow waves. The sea was so clear, the water obscured nothing.

I climbed to my feet, the sight of her naked body stirring more than just my mind. I undressed more slowly than she had, wishing my stomach was a little flatter and the muscles a little more pronounced.

The water was warm and refreshing and I swam hard to catch up with her. We swam around playfully for a few minutes and then started back to the sand, pausing together and sitting up with the water covering our laps.

She reached over put a hand on my shoulder and pulled me toward her. We fell backwards together, splashing and laughing. Her body was cool and smooth as she straightened against me, pushing hard and kissing my mouth. It felt good and I clung to her, my legs wrapping around her legs. If only all this was over, I thought.

She must have had the same feeling a moment later because she eased away from me. "Now we have something to look forward to, don't we?"

I nodded.

"So be damn careful, Julian Castle. I'd find it quite difficult to make love to a corpse."

"The same goes for you," I told her.

She nodded, gave me a last peck on the cheek and climbed out of the sea.

I lay there, enjoying the view of her body as she used the shirt to dry herself.

Then I stood slowly up and joined her, drying myself and dressing.

By the time we were back over the rocks the soldiers had dressed. McQueen and Sharpe looked up, took in our wet hair and grinned. I tried to keep a straight face.

It was Sharpe who brought us all back to reality. He reached down and picked up a web belt with a holstered .45. "I'm told you know how to use this thing." He handed it to me.

I looked at it disdainfully. "You think I need it?"

He frowned. "I wouldn't give it to you unless I did."

The radio crackled as I put it around my waist and twisted the metal clip to secure it. I watched Sharpe pick up the radio and an earpiece. He made contact with the operations centre and listened, then turned to me.

"We've got more information on your Colonel Radcliffe-Jones. Former regular army in Britain. Top regiments, including some time with the SAS, the works. Northern Ireland. Falklands. Sacked for excessive cruelty toward Argentine POWs."

It fitted what McQueen had said, with additional information. Sharpe was going up against one of his own. "I gathered that. The guy was good."

"He's still good," the captain said, "and intelligence thinks he's out there on the island with Carson, along with some of his mercenaries from Nicaragua."

We all looked around at each other. That certainly complicated things.

"They're a lot tougher than Kasilov's types," I said.

"Undoubtedly," Sharpe said. "I'm going to change a couple of the plans." He went off to talk with his men.

I took the .45 out, released the magazine and checked the bullets. It was fully loaded. I slapped the magazine back into the grip and heard it click home. I returned it to its holster and snapped shut the flap.

Jade was watching, concern showing.

"Let's go," Sharpe shouted.

We loaded into the rubber boats, five altogether. McQueen and Sharpe each went into separate boats. Jade went with me. The soldiers slid into place just as if it was an exercise. They were confident, but quieter now than before. The motors were started. It seemed strange to see the small wakes behind each boat and to hear only a brief purring from the muffled engines.

There was no sign of the island. It was beyond the horizon. The only sign of life on the nearby sea was a sailboat far off to the south.

We skimmed across the water as darkness fell. One moment there was a blue sky, the next it was bright red with the sunset, then darker, then a greyish black and then black. There was no wind and the surface swell was gentle with a long gap between each wave.

The boats stayed close together, even when the speed built up. They were like a precision flying team, maintaining the same speed and separation. There was a small blue light on a pole set in the middle of each boat. It was what each helmsman was watching. As the darkness became more complete, Sharpe's boat moved out into the lead. He was navigating.

Jade was close to me. I could feel her leg pushed against mine and occasionally her head would move toward mine and the wind pushing her hair would force the strands against my cheek and forehead. When I set aside my fears about what lay ahead, I was glad she was there; when I thought of the colonel and his soldiers, I wished I'd been firmer with her. She had no place here. But then, when I got right down to the bottom line, neither did I.

The horizon was gone in the darkness, but

Sharpe was good. There was a red blinking light from his craft: three blinks, followed by two longer flashes. It was the signal the helmsmen had been waiting for. They slowed their engines and moved into line astern. Ropes were tossed from one boat to the next and when we were finally tied together in a line all the engines were stopped, except Sharpe's lead boat. He was towing us in.

I peered through the darkness but could see very little until there was a flash in the water ahead. It was a beach. We ground ashore, the soldiers jumped out along with Jade and me and the boat was lifted clear of the water and run across the beach into the tropical vegetation. No one said anything. Within minutes the boats were covered over with camouflage netting and palm leaves.

Sharpe led the way through the night, keeping right on the edge of the beach and the jungle. He wanted to avoid the trails and the open expanse of beach, he had said, because if any alarms were set out to catch prowlers the one place that might be clear was right where the beach joined the jungle. In single file, we walked toward the compound.

I could visualise the map of the island as we moved. Thin at one end like a tear—that's where we'd landed—and then the island grew wider quickly until it rounded out with a blunt end where the main houses were located.

Two hours later Sharpe brought us to a halt and let the column bunch up around him. There was still no talking. But I knew the plan. The column would break into three groups. One group would cross the island. A couple of soldiers would swim out to the boats in the bay and disable them. The rest would advance up the beach toward the compound. A second group, with McQueen, would cross to the centre of the island and advance toward the compound, while our group continued along the beach. The three groups, when in position, would form a line cutting off the compound from the rest of the island. The fourth group, responsible for disabling the helicopter, had been cancelled when Sharpe had been told the colonel was on the island. It was, he had said, too risky. The helicopter might have been approached with just normal guards on hand, but the presence of the colonel's highly trained mercenaries made it a dangerous proposition. The chopper would now be taken out, by whatever means were appropriate, during the actual assault or if someone started the machine and tried to leave before the assault actually got under way.

Within another hour we were in position. There was concern for a few moments when a dog started barking. Soldiers who carried pistols with silencers attached were called forward but the dog stopped barking and everyone settled down in the jungle to wait. Jade was still close to me, almost like a shadow. She leaned against me as we sat in the foliage waiting for dawn. Her hand sought mine and we lay in the humid darkness listening to the insects and a gathering breeze as it ruffled the tops of the tall palm trees overhead.

I wondered if she was thinking of baby Joseph Roa. I was. The little guy had come through quite an adventure. Now he was back in Manila with some uncle or cousin. He'd never remember any of this. I played games with myself as I shifted to a more comfortable position, my shadow moving with me. One of the games was trying to remember my earliest memory. I could get back as far as my parents bringing home my new sister from the hospital, but I couldn't remember that clearly. Her first birthday was more vivid. I was five years older than she. I was jealous of all the attention that was focused on her and I blew out the candles on her birthday cake before she had a chance to do it. Lying there, three and half decades later, I felt terribly ashamed at what I had done. She was married now, with two kids and a husband who worked in a steel mill in Wollongong. It had been years since I had seen her. I vowed, there in the darkness, to tell how sorry I was about that birthday cake when this was all over.

The memory had gone on for a long time. I was brought back to reality by soldier tapping soldier. There was a faint hint of dawn on the far horizon and the light would come up as quickly as it had gone down. Sharpe had picked his time well. The plan called for most of the household to be taken in their beds. The only complication was how the colonel would have deployed his men. Did Carson have any reason to be ready for some kind of attack or a visit by the authorities? When I'd asked Sharpe the question he'd shrugged and answered simply that he would assume the worst at each step. The worst scenario, and the one he'd planned for, was the colonel dug in ready and able to repel invaders or prowlers.

Everything slowed right down. Crouched over we moved through the foliage until there was only one set of bushes left between us and the compound. Then we were on our stomachs searching the cleared ground before us, the small buildings, the helicopter pad and the tied-down chopper. There was at least one closed-circuit camera moving back and forth across our part of the yard. Sharpe assigned a man to move in on it and we waited while he slithered forward. He had a gun with a silencer and would take it out with one shot when Sharpe gave the word.

For the first time Sharpe used his palm-sized radio. He looked back at Jade and me and nodded his head, then spoke into the radio. "Check."

He had a small earpiece. We couldn't hear the other radios but his head nodded as the other groups confirmed they were in position and ready. He spoke once again. "Go!" He raised his hand and dropped it.

Out in the yard the soldier fired his silenced pistol at the television camera. The bullet shattered the lens. There was very little noise.

Sharpe stood up and started running towards the house, his men behind him. Jade and I brought up the tail. I had the big pistol in my hand, a bullet in the chamber and the safety catch off. I visualised the other two groups making their moves.

For ten paces there was no sound, then dogs started barking and I heard a shotgun blast on the far side of the house. It had started.

"The chopper," Sharpe yelled.

A soldier went down on a knee, levelled a compact rocket launcher and fired. The rocket exploded on the helicopter and it burst into flames. No one would go riding in that any more.

The soldiers peeled off into each building, covering each other and moving with practised movements.

There was more gunfire now. I saw four men in fatigues run out on a porch, all armed. They fired short bursts from machineguns and dived for cover. We hit the ground. Two soldiers sprayed the verandah while the rest spun off to the left and right. Jade and I stayed exactly where we were, sprawled on the lawn.

"The roof," Sharpe yelled over his shoulder at me. Someone had said something to him over the radio. I looked up. Two heads bobbed on the roof of the main house. A rifle came up. I lifted my pistol and fired three shots. The rifle disappeared as the bullets whined off the wall nearby.

I grabbed Jade by the arm and raced after Sharpe. He had made it to the side of the house. We crossed the verandah. There were double doors ahead. Sharpe's boot lashed out and the door smashed open. A hail of gunfire came through the hole. Slivers splashed from the wooden poles on the verandah. Sharpe and a soldier dived straight inside, rolling on the floor and firing as they came to their knees. The bursts were short and loud in the room.

The inside of the mansion was quiet. Jade and I followed. Inside there were two men in shorts and singlets. They were lying on the floor, one dead and one wounded. The soldier kicked their weapons across the room.

"He's not going anywhere," the soldier yelled, looking down at the man with the stomach wound.

"Let's go," Sharpe said, moving into a corridor that led deeper into the house.

Jade and I followed him. She was still close behind me, staying just a pace off my right side. The .45 was getting heavier but I clutched it as though it was some kind of a security blanket.

Carson sat upright in his bed at the first sound of gunfire. He recognised the shotguns and then the sub-machineguns. He heard an explosion and guessed it had taken out the helicopter. The sounds of battle didn't surprise him but he wished, for the last time, that he'd had just a few more days to get ready. Rolling quickly out of bed, he ran to the window. His bedroom was in the highest part of the building, at the front overlooking the beach. The room was the only second-level room in the largely ground-level house. He saw soldiers off to the right, going in and out of the smaller buildings. He turned, grabbed pants and shirt and pulled them on. His feet slipped into loafers and he opened a cabinet, taking out an Uzi machinegun and pocketing two magazines.

He went out the door just as there was a burst of gunfire from somewhere in the house. By the time he was down the stairs, Radcliffe-Jones was coming along the corridor.

"We're under attack," the colonel told him.

"How many?"

"Lots."

"Can your men hold?"

The colonel hefted an M-16. "We'll give it a good try."

"Do that." Carson turned away, then stopped. "Peter!"

The colonel paused.

"Take care." Then he ran off in the opposite direction. He had no doubt the colonel would give a good accounting of himself. That's exactly what the last page of December Cleanup had called for. He had hoped they would never reach this point in the plan but now that it was here, he was ready. All he had to do was stick to the final page of instructions.

The corridor led down into the kitchen set slightly below ground level. He ran past the stoves and stopped in front of a large wooden table. Reaching underneath, he twisted an innocuous-looking wooden joint. The table slid sideways, revealing a set of steps leading down into the ground. He went down the steps, then reached behind him to swing the table back. It went halfway, and locked. He punched at the handle. Nothing moved. He tried again. It was stuck. He climbed halfway up the stairs and looked into the spring mechanism that was supposed to seal the hole. Something was stuck in the spring. There were more gunshots and urgent yelling outside. Someone screamed.

He reached down and grasped the handle of a metal soup ladle. The damn thing was stuck in the mechanism. He wrenched at it. It wouldn't budge. He heaved on the table leg. It swung a short distance and then jammed tight. He took one last look at the ladle, swore and then went back down the steps. The shooting was getting closer.

The underground corridor was narrow and carefully constructed on all four sides with metal strips and strong planks. It sloped beneath the house and went off into the distance. A few light bulbs had been placed along its distance to provide dim lighting.

He ran along the planks for some distance and then paused. There was a small box. He opened its cover and looked inside. A timer was attached to wires. The explosives had been set behind the box, just enough to seal the tunnel off so that anyone following would only get so far. With the table out of position, this was a fallback position. No one would catch him now. He set the timer at one minute, turned it on and ran off down the corridor.

Jade and I were still right behind Sharpe inside the mansion. The main battle sounded like it was going on outside. There was a fierce firefight on the eastern side of the house and sporadic firing from the west. Most of our group had peeled off into various rooms and already servants were being rounded up behind us in the lounge rooms. The original plan was working. Carson's personal staff were causing little trouble. It was the colonel's men who were putting up a fight. There was a full-blown battle going on. It was a good thing we had the SAS on side. A regular police force would have been savaged up against this defence.

Sharpe was darting in and out of the rooms. He swept into a kitchen and then back out. He sprinted forward, leaving me well behind. I paused in the doorway to the kitchen. It was empty. I started to turn away when I saw the table. It didn't click for a moment. It was just a big, wooden picnic-type table but it was sitting at an unnatural angle, like someone had hastily pushed out from behind it and not slid it back into place. It just stood out as being something askew. I took one pace into the room and saw the partially hidden hole under the table. There was no question what it was.

"Get Sharpe," I said over my shoulder to Jade.

She looked at the hole, then turned away. "Wait for us," she yelled back.

I crossed to the table and pushed at it. Nothing. I put my feet against the wall and my back against the table and heaved. It moved a bit, just enough for me to squeeze down into the hole. I went down slowly, knowing I should wait for the captain. There were lights in the underground corridor. I eased all the way down the steps and started forward slowly. The passageway was narrow and I had to stoop slightly to avoid hitting my head on the plank roof. It was solidly built. Someone had gone to a lot of effort to construct all this.

The little voices were back. It had been a long time since they'd sounded off. Now they were telling me what I already knew; I was a bloody fool to go charging off down the tunnel without waiting for backup support. I paused, then went forward even more slowly.

Jade was back at the tunnel's entrance, Sharpe right behind her. I could hear them calling out to me. The explosion ahead, her scream and my own warning voices all merged together in some kind of jumbled kaleidoscope of noise. It started as a muffled sound, then grew louder and raced toward me. The blast slammed me backwards onto the rough planks.

The walls were caving in. I had to get up but everything hurt. Sand was pouring in all around me. I shielded my eyes from the dust. Coughing, I climbed to my knees. A board from the wall slammed into my legs and the corridor came totally apart. I lunged back toward the stairs, felt the bottom step and reached out. Sharpe grabbed my arm. He heaved and lifted me up through the small hole as the last of the corridor crashed down behind me.

I lay on the floor panting. "Thanks," I managed.

"Leave the hard stuff to us, eh!" Sharpe said. "Which way did the tunnel go?"

I climbed unsteadily to my feet and tried to orient myself. "That way," I said, pointing.

We both said it together. "The generator plant!"

Jade's scream grabbed our attention. "That's the colonel!" She was pointing out the window at Radcliffe-Jones. He had an M-16 pointed at us.

"Down!" Sharpe yelled, just as the colonel fired.

The bullets cut a solid path across the room above our heads. Glass slivers from the windows sprayed us. There was a pause and something solid hit the floor.

"Grenade!" I yelled as soon as I saw the ugly oval ball. It rolled a pace and then stopped.

Sharpe was fast. He was closest to it. His leg lashed out and kicked the ball toward the hole leading to the collapsed tunnel. It seemed to roll so slowly.

I held my breath, trying to slow the seconds before it exploded. We didn't stand a chance if it went off.

It exploded just after it went over the lip of the hole. The room erupted but the shrapnel went straight up, cutting dozens of holes in the high roof.

"Stay here," Sharpe yelled as he clambered to his feet and dived out through the shattered window.

Carson had gone down that tunnel. I knew it. No one would have blown it unless it had already been used. He was going to get away somehow. I could feel it. And I couldn't let that happen. I was on my feet, racing for the door.

"Julian!" Jade was yelling at me.

I didn't stop. I went through the doorway and out into the corridor. It was empty. I raced down the length of it. There were double doors at the end. I stopped for an instant and looked out. There was shooting off to one side. The way ahead was clear. Jade was by my shoulder. I knew it would be useless to tell her to stay in one place.

One kick slammed the doors open. I ran through, keeping low and running as fast as I could across the open ground. I knew she was there but I didn't pause to look. Bullets hit the ground all around me. I couldn't see where they were coming from. My heart was pounding. I needed backup but nobody was there. Everyone had their own battles to fight.

She screamed once, long and painful. The sound cut through me like I'd taken the bullet.

I swung around. Jade was on the ground holding her leg. I went to her, down on both knees. Picking her up, I carried her to a small building. The door was open. It was empty inside. There was warm blood on my hand.

She took only a minute to examine it. "It went straight through," she whimpered. "Leave me. Get the bastard, Julian. Get Carson. Don't let him get away!"

All those little voices were screaming at me, telling me I shouldn't leave her. We couldn't let Carson get away. Not now. Not after everyone had paid such a terrible price to get him.

I stood up and left. The generating plant was some distance away and the soldiers were too busy to help me. McQueen? There was no time to search for him. I was on my own if I went after Carson— if he was there. And if he wasn't? The thought scared me. Carson was too smart to let himself get cut off on the island. The helicopter couldn't be the only way out. There were no boats in the lagoon. That left only the generating plant.

Carson had made it to the end of the underground corridor. It surfaced in a small storage shed a short distance from the generating plant. He went up the stairs, carefully opening the door. There was no one around. He could make it, he knew. If he could get to the power plant he could get out to the *Anastasia* and away to safety.

His world was coming unravelled much faster than he could keep up with it but he still believed he could make it. He was still working to the cleanup plan. He had to get away. They could never put him up before the public to tear him slowly apart. If the colonel could hold them for another few minutes, he could get away with it all. The tunnel was the only link, and he had put paid to that. He'd heard the muffled explosion and felt the blast of air at his back as the tunnel collapsed somewhere far behind him.

There was still no one else around. The place was deserted. The solid crunch of grenades tried to compete for his attention, but he fought off the urge to look back.

The generating plant building was directly ahead. He fumbled in his pocket for the keys to the special locks that had been installed. He reached the door and pulled it swiftly open. The keys were ready. He climbed down a steel ladder to the ground floor. Two large turbines were whirring away in the room. It was hot and dry inside. The whole room was a miniature version of a large power plant. It had served him well and was now playing out its final use.

He crossed the concrete floor to a door marked MAINTENANCE and inserted the first of the keys. The first door swung open to reveal a workbench and an array of tools mounted neatly on the wall. Beyond the bench was another door. He inserted the second key, then reached up higher on the metal frame and put in a third key. With both hands on both keys, he turned them simultaneously.

The door swung open, revealing a small concrete bunker. There was a metal hatch in the middle of the cubicle. Another key was needed to work the hatch, but it opened easily when the key was twisted. He reached up and flicked on a light switch mounted on the wall beside the hatch. The room below was flooded with bright light.

He climbed into the hatch, found the rungs of the ladder and started climbing down. Halfway to the dock below, about ten paces away, he turned and looked at the submarine. He paused for only a moment before finishing the descent.

He untied the forward lines and ran along the quay to the stern ropes and tossed them loose. The docking bay was only a foot wider than the small submarine. He climbed up on the back of the squat little ship and unfastened the clips holding the plastic bubble hatch. The vessel was painted battleship grey. When it had been a scientific submersible for the Canadian marine company, before he had purchased the company, it had been painted bright yellow to make it more visible. The grey paint was for the opposite purpose.

The electric motors that closed and opened the

doors separating the dock from the sea were operated by a handheld remote control switch. There were two control panels, one on the dock, the second aboard the submarine. He climbed into the spacious cockpit, designed to carry the pilot plus two observers. The entire front of the submarine was reinforced plastic and thickened plexiglass, designed to withstand deepsea pressure and sudden knocks against underwater obstacles. It also provided those aboard with a clear view of whatever lay ahead in the sea.

Carson lowered himself into the pilot's seat. He'd worked hard to learn, and had practised as often as possible, the complicated procedures for operating the submarine. Run on battery power, it made slow but steady speed once under way. But flooding the ballast tanks and operating the diving planes took considerable skill. His last practice run had been only four months ago and he had successfully taken the sub out into the open sea and submerged to 30 metres and then had navigated to within 500 metres of a target 25 kilometres away—a slightly truncated version of what was required now. He only needed one more coordinate—the actual position of the *Anastasia*. But he could get that later. Once clear of the horizon he could surface and radio the cruiser to come to him, or he could get a navigational fix from the ship's beam and home in on it.

He flicked the right switches and the electric motors purred smoothly. He had power. The throttle moved at his fingertips and the submarine eased forward. Everything was working. The dock was deep enough to sink the submarine out of sight. It was for testing various systems, but this time it would be useful because it would allow him to leave the generator building under the water without being seen.

He pulled back the ballast levers that would flood the outer tanks, destroying the buoyancy and sinking the submarine. There was the hiss of escaping air and the submarine started settling in the water. He lifted the remote control and pressed the button. The outer doors to the dock started sliding back. He was going to make it, he concluded.

The gunfire was only sporadic now. For a moment as I pounded down the trail toward the generating building, I wondered whether we had won or lost. It would all be academic if Carson got away. I urged my sore legs to keep going.

Then I was there. I paused and eased into the doorway, the sound of my heart pounding in my heaving chest much louder than the sound of the generators whirring away inside. I searched the room with my eyes. Nothing. I went inside, pistol out in front of me. Was I wrong? Was this nothing but a generator room?

Then I saw the maintenance door standing ajar. I went down the ladder and quickly crossed the room between pulsing equipment. I swung the door open with my foot, gun ready. Nothing except another door. I knew I was on to something. Inside there was a worktable and a second door. I crossed through it quickly. There was great urgency now. A hatch was open in the middle of the floor. I swung my legs over it and eased down.

The sound of escaping air was the first thing I heard, then the grinding sound of some large piece of metal moving on wheels. I went down three rungs and hung there, eyes wide. I had been right. There was a submarine there—one of those deep-sea divers. And there was a set of large doors at the far end of the docking area and they were starting to slide open. I caught a glimpse of morning sky and blue sea through the widening crack as the panels slid slowly back. The escaping air from the submarine and the purring electric motor told me the worst: Carson was inside and he was going to get away.

The bow of the submarine was pointed toward the door and I couldn't see the pilot's station. It was well forward.

I climbed quickly down to the dock and ran across to the stern of the sub. I felt helpless. Nothing could be done. I knew the plastic bubble hatch on the top of the sub would be locked and sealed from inside.

The .45 was still in my hand. I couldn't stop that metal monster with the gun alone. I wished I had the rocket launcher that had taken out the helicopter. Wishful thinking. But I had to do something, or Carson was going to get away.

The door was almost open far enough for the sub to slip through. The electric engines increased their speed. Water was three-quarters of the way up the sides of the sub and it was sinking lower. I ran along the dock and jumped the gap, landing hard on the stern. Stupid move, Castle, I admonished myself. The sub sinks and you get washed away into the sea. I clambered forward to the bubble hatch and pounded on it with the butt of the gun. Nothing. But whoever was driving the submersible had heard me. The engines whined and the sub leaped forward in the water. The sudden movement unbalanced me and I slid back to a railing. Water was lapping at my feet.

I raised the pistol and aimed at the hatch. I pulled the trigger four times. Four times my hand bounced from the impact of the firing. Three holes appeared in the plastic and with the fourth the entire canopy crumpled.

The submarine was still going down. Didn't he

have warning lights showing he was no longer watertight? The sub was sliding through the doors. Then I realised the problem. The plastic cover was broken, but the hatch cover itself was still locked tight. If there was a warning light or alarm it wouldn't have been activated because the cover's trim was still set securely in place. Water was now splashing across the roof.

I couldn't move with the gun in my hand. I tucked it into my belt, slid forward and lowered myself into the submarine. I could see all the way up to the pilot's station and Carson was sitting there, staring ahead, nervous and jerky in his movements. There were two compartments, the one I was in and the pilot's compartment. I stepped forward as carefully as possible into the pilot's compartment, then slowly swung the door shut. There were four dog latches. I had only one of them done and was working on the second when he finally turned to me.

"What are you . . .?"

I spun around and watched as he paled.

"Castle . . ." he said lamely.

He might have been shocked but the Uzi I hadn't seen came up quickly, pointed right at my stomach, and he regained control of himself very fast.

I raised my hands high. "You've lost the bubble in your entry hatch. You'd better blow your tanks and surface or it's going to get very wet in here."

His eyes went to the control board, then back to me. "You're lying. I've got a green board. If the cover was off it'd show red."

"You fool. I said you've lost your bubble, not the hatch." Over his shoulder I could see that we were free of the docking bay and out into the open water. We were making good forward speed. I braced against the waves. But we were still going down.

287

There was a massive rush of water behind me. We'd gone under and the water was pouring in through the smashed bubble.

Carson looked uncertain. He'd only trimmed for water in the ballast tanks. The sudden flow of water into the compartment behind me had thrown all his calculations out of place. He seemed frozen, unable to respond.

The submarine lurched suddenly to the right. Carson was half in and half out of his seat and as we turned on our side, he lost his balance and fell sideways.

I reached up and braced against the ceiling with one hand while trying to pull out the .45 with the other hand. I wasn't going to make it.

Carson tried vainly. He squeezed the trigger on the Uzi and bullets smashed around the small compartment. Sparks flew as electrical lines were cut. The engines spluttered and then stopped.

The sub was on its side, going down much faster. It hit the sandy bottom and I finally lost my footing and fell against a bank of levers. I heard a rib crack and felt incredible pain in my right side.

Carson was still trying to get up. He'd almost made it until we hit the bottom and he'd fallen a second time. He was scrambling and reaching for the Uzi.

I'd lost the .45 when I fell. Ignoring the pain in my side, I lurched forward and grabbed the snub nose of the small machinegun. Carson had the other end. Neither of us was near enough to the trigger to make any difference.

There was water on the deck under me. As we grappled I glanced back. The hatch between the two compartments had sprung. The one latch, all I'd been able to get secured before Carson had spotted me, wasn't enough. Water was pouring in.

With my free hand I smacked Carson's face as hard as I could. He went backwards, letting go of the gun, cracking his head against the plastic dome. He crumpled up on the deck, unconscious.

Carson was no longer my problem. I knew nothing about this submarine. But the water was rising quickly. I wondered how far down we were. I didn't have any choice. But what I had in mind had already worked once.

I picked up the Uzi and aimed it at the front dome. The water was up to my waist. I sank down as low as I could, keeping the gun above the water and then pulled the trigger.

The dome shattered under the stream of bullets and water roared in, pieces of plastic spearing across the compartment. I only had time for one deep gasp of air. It was going to have to last for a long time.

I pushed forward. The current sweeping through the compartment stopped as soon as it was filled. I gripped the edge of the jagged plastic then thought of Carson.

I turned, the water blurring my vision. His body was floating. I gripped his wrist and yanked him toward the broken plastic. My lungs were already hurting and I wasn't even out of the sub.

I manhandled Carson through the dome and pushed both of us out and up. He wasn't moving. I kept going. Up. Up. I could see the surface but it looked so far away. Then my head broke free. I gasped as deeply as possible and pulled Carson to the surface. His eyes were open. I felt for a pulse. Nothing. He was dead. I felt strangely cheated but I kept getting mouthfuls of water. I couldn't hold him up any longer. Pushing him away, I looked back toward the compound.

Far up on the beach, beyond the rocks that cut off the strip of sand from the generating plant,

I spotted Sharpe. He must have seen the submarine leave the dock. He was carrying a rifle and was moving swiftly. He had seen me.

I struck out for the sandy shore nestled between the rocks. It wasn't far and it didn't take long. My feet caught the sand and I stood up and waded ashore. It was finally over but I felt nothing. My emotions, like a battery drawn on too often, were run down past the point of even registering. It had been too close and Carson had been taken away before he could be brought to account. It was not the way I had wanted it to end.

On the dry sand I hung my head and bent over, retching seawater. I'd be okay. I just need some time and fresh air.

But I wasn't going to get it.

"Castle!" The voice was cold and ominous.

I brought my head up slowly. It was such an effort.

The colonel stepped out onto the sand from behind a rock. He was holding an M-16 in one hand. The barrel wavered. His right hand hung limply. Blood covered most of his shirt and dripped from the hand.

"I've wanted you for so long, you sonofabitch," he screamed as he lurched forward, almost drunkenly. "All my life you've slandered me. You've cost me so much. Now you'll pay." The rifle wavered.

I was frozen. There was nothing I could do. For a moment I just wished it would end, be over. The little voices were at work, issuing stupid orders for me to duck, run away, fight back. I ignored them. There was nowhere to run.

"You cost me in Stanley, in Londonderry, in Managua, here today. I'm going to take great pleasure in killing you." He was weak and swayed.

He wasn't weak enough not to finish what he

so desperately wanted to do. I was going to die without a word. I opened my mouth but nothing came out. All I wanted to do was to tell him to hurry up and get it over with because I was so tired and it was such an effort to stand there and listen to him.

The rifle came up higher. I could see him fighting back the pain of his wounds and trying to pull the trigger. He would make it. He was close enough now he couldn't miss.

"You're out, Castle!"

That was it. His final announcement.

I dived to the right as he fired, making one last, almost involuntary movement. He couldn't miss the second time and I had no other move to make.

Suddenly there was the sound of another gun. The colonel took the shots square in the back. He seemed to jump forward in the air and hang there for a long moment, his mouth working frantically, the M-16 tumbling to the sand.

I couldn't get up. I just lay there as the SAS captain stepped forward and looked down at the colonel. Then he shook his head and came over and sat down on the sand beside me.

"Thanks, a second time," I managed to say.

He nodded and looked back at the colonel. "He knew his trade. He was good at that. Too bad he had to put it to use for the wrong side."

I raised myself up to a sitting position. "Jade?"

"She's okay. Superficial wound. She's already working on some of my guys who didn't duck fast enough," he said.

I nodded.

"That's why I decided to let her come. McQueen gave me the final say." He looked out at the sea. "I figured we were in for a bad time. She was a doctor. I needed her here. She had a right, too." He shrugged as if it was enough of an explanation.

291

I stood up, understanding. When you got right down to it, we all did what we had to do. There were no ironclad guarantees for any one of us. "Let's go." I walked past the body of the colonel without even looking down at it.

EPILOGUE

McQueen was standing in the centre of the office. I was at the window watching a sleek F-18 fighter bomber race down the runway and lift rapidly away to the east. I was back at the beginning, thinking of Gerry Roa, the palace filled with opulent wealth and the $50 million dollars locked away in an account in Geneva. McQueen had filled in part of the story about the money. The CIA had informed the Aquino government about the account, based on what they had gleaned from Jade and me during the earlier debriefings. The new government had already set up a commission to try and track down the wealth Marcos had secreted away all over the world. The $50 million would become another item on the list of treasure the commission was trying to track down and return to the Philippines. It would be slow, difficult work—particularly given the Swiss banking system. I sighed. In this imperfect world, perhaps justice might prevail and the money might find its way back to where it belonged, even though the numbers inscribed inside the shattered little yellow duck were now lost somewhere in the depths of the Pacific Ocean.

A giant Hercules lumbered past on a runway, engines roaring. I thought of the SAS captain. Richard Sharpe had gone back to wherever he had

293

come from. It was like that with the SAS: strike swiftly and then fade back into obscurity. He'd saved my life twice and I'd never got around to thanking him properly. I turned away from the window.

"We've tied up a lot of loose ends," McQueen said. "We can roll up some of Carson's network. He ran the place in such a way there was no one to take over. Most of it will dry up pretty soon."

Jade was sitting in a chair. Her leg wound was well wrapped and she was beginning to sound like her old self. "How much are you going to let Julian write?"

McQueen shrugged but seemed sure of himself. "Not much. National security. You know the line."

He was speaking to me as much as to her and I was listening to him.

"That's not fair," she argued. "He's been on this story from before you guys even got involved."

McQueen looked at me. There was a questioning look on his face as though he knew my answer and was waiting for my confirmation.

I let out a long breath, tilted my head and winked at him.

Jade saw the exchange. "I don't understand you two." She shook her head in disgust.

What could I say? There were some things best left unsaid—to her and, perhaps, even to that wider audience that I sometimes wrote for. Maybe I was starting to think a little too much like McQueen. What's worse, I concluded wearily, that thought didn't even seem to bother me any more.

The Painted Shore
James Cowan

Joel Cassidy resolves to investigate the events behind the violent death of Odile Leger, once his closest companion on the island of Mauritius. But he must unravel her past, and also solve the mystery that took him to Mauritius in the first place—the lost journal of explorer Matthew Flinders. Flinders' involvement with a cryptic mystical sect, his suspected espionage, caused Joel to confront his own life, revealing new betrayals, new enlightenments.

A contemporary story of discovery and an historical thriller in the rich tradition of Daphne du Maurier and Somerset Maugham.

ISBN 0 947189 30 0   AUST: $9.95
                            RECOMMENDED RETAIL PRICE

BANTAM BOOKS

Australian Eyes Only
Michael Sexton

Murchison gazed at a memorandum whose classification was TOP
SECRET: AUSTEO. It was a warning on military or diplomatic
documents that the contents were not subject to the normal
sharing arrangements with American and British intelligence
agencies.

From the moment he stumbles upon mysterious papers in the files
of a violently murdered colleague in Washington, political
journalist Jim Murchison's life is also in peril.

Travelling between Washington, New York and Canberra,
Murchison begins putting the wrong question to the right
people—and he learns that some are prepared to kill in order to
safeguard their secrets.

Michael Sexton has worked as a lawyer in Canberra and
Washington and is now a Sydney barrister.

ISBN 0 947189 04 1   AUST: $9.95
                            RECOMMENDED RETAIL PRICE

BANTAM BOOKS

The Garden House
Martin Long

A rich Sydney playboy . . . dark family secrets, and an Irish servant girl . . . It all adds up to murder in **The Garden House**.

When playboy Charles Blakewell is found murdered in the garden house of his parents' mansion, a servant girl with whom he has been having an affair is charged and imprisoned. But Juliana Pyke, crusader for the rights of women, is convinced the girl is innocent. Enlisting Wellington Cotter in her campaign to have the Blakewell case reopened, together they discover evidence of intrigue and conspiracy involving some of Sydney's most respected and wealthy citizens.

Set in Sydney during the wonderfully atmospheric gaslight era of the late nineteenth century, and introducing the eccentric retired police officer Wellington (Tom) Cotter, **The Garden House** is the first in the Gaslight Mystery Series.

ISBN 0 947189 55 6   AUST $9.95
                                     RECOMMENDED RETAIL PRICE

BANTAM BOOKS

Fragile Empires

James Crown

Introducing Julian Castle—tough, ex-war zone journalist, used to being where the trouble is; used to chasing the real stories behind tragedy and corruption; prompted by a battered but still active conscience and an obsessive urge to find the truth.

FRAGILE EMPIRES has Julian Castle searching for the threads that link stolen Nazi gold, the murder of a journalist in the Philippines, CIA subversion of foreign governments, illegal weapons research, and the apparently motiveless assassination of an industrialist. It is a story of revenge stretching back to 1943, played out against contemporary world events. It ranges from Germany to Australia, Indonesia, the Philippines and the United States, and culminates in a stunning finale of terror, action and suspense.

ISBN 0 947189 13 0   AUST: $8.95
                                    RECOMMENDED RETAIL PRICE

BANTAM BOOKS

Concertinas
Trevor Shearston

Nine years after leaving Papua New Guinea, Chris Davage thinks he's finished with that country—its beauty, its turmoil and its people. Until he meets Timii, an ex-student, in a crowded Canberra shopping centre.

Timii, now a young woman of strength and charm, is also that special kind of adventurer, prepared to risk her skin to test her conviction. Through Timii, Davage is drawn again to the country he once believed was "home" and also into a quietly dangerous cause—that of the West Papuans, twenty years under Indonesian rule.

Family, job, friendships, his whole settled life, lose their meaning in a tangle of conflicting emotions as Davage pursues a new ideal of freedom, justice . . . and difficult love.

Concertinas sets a personal story of political adventure against the controversy and tension of Australia's nearest alliances—and misalliances.

ISBN 0 947189 30 0   AUST: $10.95
                                  RECOMMENDED RETAIL PRICE

BANTAM BOOKS